Dream House

Second Edition

Dream House

Second Edition

Mike Faricy

Library of Congress Control Number: 2023917945
paperback ISBN: 978-1-962080-41-5
e-Book ISBN: 978-1-962080-42-2

MJF Publishing books may be purchased for education, Business, or promotional use. For information on bulk purchases,
please contact the author directly at mikefaricyauthor@gmail.com

Published by

MJF Publishing
https://www.mikefaricybooks.com

Acknowledgments

I would like to thank the following people for their help and support:
Special thanks to my editors, Kitty, Donna and Rhonda for their hard work, cheerful patience and positive feedback.

I would like to thank Ann and Julie for their creative talent and not slitting their wrists or jumping off the high bridge when dealing with my Neanderthal computer capabilities.

Special thanks to Ann for her patience.

Last, I would like to thank family and friends for their encouragement and unqualified support. Special thanks to Maggie, Jed, Schatz, Pat, Av, Emily and Pat for not rolling their eyes, at least when I was there, and most of all, to my wife Teresa whose belief, support and inspiration has from day one, never waned.

Prologue

The Mechanic stepped back and said, "You're good to go, Mr. Wazinski. We changed the oil and filled your window washer fluid. Tires are fine, air conditioner works. We installed a new lock on the driver's door and a new ignition. I've got two keys in the office. Come on in, and we can settle up. Looks like whoever tried to steal your truck was ready to take off. They had it all set to hot wire. Good thing you caught 'em when you did."

Ken flashed his sparkling white teeth and said, "You just can't make it up. Wouldn't that just piss you off? I'm about to drive half-way across the country, and some idiot decides to steal my truck just as I'm getting ready to leave."

"Yeah, the world's full of 'em. Come on. We'll get you settled up and on your way."

Ken followed him through one of the work bays at the gas station and into a rear office. "Here's the list of work we did. Oh yeah, and we put a padlock on that door to the back. You don't want some idiot getting into the back of the truck. They'll have you emptied out before you know it. Now is this going to be credit card or cash?"

"I'll be running it on my business credit card," Wazinski said as he pulled the card out of his wallet.

"That's fine. Now, we add on a one-and-a-half percent charge to all credit card payments."

"I don't blame you. Surprised it's not more. Here you go," Wazinski said and handed him the credit card.

Jerry looked at the card. "Able Manufacturing? You're over in Compton, right?"

Wazinski gave a slight nod and said, "That's one of our locations. We're all over California. Say, I should probably get going. I've got a lot of miles ahead of me."

"Oh yeah, sure." Jerry ran the credit card and handed Ken the keys. "Okay, you're good to go. Safe journey. Been a pleasure meeting you."

"Thanks, appreciate the quick service. I'm going to mention you to all my friends, and I'll see if the company can get in touch. We got a fleet of trucks, and there's always something that needs to be taken care of."

"Thanks. If you do that, I'm sure we could work something out, make it worth your while."

"I'll get on it," Wazinski said. He headed out to the parking area and climbed in the truck.

The mechanic stepped back from the raised hood and wiped his hands on the rag draped over the radiator. "What is with that dude? His eyes were all squinty, that forehead, the cheeks, the lips. Was he in some major accident?"

"You got me. Strange duck, that's for sure. You look inside that truck?"

"Yeah, full of boxes. I'd guess he came out here to be a movie star, and after waiting tables for ten years, decided to head back to wherever home is. I'll be finished with this one in about fifteen minutes if you want to give them a call," the mechanic said and bent down under the hood.

Wazinski checked the mirrors, and waited for two woman to walk past before he pulled onto the street. Three blocks away, he stopped at the light. A homeless man held out his baseball cap and looked hopeful.

Wazinski flashed his sparkling white teeth and rolled down the window.

"God bless you, sir," the homeless man said. His eyes were bloodshot, and he was missing his front teeth.

Ken dropped the Able Manufacturing credit card into the hat and got a questioning look in response.

"Good for only one day," he said, laughed as the light turned green, and he drove off.

One

Louie pulled his Ford Fiesta to the curb in front of the police impound lot. The thing was a faded orange color and hadn't been washed since the day he bought it back in 2016. It shuddered for a painful five seconds when he turned the engine off. "Dev, you sure you don't want me to wait for you?"

"No, thanks Louie, but I don't know how long this is gonna take."

"I thought you said you had the winning bid?"

"Not exactly, I had the highest online bid as of ten o'clock this morning. But the auction starts in twenty minutes, and there are lots of guys like those two who are probably here every month bidding on cars." I nodded at the two guys heading into the office. One wore a navy-blue sport coat and jeans, and the other had a white shirt with a button-down collar and dress slacks. I was wearing cut-offs, a faded t-shirt, and was armed with a cashier's check for two-thousand-seven-hundred-and-fifty dollars.

"You got your check?" Louie asked as a red BMW parked across the street from us. A guy in a grey suit hopped out and headed inside the building.

"Yeah, certified, I just hope some regular attendee doesn't outbid me. I've never been to a police auction before."

"Well, it's basically cars that have been confiscated in an arrest or left on the side of the road. Who knows, all these folks might be here to bid on the same fancy car. Look, I got some cash," Louie said, pulling out his wallet. He reached in, pulled out some bills, and handed them to me.

"Oh, Louie, I can't take—"

"Come on, man. Take it. I know you're good for it. Just in case some jerk tries to go ten bucks over your bid."

I took the bills and counted them, three twenties, a ten, a five and a bunch of ones. "Oh, thanks, Louie. Eighty-seven bucks. Much appreciated."

"My pleasure. Now you give me a call if you need a lift after this."

"Well, hopefully, I'll be driving back to the office within the next ninety minutes. It's the third lot on the list."

"Better hurry in there. I'll see you back at the office, Dev."

I shouted a thanks as I climbed out. Louie's car emitted a dark cloud of exhaust as it sprang to life. He gave a wave and pulled away from the curb.

"There's one for you to bid on, Jack," some guy said to his friend eyeing Louie's Ford Fiesta.

"I don't think so," the friend chuckled. They crossed the street laughing and headed into the building as Louie disappeared around the corner.

I followed them inside, up a flight of stairs, took a right, followed the arrow marked 'AUCTION,' and went down another flight of stairs. Two women in shorts, t-shirts, and baseball caps sat at a table at the edge of a large parking lot filled with cars and a few trucks.

"We'll need a driver's license, proof of insurance, and five dollars for the bid card," one of them said to me. I pulled my license out of my wallet and handed it to her. I had the insurance papers in my back pocket and laid them on the table next to the license. I tossed Louie's five-dollar bill on top of the insurance papers.

She typed my name, address, and insurance info into the computer. "Okay, you're good to go, Mr. Haskell. Good luck," she said a minute later and handed me a cardboard card with the number one-fifty-one on it along with my driver's license and insurance papers.

I wandered into the center of the lot. Over two hundred cars and trucks were parked, one next to the other. Vehicles abandoned in the April blizzard that dumped twelve inches on the city. Stolen vehicles no one had bothered to claim. Vehicles parked too long in one spot that were eventually towed, and apparently, no one missed them. They all had a number written on the front windshield in yellow marker.

I glanced at number three, the vehicle I would hopefully get. I didn't go near the car for fear of attracting attention. I wandered through the lot, looking at various cars until a loud, high-pitched squeak sounded over a loudspeaker followed by a voice that said, "Good morning, ladies and gentlemen. We want to thank you all for coming. Before we get started, the four portable units at the back of the lot will be serving as our restrooms today. All vehicles are sold as-is. All sales are final and must be paid with either a certified check or cash by four o'clock this afternoon. Now, if you'll gather round, we'll begin in just a minute."

It was more like ten minutes, but eventually, the auction started. The first lot was a 2014 Mercedes C-class, blue with a crack running across the entire base of the windshield. Bidding began at twelve-five and ended at an even fifteen hundred. The next vehicle was a 2011 Toyota Camry with a major dent in the driver's door. Four bids were given, and the vehicle sold for forty-nine hundred.

The next car up was the one I'd bid on. "Let's move on to lot number three," the auctioneer said. "It's a two thousand nine Ford Crown Victoria Police Interceptor. Black, with a hundred and sixty-nine thousand miles on it. Bidding will begin at two-thousand-seven-hundred-and-fifty dollars." The auctioneer raised his voice on the word fifty, and I could feel my heart pounding in my ears.

He waited a moment and repeated, "Lot number three. A two thousand nine Ford Crown Victoria Police

Interceptor. Black, with a hundred and sixty-nine thousand miles on it. Do I have a bid? A two thousand nine Ford Crown Victoria. We're starting at two-thousand-seven-hundred-and-fifty dollars. Do I have a bid? Going once, going twice, sold for two-thousand-seven-hundred-and-fifty dollars. Lot number four, a two thousand thirteen Chevrolet Traverse. White, with one hundred and twenty-two thousand miles…

I drowned the rest of the auction out and hurried over to the table with the two women in t-shirts. There were still people just coming into the auction, and I had to wait in line behind four people before I could pay. I gave them my check and had to wait for another hour before the auctioneer took a break, and I could drive my Crown Victoria out of the lot. Thankfully, it started on the first try.

TWO

I stopped at Rooster's Bar-B-Que just up the street from the office. I got two pulled pork bar-b-que sandwiches for Louie and me and a bone for Morton. Morton met me at the door as I stepped into the office. Louie slowly opened his eyes and sat up in his desk chair.

"I hope you haven't had lunch already," I said, as I placed the Rooster's bag on his picnic table desk.

"Mmm, no, this is perfect. I can use a little break."

I decided not to mention he'd been asleep. I set a Styrofoam sandwich container down in front of him and settled in behind my desk. The bar-b-que smell permeated the office once we lifted the lids on our carryout containers. Morton gave me an orgasmic look as he rubbed his head on the pork bone and seemed to settle even deeper onto his pillow.

There was no talking for the next few minutes as we attacked the bar-b-que. Eventually, Louie swallowed his most recent mouthful and said, "So, if you're back already, either you got the car, or someone outbid you. Which one is it?"

"I got it. It's parked out on the street, right behind yours. Before I forget, let me return this cash to you. I still owe you twenty-five bucks."

"Not a problem. So you got the car. Great," he said, standing and stepping over to the front window. "Let me just take a look and— Dev, are you kidding me? You can't be serious. That black Crown Vic? That's the car you bought?"

"Yeah, and no one else bid against me."

Louie shook his head. "There's a surprise. Really, that black Crown Vic?"

"Yeah. Why are there two out there?" I made a show of pulling my binoculars out of a desk drawer and scanning the street.

"You bought that Crown Vic?"

"Yeah. You like it?" Along with being black, it had tires with absolutely no whitewall. There was a moveable spotlight mounted just above the sideview mirror on the driver's side. The front of the car featured two large rubber bumpers running from the front bumper up to the top of the chrome grill, designed to push stalled vehicles.

"I don't know. It would just seem to me, given the business you're in, that maybe you might have thought of something a bit more understated."

"What do you mean, understated?"

"You know, for when you're supposed to be keeping a quiet eye on someone or something. When you're supposed to watch someone sneak in or out of an office or from someone's house. How many times a year does someone ask you to take photographs of a significant other they suspect of dabbling? Do you ever attempt to follow someone unobserved? Ever think about blending into a crowd?"

"Mmm, yeah. I guess I didn't really consider any of that. I was more focused on the fact that it's bulletproof, and I was so blown away by the speedometer. It can do up to a hundred and twenty-nine miles per hour and goes from zero to sixty in five seconds. A pal from the department motor pool turned me onto this one going up for auction. They did a whole revamp of the engine, everything from new battery to spark plugs and new fuel filters, added a new fuel pump. They checked the ignition, rotated the tires."

"After they did all that work they put it up for auction for two grand?"

"Two-thousand-seven-hundred-and-fifty," I corrected.

"Okay," Louie said, settling back in behind his picnic table and finishing the last half of his sandwich. He ran a finger through the bar-b-que sauce left in the container and licked it a couple of times. A half-hour later, he stuffed his laptop in his computer bag and headed toward the door. "I've got a court appearance at three, but I should be back after that, hopefully. You up for The Spot later today?"

"Yeah, I can do that. I'll buy."

Louie smiled. "Yeah, you're right. You will. See you over there," he said and headed out the door.

I tossed the Styrofoam containers in my wastebasket, picked up the binoculars, and scanned the apartment building across the street. A woman in one of the units was busy preparing something in the kitchen. Unfortunately, she was dressed. I returned the binoculars to my desk drawer and glanced out the window. A pink Mercedes convertible with a two-seat black interior parked behind my Crown Vic. The left rear taillight appeared to be broken, which didn't come as a surprise. I watched a busty blonde slide out from behind the wheel, Barbie Dahl. The last time I saw her was out in Vegas, where she'd dumped me for Goose Gander's brother, Kenny. She was still gorgeous, and I presumed still certifiable.

She waited for a car to pass, but the guy slowed down and stopped so she could cross in front of him. As she walked past, he lowered the driver's window, shouted some comment I couldn't hear, and gave a whistle that I did hear. Barbie smiled, gave him a sexy little wave, and entered the building. A moment later, I heard her on the stairs.

I quickly pulled my wastebasket behind my desk and Googled the police department on my computer. The site came up on my computer screen just as she opened the door, smiled, and gave a sexy little knock on the door frame.

She wore an extremely short, pink plaid schoolgirl skirt, thigh-high white nylon stockings, white stiletto heels, and a pink, short-sleeve tie top. Her gorgeous blonde hair hung a good four inches below her shoulders, and her enhanced attributes appeared to have gone another round or two in the enlargement department. She smiled and slowly turned from left to right as if on stage, giving me a hundred-and-eighty-degree view as she stood in the doorway. "Miss me, darling?"

Three

Morton was suddenly off his pillow. He hurried over and shoved his nose beneath her school-girl skirt. "Wow. Barbie, long time no see. To what do I owe the pleasure?""Mmm, Martin, I see you haven't changed." She gave a sexy little shrug as she spoke but didn't push him away.

"Actually, his name is Morton. When did you get back in town? Last I knew, you were out in Las Vegas living it up in the Barbie Suite. Are you just back visiting?"

"All good things must come to an end. Are you going to invite me in?"

"Oh, yeah, please, please, come on in and have a seat. Can I get you something? I think there might be some coffee left, or maybe you'd like a beer?"

"No, thank you, Dev. I'm just fine." She gave a little sideways glance, suggesting my offer sounded crazy. As she sat down, she crossed her legs. Unfortunately, my desk limited the view. "So, how have you been, big boy?"

"Who, me? Well, I've been pretty good. You know me, I remain the most boring guy in town. So, you never said, are you just back for a visit?"

She shook her head. "No, as a matter of fact, I moved back almost two weeks ago. I bought a townhouse out in the burbs. After working in Vegas, I went out to California for a while and made some movies. I toured the country on a promo tour, dancing." I had the feeling the term XXX might be in there right before the word 'movies'. "I came back because I want to follow my true vocation."

"Your vocation? What are you planning to do, Barbie?"

"Hospital work."

"Really? You thinking of going to nursing school or trying to get into med school?"

"Don't be silly. I've built a following all across the country. I'm planning on opening up a Barbie hospital."

"A Barbie hospital?"

"Yeah, you know, Barbie has an ambulance and a hospital playset, and so I figure the next logical thing is for me to open up a Barbie hospital, except I'm going to call it the Dream House. I'll repair the various dolls, replace hair, maybe an arm or a leg."

"The Dream House?"

"Yeah. The market's ripe, and I've got over two million followers."

"Two million followers?"

"Yeah, between Facebook, Twitter, and my Pod-casts."

"You do Podcasts?"

"Oh, yeah, Barbie Podcasts. I do them weekly. I've got a number of virtual Barbie backgrounds I use. My fans just love them. It would only seem logical that they'd all want to refresh their dolls. Don't you think?"

"I, umm, guess I never quite thought of it like that. Good for you, go for it."

"Well, thank you. Now, there just seems to be one little problem."

Here it comes, I thought. I figured she was about to ask me for money. I learned my lesson four years ago when we were out in Vegas. No way, not a cent. "So, you've got a little problem?"

"Yes, Ken's missing, and he's driving a truck filled with my entire Barbie collection."

"Wait a minute. You mean Kenny Gander, the IT guy from Vegas. He was, or is, my friend Goose's brother. He's missing?"

"Oh, I haven't seen either one of those two in years. No, this is my Ken, Ken Carson Wazinski. Although he's in the process of getting his name changed, I'm sure you can understand why."

I nodded and had no idea what she was talking about. "So, this Ken Carson guy is missing?"

"Yes. I flew back here from L.A. after I purchased the townhouse. I had my car and all my furniture shipped, and everything was delivered on time. But I didn't want to risk having anything happen to my Barbie collection. It's been appraised for between one-point-five and two-point-five million dollars."

"Of course," I said and nodded.

"Anyway, Ken graciously offered to drive it out here. We loaded everything in the truck. Packed it carefully, secured it so things wouldn't be bouncing around on the cross-country trip, and now he's nowhere to be found. I can't reach him on his cell phone. I'm not getting any responses to my text messages or my emails. It's like he's simply vanished."

"Did you ever think he just might be in an area where he's unable to get internet service? You know somewhere in the mountains or the middle of Nebraska."

"It's been over eight days."

"Hmm, do you know the route he was planning to take?"

"The route? More or less. L.A. to Vegas going up into Utah. From there, he would drive across Colorado and Nebraska and come up through Iowa and into Minnesota. He figured five days at the very most, you know driving a truck and all."

"So he's a day or two late. Maybe he had to stop for a repair or—"

"But I haven't been able to contact him since he left L.A. Certainly he would have stopped somewhere along the way and called me. I'm really worried something may have happened to my Barbie collection. Oh, yeah, and I guess Ken too," she added as an afterthought and not sounding all that convincing.

"Do you know who he rented the truck from?"

"He didn't rent it. He borrowed it."

"Do you know who he borrowed it from?"

"No, I don't. I can't locate him. I've called the highway patrol in all seven states, and they all say the same thing. They need more information."

"I don't suppose you have the license number of the truck."

"No, I don't. To be honest, at the time, I never even thought about it. He paid for the taxi to take me to the airport, said he would be leaving in a couple of days, and that's the last time I saw or talked to him. I'm worried about my collection. It's almost every Barbie item I own."

"Is your collection insured?"

"That was one of the benefits of having Ken drive everything up here, so I wouldn't have to pay insurance."

I took out a pen, pulled the bag from Rooster's out of the waste basket, and asked, "What's Ken's phone number?"

"She pulled her cellphone from her pink purse and moved her thumbs at lightning speed until she arrived at Ken's number. I found it interesting she didn't know it off the top of her head. I wrote the number on the Rooster's bag along with Ken's full name, Barbie's address, phone number, and email address. I opened a desk drawer, pulled out two business cards, and handed them to her. "Let me do a little checking, and I'll get back to you. Did you have any of Ken's personal items packed in the truck that brought your furniture and things?"

She nodded and said, "I've got maybe a half-dozen boxes and two suitcases with some clothes."

"Okay, I'll get on this right away. I'll call you in a couple of hours. Don't worry. We'll find him."

She pushed the chair back, stood, and slowly leaned over my desk. Her pink, short-sleeve tie top left nothing to my imagination. She gave me a lingering kiss on the lips, slowly stood and said, "Mmm, I really missed you. Don't forget to call me, Dev."

With that, she picked her purse up off the floor and sashayed out of the office. I watched out the window as she strutted across the street. Some guy drove down the street and tooted his horn as she climbed into the pink Mercedes. A moment later, she drove up the street and disappeared.

Four

I punched in the phone number Barbie had given me for Ken. The phone rang a number of times, before it dropped me into voicemail without having to listen to a recorded message. Once the beep sounded, I said, "Hi Ken, my name is Dev Haskell. I'm a friend of Barbie's. Just calling to make sure everything is all right. She was worried about you and stopped by my office. Please give me a call, so we know everything is okay, or in the event you need some assistance, we can get moving on that. Thanks, my number is six-five-one, blah, blah, blah. Looking forward to hearing from you."

Next, I Googled Ken Wazinski, and a message immediately popped up, 'There are no results matching your search.' I came up blank on a half-dozen other searches and called Aaron LaZelle, my pal heading up the homicide division in the St. Paul police department. I ended up leaving a message. "Hi Aaron, this is Dev. Would you give me a call when you have a minute? I'm trying to find a guy, and I'm drawing a bunch of blanks."

I brought up a Google map of routes from Los Angles to the twin cites. There were basically two, one of which listed all the states Barbie had mentioned. I Googled state by state car accidents but only came up with legal firms looking for clients. Iowa looked like it had a site that listed accidents by date and county, but when I filled in the information, I got the notice that the site had been out of service since 2015 with no restart date available. No wonder Barbie was having a hard time finding this guy.

It was about half-past four when I heard the stairs creaking, and a moment later, a red-faced Louie opened the door and collapsed in his chair behind the picnic table. I knew better than to ask him a question at the moment. A couple of minutes passed before he said, "Oh, man. I wish there was an elevator I could take in this place."

"Yeah, I know what you mean. Climbing all the way up to the second floor can be a lot of work," I said.

Louie looked at me for a moment but didn't say anything.

"Everything go okay at your court hearing?" I asked.

"Yeah, other than they were running behind schedule. We weren't even called until almost half-past three. But in the end, we got what we wanted."

"Charges dropped?"

"If only. No, nothing quite that good, but a suspended sentence with charges expunged from her record after twenty-four months as long as there's not another incident."

"Will your client be able to do that?"

"Yeah, I think so. She's a grade school teacher. Got in a fender bender that actually wasn't her fault. Unfortunately, the cops happened to show up. She'd been drinking and blew over the legal limit. Cost her twelve hundred in repairs, a five hundred dollar fine, and she'll be in a risk insurance category for the next seven years. Even with the charges dropped, it's going to cost her eleven to twelve hundred bucks over the next seven years. Anything happen in your life?"

"Well," I said and proceeded to give him my Barbie update.

Louie just shook his head as I described her situation, what she looked like, and the fact that I had found absolutely nothing on her close personal friend Ken. "So let me get this straight. She still thinks she's the real-life Barbie. She's ended up with some fruit cake who's going to change his given name, whatever the hell it is, to Ken Carson. She does Barbie podcasts and is going to open up a Barbie Hospital and call it the Doll House, or Dream House, or something. Does that pretty well sum things up?

I nodded. "Yeah, pretty much. Don't forget, this Ken character is missing in action."

"Oh yeah. How could I forget? Barbie can't seem to find Ken. I'm thinking it sounds like he maybe absconded with all her Barbie stuff. What'd she say that junk was worth? The dolls and all the other crap?"

"She wasn't that specific. What she actually said is the stuff has been appraised at between one-point-five and two-point five million."

"Maybe it is. I'm certainly the wrong guy to ask about it," Louie said. "Could be this Ken character, or whatever his name really is, took that appraisal for hundreds of thousands to heart and headed somewhere else with her Barbie collection. Nowadays, with eBay and the like, he could be selling that stuff all day, every day, and it would be damn near impossible to stop him."

"God, I never even thought of eBay," I said. I Googled eBay and entered 'Barbie Dolls.' The site had fifty items per page, and I don't know how many pages. The first item on the page was Flash Dance Barbie for a hundred and seventy-five bucks, and the second item was Barbie the Rose for seventy-five dollars. "This is crazy. There are people out there paying this kind of money for these things?"

"Collectors, Dev. Is it that much different from collecting stamps or coins?"

"I don't know. It's just, oh man. Check this out."

"What is it?" Louie asked.

"There's two pictures of Ken, the doll. I completely forgot that was the guy doll Barbie was having an affair with. Interesting, they're only going for twenty-four bucks. I'll bet that's why I couldn't find him online. His name isn't really Ken. She told me he was changing his name, but I figured it would just be his last name. Oh man, if he's changing his name, I wonder if he's done any plastic surgery to make him look like the dolls."

"I'm guessing they're handsome," Louie said.

"Actually, they kind of look like the guy you'd want to punch in the nose just because. One of those privileged jerks everyone thinks the world of. If he looks anything like these things, no wonder we can't find him. The first guy who saw him probably just beat the crap out of him."

"Maybe ask your pal Barbie if she's got a picture of him. Just for starters. You could always put something online. You know, a missing Ken doll report." Louie laughed. "You know it would be interesting to do that. Just to see if you got a bunch of women replying saying the picture looks just like their Ken doll."

"Actually, Louie, that's not a bad idea. Hang on." I punched in Barbie's number. She answered on the third ring. "Hi Barbie, it's Dev."

"Did you find Ken already?"

"No, at least not yet, but I'm chasing down some leads. You said you have some items of his at your place?"

"Yeah, a couple of suitcases and some boxes."

"I'm just about to go into a meeting. Once that's over, I'd like to head out to your place, if that's okay, and go through those things. Might be an hour or two before I get there."

She seemed to think about that for a long moment.

"Barbie, you still there?"

"Yeah, umm, I guess that would be okay if you think it would speed things up."

"You're at the address you gave me in Oak Park Heights?"

"Yes, my townhouse."

"Okay, I'll see you in ninety minutes or so," I said and hung up.

"You've still got a meeting this afternoon?" Louie asked.

"Yeah, with you. Remember, I'm buying over at The Spot."

Five

Louie headed across the street to The Spot bar. I clicked Morton's leash onto his collar and took him for a quick walk. After checking out every other tree and three fire hydrants in a four-block area, we made our way into The Spot. Louie was one of six people in the bar. He was seated at the far end of the bar on his usual stool, talking to Mike, the bartender.

As we stepped in the front door, Mike glanced back, saw it was us, and pulled a bag of pork rinds from the rack. He tossed the bag in front of Louie, causing Morton to strain on his leash in an effort to hurry over to Louie.

As Morton rounded the corner, Louie reached down with a generous handful of pork rinds and said, "Oh, Morton. Thank you for bringing Dev over. I've got a tab going in his name, but I wasn't sure he would be able to find his way across the street. You know how he is."

Morton inhaled the pork rinds and proceeded to lick Louie's hand clean.

"I'll have a beer, and you better get another of whatever Louie's having," I said as Mike made his way down to the beer taps. He took another order along the way before he started pouring beers. I hopped on a bar stool, two away from Louie just to keep the distance but close enough so we wouldn't have to yell at one another.

Louie picked up his glass, drained the remainder of the dark liquid, and said, "What are you hoping to find out at Barbie's place?"

"Anything that will help me locate this Ken character. The more I'm thinking of it, the more the whole thing isn't sounding right."

"What, you mean her idea of a Barbie hospital? Actually, with two million followers across the internet and a number of collectors out there, it just might be a gold mine. You saw how much of that stuff was on eBay. Think of all the women out there who would love to drag a box of dolls out of their attic if only there was a way to get them repaired."

"Oh, yeah. I get what you're saying, Louie. In fact, I'm with you. I think it could be one hell of a good idea. My only concern is that Barbie is such an absolute flake she's bound to screw this up somehow."

Mike delivered our drinks. Louie was drinking whiskey. It looked a little too dark to be Jameson Irish, so I guessed Makers Mark bourbon. I was drinking my standard Summit IPA. Mike smiled, raised his eyebrows, and stood there waiting.

"Oh, sorry, Mike. Let me just get some cash from the ATM, and I'll be back."

"Amazing the things I put up with," Mike said to Louie and headed back down the bar as I ran over to the ATM that sat between the restroom doors.

I inserted my card, requested sixty bucks from the ATM, and crossed my fingers that the request would go through. Fortunately, it did. I walked down to the far end of the bar and handed Mike a twenty. "Keep the change, Mike."

"Much appreciated," he said and rapped the twenty on the bar.

I headed back to Louie. He was in the process of pouring a third of the pork rind bag into his hand, leaning down and giving it to Morton who was waiting patiently at his feet. Once Morton licked his hand clean, Louie repositioned himself on his barstool and said, "So, you were telling me what an absolute flake Barbie is."

"Yeah, and now that I'm reminded about the Ken dolls, I'm wondering if the guy supposedly driving her collection up here in a truck isn't the male version of a Barbie flake. He's apparently in the process of changing his name to Ken Carson, which is the Barbie doll guy's name. It isn't a huge leap to think he's maybe done all sorts of reconstructive surgery to actually look like the doll. He's probably taken a wrong turn somewhere in Nebraska and has been lost for the last three days. God, how do I end up with these cases?"

Louie laughed and said, "You ever think it might be something along the lines of 'Birds of a feather flock together?'"

"Thanks for that compliment." We sat and chatted about everything and nothing for the next forty-five minutes. I drove Morton home, let him out into the back-yard for a bit. I pulled a bottle of white wine from the refrigerator, and hurried over to Barbie's townhouse.

Oak Park Heights is east of St. Paul along the St. Croix River, set between the towns of Bayport and Stillwater. It's a nice enough area, although if you google the place, the biggest attraction seems to be the Oak Park Heights Correctional Facility. It operates at the highest custody level of any facility in the Minnesota Department of Corrections system. My GPS directed me through the area to a series of two-story structures with built-in double garages and a black mailbox on a wooden post next to the end of every driveway. I counted an even dozen units. Barbie's was number 405, third from the far end. I spotted it from nine units away, the only place painted pink. I pulled into her driveway and parked. The pink metal siding had blue trim, and black address numbers tacked on the siding next to the front door.

I rang the doorbell and heard it chime inside. Barbie answered the door a moment later. At least I thought it was her. She answered the door in a white terrycloth bathrobe. Her blonde hair was pulled back in a ponytail, and she had thick blue cream smeared across her entire face with the exception of her eyes and mouth.

"Oh, hi, Dev. Come on in," she said as she opened the door. I stepped inside and was immediately hit with a visual assault from the pink walls in the living room.

White carpet seemed to cover the first floor. A pink recliner and footstool were positioned next to the fireplace. A plate with what looked like two slices of cucumber rested on the granite hearth in front of the fireplace. A light purple couch and glass-topped coffee table faced the fireplace. What looked like an impressionist painting of Barbie framed in black hung over the fireplace. Beyond the living room was a dining area painted a lighter shade of pink. A staircase with more white carpet and an oak railing rose up to the second floor.

I took it all in over the course of two or three seconds, before I stared at the blue cream covering her entire face.

"Oh, don't mind me. It's just plum and sour cream. I'm doing my podcast in the morning, and I always want to look my best."

I nodded like that made sense and handed her the bottle of white wine. "Here, a little housewarming gift. Welcome back to Minnesota. I see you've been doing some painting," I said, looking around at the pink walls. I tried to remember if I had any aspirin in the car to deal with the headache I could feel coming on.

"I had a painting crew in to do it. They finished everything in a week and didn't spill. I've got another seventeen minutes on this mask. Ken's stuff is all downstairs in the basement. The door is through the kitchen," she said, pointing toward the dining area. "Oh, and if you wouldn't mind, put this in the refrigerator." She handed me the bottle of wine.

I headed toward the dining area as she settled back into the pink recliner. She pressed a button on a remote, and the flatscreen brought up an image of an ocean beach and the sound of waves. She placed the cucumber slices over her eyes, undid the belt on her bathrobe, and crossed her hands over her stomach. I waited a moment to see if I might be treated to a peek but no such luck.

I stepped into the dining area and took a left into the pink kitchen. Thankfully, the refrigerator and stove were white. I set the wine bottle on the bottom shelf of the refrigerator and headed down the basement stairs. The basement walls were painted a light gray, and I breathed a sigh of relief at the bottom of the stairs. In the far corner, opposite a washer and dryer, were a half-dozen boxes stacked against the wall. Next to the boxes were two black suitcases and one smaller red suitcase.

I started in on the suitcases first. They held nothing unusual other than nice clothes. One black suitcase held trousers, five belts, and six pairs of shoes. The other black suitcase held four folded starched shirts in plastic bags from a dry cleaner and six sport shirts. Three more pairs of dress shoes, one pair of sandals, and two v-neck sweaters topped it off. The red suitcase held boxer shorts, t-shirts, socks, and shaving paraphernalia.

There was absolutely nothing of note in the suitcases, so I started in on the boxes. The term junk immediately came to mind. A whistle, bedroom slippers, a waist trainer sweat belt, tubes of sun cream, and all sorts of worthless nonsense. I was in the middle of the third box when I heard the shower running upstairs. The third, fourth, and fifth boxes were just as ridiculous as the first two. The sixth box was a different story.

It was the heaviest of the boxes, and when I opened it, I stared at files and lots of receipts. I paged through the files and started taking notes. After a few minutes, I found an empty folder and began pulling items of interest and placing them in that file. The first thing I noted down was Ken's real name, Arnold Rudolph Wazinski. A number of credit card bills with red stamps across the front shouted 'Overdue' or 'Service Halted.' I counted seven different credit cards that had apparently been canceled over the course of thirty-six months. Interestingly, there were two credit card bills where what looked like the complete card number, security code, and password had been handwritten on the bill. I placed both bills in the folder. There was a notice of a hearing from the Los Angeles City Attorney's Office. The notice was dated July 7th, and the hearing was held July 28th. No indication if Arnold Rudolph Wazinski had attended or what the hearing had been about. I placed that in the folder.

There were a number of past due bills and collection letters over a three-year period from doctors' offices and surgery centers. Reading through the bills, they were from a variety of plastic surgeons doing multiple nose jobs, Botox injections, chin tucks, six-pack ab implants, a buttock lift, chest implants, and hair implants. I added the bills and collection letters in the folder. I was in the process of returning the rest of the files to the box when

Barbie called from upstairs, "How's it going down there?"

"Fine, fine. I'll be up in just a minute," I said, pushing the box back against the wall and tucking the folder under my arm. I glanced around the empty basement. There was nothing else to look at, so I headed upstairs.

Six

There were two empty wine glasses arranged on either side of an ice bucket holding the bottle of white wine I'd brought. A plate next to the wine glasses had Oreo cookies arranged in a circle.

"I'll be out in just a moment, Dev," Barbie called from behind a closed door, either the bathroom or a bedroom. I thought it might be a good time to toss the file of credit card statements, collection letters, and notices from the Los Angeles City Attorney into my Crown Vic, so I headed out the door. I had just stepped back into the kitchen when I heard a door open, and a moment later, Barbie appeared.

She wore a short, tight, pink-sequin dress with spaghetti straps. What looked like a pink see-through plastic dog collar was wrapped around her neck. A large chrome ring hung from the middle of the collar.

"You like?" she asked as she slowly turned a full three-hundred and sixty degrees, accentuating various attributes as she did so.

I made an audible swallow and stuttered, "Ye-ye-yeah. Very nice. I mean, you're gorgeous."

She grinned and said, "Of course I am. Why don't you pour me some wine."

I shook my head back to reality and said, "Oh, yeah, sure. Sorry about that." I poured two glasses of wine and raised my glass in a toast. "Here's to you, Barbie. You look beautiful."

She shrugged as we clinked glasses and said, "That's what everybody says." She took a sip, set her glass down, and reached for an Oreo. "So, did you learn anything?"

"Oh, maybe some general information. We'll see how it goes. It may help me do a little more research. Still no word from him? You didn't get a call or a text message?"

She shook her head and took another sip. "No, nothing. It's just not like him. He's usually so attentive. of course, I was paying the bills, just until he got the business up and running."

"He's starting a business?"

"A division of my hospital. We're calling it Ken's World. He's going to be doing a weekly podcast. We'll interact occasionally," she said and took another sip of wine. She set her glass on the counter, picked up another Oreo, and took a small bite, placing maybe ten percent of the cookie in her mouth.

"Ken's World? You think there's a market for that?"

"Oh, you'd be surprised. With all my followers, even if he got just a quarter of them, that would be …" She seemed to think for a long moment before she shook her head and said, "Well, it would just be a lot of people. So would you like a tour of the place?"

"Yeah, absolutely. Looking forward to it," I lied.

"Follow me," she said, wiggling her index finger at me and raising her eyebrows. "You can bring my wine glass, too."

I picked up her wine glass and took three steps into her living room.

"This is the living room," she said, cranking her hips to one side and striking a pose. I noticed the plate with the two cucumbers was no longer in front of the fireplace. "Come on. You can check out the upstairs."

She led the way up to the second floor. I slowed with each step and confirmed the fact she wasn't wearing anything beneath the sequined dress. There were two bedrooms and a full bath on the second floor. All three rooms, along with the hallway, were painted pink. One bedroom had twin beds. The other had a double bed: pink bedspreads, shades, and curtains decorated both bedrooms. The bathroom had a pink tub, sink, and toilet. Two pink towels and a washcloth hung on the towel rack.

"Really nice. You've done a great job, Barbie," I lied. I handed her wine glass to her. She took a small sip, and we headed back downstairs.

She walked down the short hall next to the pink recliner and opened the door on the right. "This is the master bedroom. Home to all sorts of adventures," she said and raised her eyebrows.

I nodded and pretended that made sense. There was more pink on the walls and a four-poster bed with a pink canopy top. Little sparkly white Christmas lights were wrapped around all four sides of the bed canopy. Three framed 8 x 10 photos of Barbie in front of what looked like crowds of adoring Las Vegas fans rested on a double dresser with a large oval mirror hanging on the wall. A dresser with five drawers stood about chest high against the wall behind me. Both dressers, along with the four-poster bed, appeared to be walnut.

"Lovely, Barbie. Really nice," I said, neglecting to add, *'too bad it's pink.'* "I like your photos. Were those taken in Vegas?"

"Yeah, I'd do the walk twice a day. They couldn't get enough of me."

"That reminds me, would you happen to have a photo of Ken? I didn't find any in the basement. It would help in our search."

"Mmm, I don't have any here. I do have some stored in the cloud. If I email them to you, would that help?"

"That would be perfect. Speaking of which, I'd better get back. I'd like to touch base with a number of agencies across the country and have them aid us in our search for Ken."

She looked confused and said, "Don't you want to stay for another glass of wine?"

"Oh, I'd love to, but right now, time is of the essence. The sooner I get this information out there, the sooner we'll know where he is."

"So, you think something happened to my collection?"

"No, right now, I'm hoping it's nothing more than a problem with the truck in some remote location, and they had to send for a part or something."

"Well, I suppose. You're going to miss out on all the fun, but my collection is more important. I'll send you those images tonight. Call me tomorrow."

"I'll be sure to do that, Barbie." I drained my wine glass and set it on the double dresser. I gave her a friendly nod and beat a hasty retreat.

As I climbed into my Crown Vic, a couple next door was just getting out of their car. "Glad to see you here, officer. We had a feeling the police would be on to her sooner or later. She's a piece of work," the guy said.

I pulled over a block away from Barbie's and phoned Louie.

"Everything okay?" was how he answered.

"You still at The Spot?"

"Yeah, just running up your tab."

"I'll see you in a half-hour," I said.

Seven

I pulled alongside The Spot twenty-five minutes later. I went in the side door. Two more guys had come into the bar since I left not quite two hours ago. Both were seated at the bar with maybe a half-dozen stools between them. Neither one bothered to look up as I entered. They remained staring at their half-empty mugs of beer, no doubt contemplating life in general.

"I didn't expect to see you until tomorrow morning," Louie said. "What happened? Did she have a customer?"

"Barbie? No, it's just that between everything painted pink and all the surgical enhancements, I'd be afraid to touch her. Not to mention the fact that she's nuts."

"You get any information on this character that's missing?" Louie asked and signaled Mike for another round.

"You must be referring to Arnold Rudolph Wazinski, also known as Ken."

"That's a step in the right direction. She told you his name?"

I shook my head and went on to give Louie an update on me going through the suitcases and files.

"You think he just had a mechanical breakdown?"

"That's what I told Barbie I hoped happened. Based on the history I learned, I'm afraid he might have headed somewhere with this truckload of Barbie stuff and is looking to sell it to someone. He may have had some company or some collector lined up before he even left.

"Barbie more or less alluded to the fact that the guy owes her money. Apparently, she was footing all the bills while he was between things. She said she'd email me pictures of him. I came across a lot of collection notices from places that did plastic surgery on the guy. She could well be looking at a complete loss and never see this character again. I'd say there's a pretty good chance he's either still in L.A., or he's headed to somewhere like Florida."

Louie shook his head as Mike delivered a beer for me and another glass to Louie. I pulled a twenty from my wallet and handed it to Mike.

He smiled and said, "I'm afraid it's gonna take another one of those."

"Forty bucks?" I said and looked over at Louie.

"Well, you should have come back sooner," Louie whined. "I was sitting here all by myself for the better part of two hours."

I pulled out another twenty and handed it to Mike. My wallet was now empty, and out the sixty bucks I got

from the ATM little more than two hours ago. I'd purchased two beers for me. One of which I hadn't even
started.

"I told you I was running up your tab," Louie said.

We continued on for the better part of another hour.
Louie even bought a round. I was home before nine and
let Morton out. I turned on my laptop to see if Barbie
might have sent the images of Ken, but she hadn't. I let
Morton back in, settled in to watch a movie, and
promptly fell asleep. I headed up to bed a little after midnight. Fortunately, Morton was asleep on his pillow. I
climbed into bed, and my alarm woke me in the morning.

I'd been on my laptop for the better part of an hour
before I heard Morton upstairs. He appeared in the
kitchen a few minutes later, stretched, and wandered
over for the first of a number of head scratches. I let him
outside, poured another cup of coffee, and when I returned to my laptop, there was an email from Barbie.

I opened the email, and she almost sounded sane.
*'Three Ken images attached below. Podcast at 9:30 just
click on the link. Gotta go!'*

I clicked on the first image. Arnold Rudolph Wazinski, AKA Ken Carson of Barbie fame, looked like an
absolute idiot. If his intention was to look like a plastic
doll, well, I guess he achieved that goal. I wanted to
punch him just because. His hair, dark along the sides,
was closely trimmed, longer and blonde on the top and
combed back. There wasn't a wrinkle on his face.

Whether that was from pulling the skin tight or stuffing his face with Botox, I could only guess.

The bridge on his nose appeared in an unnatural razor-sharp line. His chin must have had some plastic piece inserted to give it the look of a 'Y' shape with a dimple in the middle. If you took a photo of it and isolated the chin, you'd swear it was someone's butt.

His eyes were little more than slits. I went through all three images. Each one worse than the previous. The one with the swimsuit was by far the worst. It had been taken on a beach with him holding a surfboard. I enlarged the image and confirmed my suspicions. The surfboard was Styrofoam. I studied the blonde hair, clearly implants. Small groupings of blonde hair were arranged in evenly spaced lines all across the top of his head. He sported six-pack abs, and I remembered one of the collection letters had listed a down payment of a thousand dollars and an outstanding balance of forty-eight hundred for the stomach surgery.

Now, I wanted to hit him in the stomach.

Eight

orton and I were in the office before Louie arrived. I was on my second cup of coffee when I saw Louie pull in behind my Crown Vic. I dumped the remnants from his coffee mug, refilled it, and settled into my chair as the stairs began to creak. A minute later, Louie entered the office. He gave a nod, settled in behind his picnic table desk, and pulled the coffee mug closer.

I brought the Ken pictures Barbie had sent up on my laptop. Once Louie had his requisite three or four sips of coffee, he asked, "So what's new? You ever get any images of this friend of Barbie's driving the truck?"

I set my laptop on the picnic table and said, "See for yourself."

Louie spun the laptop toward him, took a sip of coffee, and proceeded to spit coffee all over my laptop screen. "Oh, man, sorry about that," he said, wiping the screen with a napkin he pulled out of the wastebasket. The napkin was from Rooster's and was covered with bar-b-cue sauce.

"This is the Ken guy?" Louie asked.

"Yeah, in all his plastic surgery glory."

"What did it cost him to have all of that done? God, it's awful. He looks absolutely ridiculous."

"It cost a lot of money over the last three years. Most of which he hasn't paid, based on the invoices I've got." I placed the file with the invoices and the letter from the L.A. city attorney's office next to the laptop.

Louie opened the file and did a quick page through. "You weren't kidding. This guy really is a nut job."

"Yeah, what do you think the odds are he's trying to sell her Barbie collection right now?"

"I'd say there's a very strong possibility," Louie said. He didn't bother to look up but continued to page through the stack of past due notices, all the while shaking his head. "Even if he's financially solid now, he's screwed for the next seven to ten years as far as a credit rating goes. Absolutely incredible. And no idea where in the hell he is?"

"No, but two of those credit card bills have what looks like a card number and maybe a password written on it. I'm going to see if I can access that information online."

Louie pushed the laptop toward me, took another sip of coffee, and said, "Good luck with that."

I settled in at my desk and brought up the credit card site. I typed in the email address for Arnold Wazinski. The email address appeared again, and when I clicked on it, the password appeared. I held my breath. After a long moment, amazingly, the site came up, and I was in. I clicked on the recent activity box, and a number of debit listings popped up—eight different gas payments from L.A. up to Minnesota along with six McDonalds payments.

The credit card payments literally tracked the guys' movements along the route he told Barbie he was going to take. The last gas payment was at a BP gas station four days ago in Woodbury, Minnesota, a St. Paul suburb. Which meant he'd made it up here at least four days ago. That pretty much corresponded to a normal time frame for driving the two thousand miles from L.A. to St. Paul. The question was, where was he now?

It was almost nine-thirty, and I went back to Barbie's email with the images and clicked on the link she'd sent to her Barbie Doll website. I waited maybe thirty seconds to be admitted to the group, and suddenly, there was Barbie's head filling my screen.

"… take Taffy for a walk with Ken. Okay, and now let's talk with Christine in Seattle. Good morning, early bird it's only seven-thirty out there. Thanks for joining us."

"Thanks for having me, Barbie. Just wanted to brag that I ran across a complete Barbie Nurse set at an estate sale last week, all original from 1961."

"Oh, how exciting," Barbie said. "Now, you're sure it's original? Because they rereleased it, I think in two thousand ten."

"It's original, in the original box. Absolutely gorgeous."

"What in the hell are you listening to?" Louie asked as he shoved his laptop in his briefcase.

"Barbie's podcast. It says she's got three hundred and nineteen people watching right now."

"Yeah, including you. We'll see how much of that you can stand," Louie said. "I've got to meet with a client in fifteen minutes. You going to be around this afternoon?"

"I'm not sure. It depends if I can locate this character for Barbie. According to his credit card activity, he's been up here for at least four days."

Louie shook his head. "And I thought I had crazy clients."

"Yeah, afraid I have to agree, it's really starting to go that way."

Louie couldn't have been out of the office for more than a minute or two when I heard the stairs begin to creak. I glanced over at his picnic table, wondering what he'd forgotten. My phone rang as the creaking seemed to grow louder, Louie calling.

"Louie, I can hear you coming back up the stairs. You okay?"

"That's not me, Dev. I'm in my car. Just a heads-up. It's Tubby Gustafson and that other fat guy with him. They pulled into my parking place as I pulled away."

"Shit." I turned off the Barbie podcast just as the door opened, and Fat Freddy Zimmerman waddled in. Tubby Gustafson appeared a moment later. Red-faced and gasping for breath. Both of them wore blue face masks, which only made their faces appear even more red.

Fat Freddy pulled a client chair back for Tubby to sit in. Tubby collapsed into the chair, pulling what appeared to be a silk cloth from the front pocket on his suit coat and proceeded to pat his forehead and the area beneath his chins.

"Haskell, you'd think at some point you'd learn. But typical, I'm probably giving credit where it's not due."

"Wonderful to see you, Mr. Gustafson," I lied. "To what do I owe the pleasure?"

"Take my word for it, Haskell. This is anything but a pleasure for me."

Nine

Fat Freddy pulled out a client chair and sat down. Tubby said, "Honest to God, Haskell. Why do I bother?" Tubby closed his eyes and took three or four deep breaths. He appeared to be a bit calmer when he opened his eyes and shook his head. "When do you intend to find someplace more suitable for your clientele, Haskell. You will continue to fail if you remain here. The look of this place, that staircase. I'm lucky the thing didn't collapse on us as we made our ascent."

Actually, Tubby had a point. I figured seven hundred plus pounds between the two of them, and the building was close to a hundred years old. I was lucky the staircase wasn't in splinters.

"Thank you so much for making the effort, sir. How may I help you?"

"A bit of a problem has developed in my real estate locations, and against my better judgement, I'm thinking this might be an opportunity for you to improve your skills."

"My skills?"

Tubby snapped his fingers at Fat Freddy, who pulled out a stack of paper stapled together and handed it to Tubby. Tubby glanced at the first two sheets and tossed them onto my desk. "See for yourself, Haskell."

I reached for the sheets of paper and began to page through them. A black and white image was on each sheet. There were five pages in all. I recognized the images as the interior of one of Tubby's clubs. Nasty's as a matter of fact. Not just a bar but a pretty popular strip club as well. The first image was a giveaway because it was an interior shot of the entrance, and above the door was a sign that read, 'Thank you for being Nasty. Hurry back!' Someone had spray-painted in black a rough image of a hand giving the finger over the sign.

"I looked up at Tubby and said, "Who did this?"

Tubby shook his head and said, "You see, Haskell, if I knew that, I wouldn't be forced to waste my time talking to the likes of you."

"Is there a way you think I can help?"

Tubby let off a sigh. "Yes, Haskell. Against my better judgement I would like you to catch the individual responsible for this attack on my business. You can see the damage they created. Go ahead, look at all those pages. There's a different image on each page. It cost me money to get everything taken care of and back to normal. I hasten to add, protecting all of my customers from the heartbreak of seeing their favorite establishment defaced."

"Thank God you had your customers' best interests in mind. So, I'm not quite clear, here, sir. Exactly what do you want me to do? Investigate and try to learn who's responsible?"

"No, Haskell, I have a difficult time believing you would be capable of conducting a responsible investigation. What I want you to do is prevent this from happening again."

"I'm still not quite following, sir."

"Which is exactly why you won't be conducting an investigation. Haskell, I want you to be there during the night, so this can't happen again."

"During the night? But, don't you have customers, bouncers, security people? People who would be there during business hours and by their mere presence would eliminate anyone from—"

"Haskell, what in the world does it take? I'm not talking business hours. I need someone on the premises after business hours when these places are closed. I need you there from two until seven in the morning when my cleaning crew arrives. If someone should venture in with a can of spray paint, you have my permission to shoot on sight."

"That may be a little harsh."

"Not compared to what I'd like to do to them. Now, Nasty's has already been attacked. We'll position you at the Lumberyard, Dolly's, Tootsies, Scuttlebutt, or the Landing Strip. I'm thinking we'll move you to a new locale every night. That way, we'll keep them guessing.

Whoever did this is bound to attempt to assault my good name again, and I want to be prepared. That's where you'll come in. Which location do you think is most susceptible to an attack?"

"I really have no idea, sir, and I'm just wondering if perhaps Freddy's crew wouldn't be a better choice from a security standpoint. You could cover every place, every night. If it's just me working, there's a very good chance I could be on-site, and whoever did this would just damage another locale."

"All of which suggests you should chose where you plan to be tonight carefully," Tubby said and gave Freddy a nod. Freddy pulled back the chair as Tubby rose to his feet. "I'll expect to hear from you before five this evening. Let me know where you plan to be, and I'll have Frederick alert the staff."

Freddy flashed a quick smile.

"But I really have no idea where I'm—"

"Silencio," Tubby shouted. "Honest to God, if I wanted to hear the problems involved, I would have done this myself. But, once again, foolishly, I've provided you with an opportunity for success. Do you even know what success is? What it means, Haskell?"

"Umm, I think it means getting whoever painted graffiti on the walls of your establishment, sir."

Tubby slowly clapped his hands a half-dozen times. "Very good, Haskell. I'll expect to hear from you no later than five this evening. Frederick, the door."

Fat Freddy waddled over to the office door and opened it. Tubby stepped out of the office, and a second later, the staircase began to creak. Freddy gave me an evil looking grin, flashed me the finger, and left. I watched out the window as they waddled across the street. No doubt the longest walk either one had made in days. Freddy held the rear door on the Escalade open as Tubby oozed into the back seat. He closed the door once Tubby was seated and took a moment to give me the finger again just in case I'd missed it the first time.

Once their car was out of sight, I picked up the images of the graffiti spray-painted on the walls of Nasty's. The walls had all been painted an off-white color. After all, who would be looking at the walls when there were dancers on stage. But, apparently, the walls represented a blank canvas to someone. For the first time, I noticed that Tubby's name was included in most of the graffiti. His name was spray-painted on every wall. 'Tubby spreads disease! Tubby is endangering the public! Tubby is cheating you! Tubby Gustafson — Criminal mind!'

That more or less left the door open to all segments of society. First, they had to know Tubby owned the business, and they had to be able to get in there after hours, undetected. Or, maybe it was someone who wandered in forty-five minutes before closing and hid in the men's room or under a table until the place was empty.

God, I didn't want to do this. I set Tubby's images aside and went back to my laptop and Arnold Wazinski's credit card activity. I printed off the list of purchases running across the country and the three images that Barbie had sent me of Arnold Rudolph Wazinski, AKA Ken Carson. I clipped Morton's leash on his collar, and we drove out to the Woodbury BP gas station.

Ten

The BP station had six gas pumps, all positioned beneath a large white overhang edged in green and gold. I parked alongside the station next to the ice machine and went inside. Along with buying gas, you could purchase all sorts of overpriced snacks and sodas.

There was one woman ahead of me in the process of paying four dollars for a black coffee. Once she left, the kid behind the counter gave me a look that suggested, 'What do you want?'

I pulled out my P.I. card, flashed it at him, and proceeded to tell him I was tracking a credit card scam that had been used in a purchase at the location four days ago. Nothing seemed to resonate with him until I mentioned I wanted to view their security tapes. He thought about that for half a second and before he said, "You better talk to the manager. Hang on, and I'll call her."

A moment later, a woman stepped out of an office in the back and walked over. I figured her for late forties or early fifties. She had salt and pepper colored hair tied in a bun. She was maybe a few pounds overweight, but you'd never call her fat. A name tag that read Marie was pinned over her left breast. "What is it, Dennis?"

"This guy has something about a credit card scam and wanted to look at some tapes."

"Hi, Marie. My name is Dev Haskell. I'm working on an investigation with the state," I lied. "There's been a fairly large effort to use illegal credit cards at a series of stations. We've been tracking the purchases across the country, one of which happened at your operation four days ago."

I pulled out the list of purchases I'd printed off and said, "Yeah, happened just a little after three in the afternoon. I'm wondering if you've got security tapes I could look at."

"A credit card scam?"

"Yes, a number of individuals purchasing thousands of dollars of fuel and supplies using bogus cards. I've got a list of purchases this individual has made across the country, along with some images we've been able to obtain."

"Come on back to my office. Actually, we don't store those images on tapes anymore. We stopped doing that a few years ago. Nowadays, everything is stored digitally up in the cloud." She raised her eyebrows as if to suggest 'the cloud' was some magic place, which I guess it more or less is. "If you have a date and a time, I should be able to locate the individual relatively easy."

"That's very kind of you. Thank you for taking the time. Hopefully, we can get these guys before they do some real damage," I said.

"I'm just surprised card access was approved. The company has a very good system. We probably have two or three people daily that are denied for whatever reason, and we just tell them there's nothing we can do, and they should contact their credit card company."

We walked down a little hall, past the two restrooms to a door labeled manager. She slipped a key in the lock and opened the door. "Excuse the mess. Grab a chair, and I'll see if I can't get the image up."

Her desk had a half-eaten sandwich resting on top of a manila folder. A number of black, three-ring binders were lined up along the front of the desk. Just behind the desk were twelve black and white screens with images of all the gas pumps, the sides of the building, and three different angles covering the inside of the store. "Tell me that date and time again," she said.

"I believe your operation is the sixth one listed," I said and handed her the list of credit card activity. She sat down in her desk chair, spun around facing the screens, and began typing on a keyboard. The images weren't a smooth running film but rather jerky frozen images, taken maybe every three or four seconds. The screen in the upper left corner flashed a blank image of a pump with no vehicle next to it, same thing on the next two screens.

On the fourth screen, a truck pulled in, and there he was, Arnold Rudolph Wazinski, Barbie's Ken Carson, in all his glory. He climbed out from behind the wheel of a white truck, larger than a panel van, but by no means a semi. He inserted his credit card, and waited a few seconds before he removed the nozzle and began pumping gas. In the black and white image, he wore what looked like blue plaid shorts and a dark short sleeve shirt with a v-neck edged in white.

"Oh my. You know, in a strange way, he looks familiar, maybe. What an odd duck. I wonder if he's been in here before. What's his name?"

"Arnold Rudolph Wazinski."

She began writing on a yellow legal tablet. "Can you spell that last name for me, please?"

I spelled it out for her.

"I'm sure I've seen him somewhere, but I don't know. Just very strange looking."

"He's had a good deal of plastic surgery."

"Injured in a fire or an accident? You know, now that you say that, it's evident, even in this grainy image. He doesn't have any wrinkles," she laughed.

"There wasn't an accident. He's had thousands of dollars of plastic surgery, all in an effort to appear more like the Barbie doll Ken. In fact, he's in the process of changing his name to Ken Carson."

"What? You're kidding. Although now that you say that, yeah. That's where I've seen him before, with Barbie. Oh, my God," she said and laughed. "You know, after a couple of martinis, he could get interesting."

"Any chance you could get the license number on that truck?"

"I can't believe it, Ken, at my station. Let me bring that vehicle up." She typed in some code, and the screen on the far end began flashing an image every few seconds. For maybe twenty seconds, the lane leading back out to the road was blank, and suddenly there it was, the white truck. It flashed three times across the screen. Marie halted the program, enlarged the screen, and focused on the license plate. "There it is, California plates."

The plate was white with a blue number across the center of the plate. California was written in script across the top and dmv.ca.gov at the bottom, both in red. A tag in the upper left corner read AUG, and an orange tag in the upper right corner read 2020. I pulled out my notebook and wrote down the license information." Any chance you can print that plate off?"

She hit a button on the keyboard, and the printer suddenly started up. "Let me get you a couple of images of this Ken character, too. I'm going to print a set off for me. I can't wait to show the girls. Absolutely crazy." She brought up the images of Ken placing the nozzle into the gas tank and hit the button. She handed me the images and kept three for herself.

"Here's my card," she said. "Please give me a call if anything develops. I'll alert the home office. In six minutes, he'll be unable to purchase from our pumps anywhere in the country."

I took her card and said, "Anything happens, I'll let you know. Thanks for your time, Marie."

"Oh, thank you, Mr. Hassle. You've no idea. You've really made my day. Let me just alert Dennis. The least I can do is give you a coffee on your way out. I can't believe it. Ken was actually here," she said and laughed.

I grabbed a decaf coffee from Dennis on the way out. I climbed into the Crown Vic, and Morton and I headed back to the office.

Eleven

I stopped at a McDonalds on the way back to the office and got a Bacon Cheeseburger and a strawberry shake. Morton stuck his head between the front seats and stared at the McDonalds bag for the next ten minutes. Once we were in the office, he followed me to my desk, never taking his eyes off the bag. I opened my bottom desk drawer and tossed him a biscuit. He seemed happy enough to settle for that and headed back to his pillow so he wouldn't have to share.

I phoned Barbie and ended up leaving a message. "Hi Barbie, this is Dev. I've picked up some information. Give me a call when you have a moment. Oh, I was able to catch a couple of minutes of your podcast this morning. Very good. Talk to you later."

I pulled the Bacon Cheeseburger out of the bag, and Morton gave me a look just in case there might be a chance for him. There wasn't. Louie parked behind my car just as I finished my lunch. A moment later, I could hear him making his way up the stairs.

He entered the office red-faced, although not as bad as Fat Freddy or Tubby Gustafson earlier in the day. I waited patiently for a couple of minutes before he was able to talk.

"How'd things go with Tubby?"

"Not well," I replied. "Some nutcase got into one of his strip clubs, Nasty's. They spray-painted Tubby's name all over the place, saying he's cheating people and stuff like that." I tossed the images of the graffiti from Nasty's onto the picnic table.

Louie paged through the images. "Cheating people. No doubt that's true, and you know as well as I do that's the least of his activities. So who did this?" Louie asked, and chuckled as he paged through the images again.

"That's what I'm supposed to find out, I think."

"You think? What's that mean?"

"He wants me working as an overnight security guard from two in the morning until the cleaning crew comes in at 7:00 or 8:00."

"You mean you're just going to sit there in the dark and what? Hope someone knocks on the door and they've got a can of spray paint? He's got more than one location, doesn't he?"

"Yeah, and as far as I know, there won't be anyone else at the other locations. He's got six clubs."

"That doesn't make any sense. What happens when one of the other places is defaced and you're cooling your heels in some joint across town?"

"They plan to have me in a different location every night."

"That makes no sense at all. Can't you just tell him you don't want to do this?"

"I tried that. Told him he should just hire someone to sit at each place, but he didn't want to hear it. He's convinced moving me around every night will keep whoever did this off-balance, and the problem will somehow be solved."

"Does that mean you're going to be working for Tubby from now on?"

"No, nothing like that. I don't want to work for Tubby. Just for starters, I know he doesn't plan to pay me. When it's time to pay me, he'll say something like I owe him money for getting the job opportunity and the chance to update my résumé."

"It sounds crazy," Louie said.

"You're telling me."

"So why don't you just tell him no?"

"Probably because I'd end up in traction over at Regions Hospital within the hour."

"Oh, yeah, I suppose. I guess I didn't consider that aspect."

"I don't know. I'll come up with something. I just don't know what."

Louie paged through the graffiti images again. "You know, this stuff doesn't look like some protest against a strip club. This is targeted specifically at Tubby. There's no mention of women's rights, the Me Too movement, or some right-wing religious group. There's nothing like that. How many people even know Tubby owns these clubs? He's got a series of shell companies listed as owning the places, doesn't he?"

"Yeah, he does, but someone apparently found out about it and tracked Tubby down."

"Let me know if I can help," Louie said.

"Well, my standard advice to everyone is to stay away from anything that involves Tubby Gustafson. I'll just have to figure something out."

In reality, over the course of the rest of the afternoon, I tried to figure out an angle and kept coming up empty-handed. I phoned Tubby at ten minutes before five. The phone rang a half-dozen times before someone answered.

"What?" whoever answered growled. It clearly wasn't Tubby.

"Tub, err, umm, Mr. Gustafson please."

"Who's calling?"

"Dev Haskell. He wanted me to call him before five."

"Hang on. I'll see if he wants to talk to you."

Tubby came on the line a couple of minutes later. "Haskell, I'd say I'm sorry to have kept you waiting, but I'm not. What did you decide?"

"I've really thought this over, sir, and as much as I would like to help you, I really can't see this particular action working for you."

"Correct me if I'm wrong, but are you telling me no?"

"No, sir, not at all. I'm merely suggesting that, if your intention is preventing another graffiti incident, wouldn't it make sense to have someone at every location? You've got six locations. I can only be at one place at a time. The odds are stacked against us, sir. If we take Nasty's off the list, that still only gives us a twenty percent chance of catching whoever is responsible. I think this would work best if you had someone stationed at every location. I'm more than willing to play my part and help, but it seems like you're taking an awfully big chance, sir."

"Haskell, I expect you to be at the Lumberyard no later than one-thirty this morning. Remember, they're on bar time, so the clock is set fifteen minutes ahead. Be sure you're there."

"But Mr. Gustafson, what if… Hello? Hello? Anyone there?"

Apparently, I was going to be working the night shift. I placed a call to Barbie and left another message. "Hi Barbie, let's talk tomorrow morning. I'm investigating some things for you tonight," I lied and promptly hung up.

Twelve

I let Morton out into the backyard a little after eight. We settled down in front of the tv. I set the alarm on my phone for midnight and fell asleep at some point. When the alarm woke me, Morton was already upstairs and asleep in the bedroom. I made myself a sandwich and went online for a few minutes checking for any Arnold Wazinski credit card transactions. Nothing came up, and at a little after one, I headed over to the Lumberyard.

The Lumberyard is set on the northern edge of the city, literally. It's on the corner of Larpenteur Avenue and Rice Street, facing Larpenteur. The city limits run down the middle of Larpenteur. The Lumberyard is located in St. Paul. Just a snowballs throw across the street is the suburb of Falcon Heights. At one-twenty in the morning on a weeknight, the traffic was pretty light, and I made the drive in ten minutes.

I pulled into the parking lot. The Lumberyard was the middle business in a five-unit 1960s strip mall. The two units on either side had signs in the window that read, 'Commercial Space Available.' The Lumberyard had a white front with a sign on the roof, spelling out THE LUMBERYARD in blueish neon letters the length of the unit. At the end of the sign, the word DANCERS in red neon flashed off and on.

With the pandemic still going on, I pulled on a surgical mask, grabbed my sandwich, and headed into the place. The entrance was a steel door, painted white. Including me, the girl dancing onstage under colored lights, and the bartender, there were now six people in the place. One of the three customers was just finishing up sending someone a text message, and as I approached the bar, he slid off his stool and headed for the door.

The bar was rectangular and built maybe six feet from the back wall. It left just enough room to climb off your stool and not disturb other customers when you left. There were maybe twenty small tables between the bar and the stage. A row of chairs all along the front of the stage allowed you to sit and lay dollar bills on the stage for some 'special' attention from the dancer. The far wall had five booths along it, all empty.

The girl on stage looked bored out of her mind as she slowly swung back and forth on a brass pole. The two remaining customers were ignoring her and apparently telling one another jokes, based on their laughing.

I waited for the bartender to finish putting away beer bottles in a cooler behind the bar. When he stood up, he seemed surprised to see me and said, "I'm sorry, sir. We're closing down for the night, and we're no longer serving. She's just finishing her last number," he said and flashed a two-second smile.

As if on cue, the music suddenly stopped, and the woman on stage picked up a pink lace negligee in the corner and sauntered off stage in her silver sequined platform heels.

The two guys at the table laughed, and one of them said, "No, I don't believe it. That's crazy."

"Honest to God's truth, that's what happened," the other said, and they laughed again.

The bartender got a frown on his face, walked down to the end of the bar, turned a dial, and the lights came on in the room.

The two guys looked around, seemed surprised they were the only people left, and slowly headed toward the door, still laughing.

"Time to go, sir. We're closed for the night," the bartender said, this time a little more forcefully, and he didn't bother to smile.

"I've been hired to work security here tonight."

"Security?" He half-laughed and picked up a note from behind the bar. "You're Hassle?"

Why even argue. "Yeah, that's me."

"Got the call earlier tonight. Can't say as I envy you. I doubt we had a dozen customers the entire night. I'm looking forward to getting the hell out of here and going home. You been here before?"

"Yeah, but it's been a while."

"Let me lock that front door, and I'll give you the quick tour." He stepped out from behind the bar, hurried over to the steel front door, and locked it. "Follow me," he said, and we walked down a hallway past the two restrooms. He stopped at the door marked private, knocked a couple times, and opened the door. The dancer was sitting in a chair in front of a large mirror, naked and smoking. The smell from whatever she was smoking drifted out of the room; it clearly wasn't tobacco.

"Hey Tracey, get dressed. I'm shutting it down and want to get the hell out of here. Five minutes, darling."

She took a long drag and blew another cloud of smoke at the mirror.

He pulled the door closed, shook his head, and walked ten more feet down the hall past a door marked office and to a door marked 'Emergency Exit.'

"Here's the back door. You push this handle marked emergency exit, and the door will open to the alley, and it'll also call the cops and fire department. Don't open it. If you do, the cost for cops and the fire department will be coming out of your pocket. Last time I checked, it was something like eight hundred and fifty bucks. The dressing room and the office are locked. We monitor all the beverages at the bar, so don't get any ideas about helping yourself to the liquor. Somewhere between seven and eight, the cleaning crew comes in. They'll knock on the door and let themselves in with a key. My understanding is, once they're here, you're free to go. Questions?"

I shook my head.

"Good." We headed back toward the bar and stopped at the dressing room door again. He knocked, and he opened the door. Tracey was just stubbing out whatever she had been smoking. "Let's go, Tracey. I want to get out of here," he said and pulled the door closed.

"Might as well make yourself comfortable, Dude. Grab one of the booths or stretch out on the stage."

I walked over to the booths, set the bag with my sandwich on the table, and stretched out. The bartender grabbed the two beer bottles off the table where the last guys had been sitting. As he walked around behind the bar, Tracey strutted out into the main room. She wore a light-colored t-shirt with some logo I didn't recognize, tight jeans, and what looked like running shoes.

"Any chance for another beverage before I go?" she asked.

"Wish I could darling, but I gotta get out of here. Come on. I'll let you out."

She grew a disappointed look on her face, which seemed to have no effect on the bartender.

He hurried over to the door, opened it, and said, "Have a nice night." He quickly locked the door the moment Tracey stepped outside. He shook his head, walked back behind the bar, and grabbed a set of car keys. "Any questions before I go, Hassle?"

"No, thanks for the tour."

"Enjoy. I'll lock the door from the outside," he said. He gave a quick look around, flicked some switches behind the bar that turned most of the lights off, and quickly headed for the door. A couple of seconds after he closed the door, I heard the lock click in place.

I slid out of the booth and looked around the place. The lights were off on the stage, and it actually looked a little grim. I noticed four cameras, one in each corner of the room with a small green light, which meant they would be recording any movements I made. I settled back into the booth, unwrapped my sandwich, and took my time eating it.

Once I finished eating, I crumpled up the cling film and walked over to the bar. I tossed the film in a wastebasket, walked back to the booth, and checked the time on my cellphone. Not quite 2:30. Five and a half hours to go, it was going to be a long night.

Thirteen

Two voices speaking what sounded like Spanish woke me from my sleep. I gradually opened my eyes, turned my head from side to side, and heard my neck crack. I slowly sat up in the booth and glanced toward the empty stage. I rolled my shoulders, cleared my throat, and looked toward the bar.

A short woman with dark hair wearing jeans and a t-shirt was holding a mop and staring wide-eyed at me. I guessed she was maybe mid-twenties. Her lips were moving, but no sound was coming out. She dropped the mop and ran toward the restrooms shouting, "Luis. Luis. Ayuda, un hombre. Un hombre está aquí afuera. Luis!" Since it was in Spanish, I had no idea what she was shouting.

A moment later, the door to the men's room swung open, and a guy stepped out carrying a long-handled white brush, the kind used for cleaning toilets. The woman shouted again and pointed at me as I slid out of the booth.

"What the hell are you doing here?" he asked and headed toward me.

He was a couple of inches shorter than me, but what he lacked in height he made up in muscle. His wide neck flowed into muscular shoulders and arms with large biceps and forearms. He headed toward me, holding his arms in a half-cocked position that left no question as to what his intention could be. "How in the hell did you get in here? I locked the damn door."

I had my hands up in surrender mode. "They had me doing security in here last night after they closed. Someone broke into one of their places the other night, Nasty's, and spray-painted graffiti on the walls."

"Oh, I heard about that. Matter of fact, one of my nephews was on the crew that repainted the place. Had it done in three hours, got paid double time."

"Yeah, well, they're kind of worried about something like that happening at the other places, so I was here last night, and I'll probably be at some other place tonight. My name's Dev Haskell. Sorry to have upset your partner there. I must have dozed off at some point and didn't hear you guys come in."

"You must have really been out. We've been working for the better part of an hour."

"An hour. What time is it?" I asked and reached for my phone.

"It's a little after eight."

"After eight? Oh man, I better hurry home. My dog is probably clawing at the back door to get outside. Nice to meet you. Your name is Luis?" I asked.

"Yeah, Luis Ortez. This is my partner, Mariana," he said, nodding toward the woman standing off to the side and still clearly keeping her distance from me.

"Hola," I said, nodded, and smiled.

She gave a slight nod in response and took a half-step closer to Luis.

"I had better get going. Sorry to have just suddenly appeared. Is this the only place you clean in the morning or do they have you moving around to all the different locations?"

He shook his head and said, "This is the one we clean. Let's go. I'll let you out, and you can get home and take care of that four-legged friend of yours." He headed to the door, unlocked it, and held it open for me. As soon as I stepped outside, I heard the lock click behind me. I hurried over to my car, the only vehicle in the lot other than the blue van I guessed belonged to Luis.

I headed home, and Morton greeted me at the front door. I hurried back to the kitchen and let him out into the backyard. I closed the door and stood studying the mess in the kitchen.

He had somehow managed to open the door beneath the sink and drag out the wastebasket. Napkins, paper towels, cellophane wraps, a chewed up Styrofoam tray that once held a chicken, and an empty spaghetti sauce jar were scattered around the kitchen. Interspersed with all that were the remnants of the meatloaf I had apparently left out on the counter. Even if I'd made it home an hour earlier, I didn't think it would have prevented the mess I was staring at.

Once I finished cleaning up and mopping the floor, I filled Morton's food and water dish and let him back into the house. He didn't even look guilty after leaving the mess in the kitchen. I gave him a good scratch behind the ears before I headed up to take a shower. Once I was showered, shaved, and dressed, I put Morton into the Crown Vic, and we headed down to the office.

Fourteen

Louie was already in the office when we arrived. He was on a phone call and gave me a wave as I opened the door. Morton headed over to his pillow and settled in. I wandered over to my desk, turned on my laptop, and stared out the window at two women waiting for the bus.

"How'd your late night activity go?" Louie asked once he was off the phone.

"In a word, boring. A complete waste of time. I fell asleep at some point and didn't wake up until the cleaning crew had arrived. Scared the hell out of a young woman cleaning the floor. Her boyfriend was cleaning the men's room. He wasn't too happy seeing me in the place."

"No one tried to break in?"

"Let's just say, if they did, I slept through it. At least the walls weren't spray-painted when I woke up this morning."

"I hope for your sake it stays that way. You done with that routine?"

"I wish. I expect to get a call from Tubby sometime this afternoon, sending me to another place. It's just stupid. There's a big part of me that hopes whoever did the spray painting at Nasty's hits another place, and maybe dumbass Tubby will finally figure out that he has to have someone at every location. I think I'm gonna—" My phone ringing interrupted my train of thought. "What do you know? That's probably Tubby calling me now. Why wait for this afternoon when you have the opportunity to ruin my entire day? Haskell Investigations," I answered, trying to sound professional.

"Hi, Dev, sorry I didn't call you back sooner I, umm, had a meeting last night. What did you find out?" Barbie asked.

"Hey, Barbie, nice to hear your voice. How are things?"

"Well, they'd be a lot better if you could find my collection. Your message said you had some information. What have you found out?"

"I learned a couple of things. I don't know where Ken is exactly. But I—"

"He has to be somewhere. He can't just up and disappear, can he?"

"No, he can't, and he hasn't. He's somewhere in town. He used his—"

"Somewhere in town? You mean he finally made it up here. Oh, thank God. He could be here at any moment. Oh, I can't wait to see—"

"Barbie. Barbie, stop interrupting and just listen for a minute, will you?" Dead silence. "Okay, much better. I was able to follow Ken's credit card receipts from L.A. up to Minnesota. He—"

"Minnesota? So he did finally make it up here. Just where in the hell is he? He has my collection, and I need to get going on that, or I might as well forget about my business idea. Hello? Hello, Dev, are you there?"

"I am. But if you interrupt me once more, I'm going to hang up. I want you to be quiet and just listen. Once I'm finished, we can come up with a plan."

"A plan? Oh Dev, what's happened? Is Ken all right? Where's my collection?"

"Are you finished, Barbie?"

"Okay, okay. It's just that… No, wait. Okay, I won't say a word. I promise. Go ahead. I promise."

I shot Louie a look and rolled my eyes. He appeared to be enjoying the situation, and he leaned forward, rested an elbow on the picnic table, placed his chin in his hand, and gave me his undivided attention.

I waited a long five seconds before I said, "Here is what I've learned. Arnold Wazinski, your Ken, arrived up in St. Paul four days ago. He purchased gas out in Woodbury using a credit card. That was the last purchase he made with that particular card. I have images taken from the security camera at the gas station. It was definitely him. I also got the license plate number on the truck, California plates, by the way. As soon as I get off the line with you, I'm going to talk to some folks I know, and hopefully, they'll put a BOLO out on the truck."

"What's a BOLO?" she asked.

"It stands for, Be on the Lookout. If an officer some-where sees the vehicle, they'll probably pull it over. We'll describe the vehicle as stolen and carrying stolen merchandise, and with any luck, maybe someone will see it in the next few days."

"But, if he's finally made it up here—"

"Barbie, he's been up here for four days. Actually, as of this morning, it's now officially five days. Has he contacted you? Have you heard anything from him?"

"No, at least not yet. But why hasn't he called? He's got my phone number."

"If I had to hazard a guess, I would say that, unfor-tunately, he wants to be paid something before he returns the collection to you. And, if he has any brains, he's probably also looking for someone who might be willing to pay more than you to get hold of the collection." Now it was my turn to ask, "Hello. Hello? Barbie, are you there?"

"Dev," she half-shouted, crying. "You're telling me she's been kidnapped. They all have, Barbie, Ken, Skipper, Anastasia, Todd, Tutti, Chelsea, Kelly, Kristine, even Taffy. Oh, my God. Oh, my God. Dev, you have to do something. You have to—"

"Barbie, what are you talking about? Who in the hell are these other people?"

"Who are they? Dev, they're Barbie's family, for God's sake. Well, except for Ken, I mean he's, well, you have to do something. What are you going to do?"

"I think the first thing we're going to do is to find out where, exactly, Arnold Wazinski, AKA Ken is. Do you know, does he have any contacts up here, say in a five-state area?"

"I, I have no idea. As far as I know, he never mentioned anything or anyone. But you know, I guess I maybe never asked him." No surprise there.

"Okay, let me do some more checking. I want to get that BOLO out there. Here's what I want you to do. If Arnold contacts you, try to learn where he is. Invite him to your home, tell him you'll cook him dinner, do anything he wants, but see if you can entice him to your place. Call me if you get in touch with him. I'm not kidding. I don't want you trying to get your collection by yourself because, whatever you try, it's not going to work the way you planned and hoped. Okay? Are you with me?"

"Yeah, yeah, I got it. If he contacts me, I'll call you immediately."

"Good. That's the plan. I'll be doing some other things on this end, and I'll keep you posted. You just stay close to the phone, keep up your podcasts. The key now is to make everything look like it's working just the way you want. If he gets the idea that you're anxious or that you're worried, he's liable to try and charge you all kinds of money, and you don't want that."

"You'll call me the moment you find out where he is?"

"Absolutely. It's going to take some time, but the sooner I get on this, the sooner you'll get your collection back."

"All right, Dev. Call me when you find out where this fool is hiding. Oh, I can't believe I trusted him. I can't wait to get my hands on him."

"Let's make sure you get the collection back before you take that next step."

"I'll be the picture of patience," she said, sounding like she didn't mean a word.

Once I hung up, Louie said, "Gee, that sounded like it went well."

"I can't blame her for being mad. This Ken nutcase has her collection, the one thing, well other than all her plastic surgery, that adds credibility to her podcast and her plans for her Barbie hospital. If I were her, I'd want to kill that idiot, too. I just hope I can find him. I better see if I can get that BOLO lined up now."

I called the general number for the St. Paul Police and asked to speak with Lieutenant Devan Riley. I'd worked with him a couple of times over the years, nothing special. Spent ten minutes talking to him once at a wedding until his wife dragged him away. My call went through to voicemail.

"Hi, you've reached Devan Riley. I'm unable to take your call at the moment. Please leave a brief message, and I'll return your call as soon as possible. Thank you."

"Hello, Devan. This is Dev Haskell. We met a year or two ago at your nephew's wedding. I worked on a cold case for Aaron LaZelle in homicide that I believe you were involved in. I've been tracking an individual who has absconded with a collection valued at somewhere between one-point five and two-point five million. I have his name, his alias, pictures, and a license plate number. If you would give me a call, I'm hoping you could put out a BOLO on him. He's somewhere in the city. I just don't know where. I look forward to hearing from you," I said and disconnected.

"You think Riley will actually do that? Put a Bolo out."

"I know he won't if I don't ask for it. I'm hoping I can get him at least interested."

I was debating my next move on Arnold Wazinski when my phone rang. I was thinking it was probably Barbie calling back with some hair-brained idea. If only!

"Shit," I said to no one in particular. "Tubby Gustafson."

Fifteen

I answered the phone, "Haskell Investigations."

"Haskell, damn it. That same bastard got into Dolly's sometime this morning and spray-painted graffiti on all the walls." Dolly's was Tubby's strip club up in Rosemount, in the next county, actually. About as far away from the Lumberyard as you can get.

"Sorry to hear that, sir. I was on duty at the Lumberyard from close until the cleaning crew arrived early this morning. There was absolutely no activity at the Lumberyard, sir."

"Damn it, Haskell. You've got to do something. How in the hell are they getting in? There's no sign of illegal entry, nothing broken. They must have a damn key."

"What did the police say?"

"The police? I don't want them prowling around in my businesses. Damn it, Haskell, you're supposed to catch whoever in the hell is doing this."

"With all due respect, sir. It was my suggestion to have one of your, umm, employees stationed in each of your facilities. Now, with another one of these attacks, it appears you are being targeted by an individual or individuals who know what they're doing."

"What they're doing is costing me money. I've got a crew up there now, repainting the interior walls."

"Were the graffiti comments directed specifically at you again? Did they mention the adult business, or women's rights, or anything along those lines?"

"Of course they were directed at me, you moron. What? Did you think it would be a complaint about the entertainment?"

"No, sir, I just find it interesting that the comments don't make any suggestion about women's rights or sexual harassment. It's all directed at you, so somehow, this individual knows that you own these businesses. Despite the efforts you've put in place to more or less disguise the fact." I cringed, waiting for Tubby to explode.

"Wait a minute. Couldn't you get a handwriting sample from this nonsense painted on the walls?"

"No, sir, that might work if we had a note on paper, but the characteristics are ill-defined with spray-painted graffiti. Even so, they would only be helpful in pointing the finger at a suspect already in custody." I held my breath and waited for the next stupid idea.

Instead, Tubby said, "So what do you suggest?"

"The same thing I said yesterday. Have someone stationed in every facility after they close."

"I'm not going to do that. I'm dealing with an element of, shall we just say privacy for the time being. I don't want the word out that this is happening. That's why you're involved. If word of this gets out, I'll know it was you who leaked it, and let me just remind you, there will be hell to pay. I want you over at the Landing Strip tonight. Get there before close, and you can leave once the cleaning crew arrives."

"But again, if this individual attacks another location, there's nothing I can do about that, sir."

"I suggest if you value your life, you had better figure out something and fast, Haskell. The Landing Strip, tonight. Be there, or you'll pay the price!" Tubby shouted and disconnected.

"That didn't sound like it went your way. I could hear him shouting over here," Louie said.

"Mmm, there's more going on here than he's letting me know. Someone has access to these places. It's gotta be a manager or a connection with the cleaning crews or something."

"You ever think it might be the painters?" Louie asked.

"Mmm, I don't know. If you did this and Tubby got ahold of you, it wouldn't be worth it. I'm not kidding. Given half a chance, he's going to kill whoever is responsible. I almost hope we don't catch whoever is doing this. That's probably one of the reasons he doesn't want the police involved. Last night, when I was at the Lumberyard, there were four security cameras in the main room. I'm guessing there's another one in the dressing room and in the office." A thought suddenly popped into my head. "Funny Tubby didn't mention his security cameras recording someone spray-painting graffiti in the middle of the night."

"Like you said, Dev, there seems to be more to this than meets the eye."

Louie left for the courthouse about an hour later. I took Morton for a walk, came back to the office and promptly fell asleep in my desk chair. The stairs creaking woke me, and a moment later, Louie entered the office. He gave me a nod and settled in behind his picnic table. I checked my phone. It was after four, and I'd slept for the better part of the afternoon. The good news was I'd had a dream about Barbie and Ken, and I had an idea.

I phoned Barbie. She answered on the third ring. "Please tell me you've found my collection."

"I wish that was the case. But I have an idea. You mentioned that Ken was going to open up a division in your hospital."

"Yes, the Dream House. At least that was our plan. Now I don't know if that would be a very wise move on my part."

"Were you going to do this legally? You know, with paperwork, insurance, and everything?"

"Oh, yeah. Because I'll be advertising online, I have to provide all that information. I had to provide them with my tax number, social security, the business address. You either give it to them, or you're relegated to the dark side of the internet, and there's no money in that."

"You wouldn't happen to have Arnold Wazinski's social security number and his birthdate, would you?"

"Well, yes, I do, but what good will that do? I'm afraid he's just going to ignore the work I plan on doing, and he'll establish his own organization."

"Does he have your information, social security, bank accounts, that sort of thing?"

"No, I wouldn't give that to him, Dev. Why? What are you thinking?"

"I'm thinking he's purchasing fuel and food with a credit card. He's either sleeping in the truck or he's at a motel somewhere. If we could get that card canceled, it would add a degree of pressure and might force him to get in touch."

"Mmm, I kind of like the sound of that."

"Find that information and send it to me."

"I know right where it is. I'll have it coming your way in just a moment. He also gave me passwords. Actually, we exchanged them. I changed mine the other night."

"Has he been in your accounts?"

"Not that I could see, and now he doesn't have the current password, so he can't. I should never have given him that information."

"Send that stuff to me. I'll be waiting for it."

"Give me ten minutes," she said and disconnected.

"Your afternoon go okay?" I asked Louie.

"Yeah, took a lot longer than I expected, but in the end, we got most of what we wanted, so I'm a happy camper. You go anywhere?"

I shook my head and lied, "No, just worked here."

A few minutes later, I got an email from Barbie. Along with listing Arnold's social security number, birth date, and bank account, she gave me five passwords, one more ridiculous than the next; 'Im*Arnold, Arnold12345, Open-UP, password, barbiedoll.'

I pulled out the invoices I had from his credit card companies. The card number, expiration date, and security code were handwritten on the invoice. I called the customer service number, went through about five different recorded messages, each offering a half-dozen different choices before I got to a live body.

"Hi. Thank you for calling. My name is James. How may I be of service?"

Based on the heavy accent, I had a tough time believing his name was James. "Thanks for taking my call, James. I lost my credit card, and so I need to cancel it. Actually, I need to cancel both of them."

"I am sorry to hear this. I can do this for you immediately. Before we begin, may I please have the last four digits of your social security number?"

I gave him Arnold's last four digits.

"Excellent. Thank you, Mr. Arnold. Would you please give me your date of birth?"

I did that.

"This is excellent. Both cards have now been canceled. We will be emailing you a list of recent activity. There is an outstanding balance of six hundred and ninety-one dollars on one card and five hundred and eleven dollars on another. Would you prefer to make a payment today?"

"You have my bank account information there? The one I pay from monthly?"

"Yes, I do, sir. Shall we debit the account?"

"Yes, that will be perfect. Please pay the bills in full, and I'll be calling tomorrow to order a new card."

"Very good, sir. Is there anything else I can help you with?"

"No, it's been a pleasure dealing with you. Thank you for your help, James."

"Thank you for contacting us, Mr. Arnold. Please enjoy the rest of your day."

"I intend to. Thank you, James," I said and disconnected.

"Credit card problems?" Louie asked.

"Not for me," I said.

Sixteen

I took a pass on joining Louie over at The Spot. If I was going to be sitting around in the Landing Strip from 2:00 until 7:30 in the morning, the last thing I needed was a couple of beers under my belt. I brought Morton home and let him out in the backyard, cooked up a couple of boneless chicken breasts, and ate one out on the back steps while throwing a tennis ball to Morton.

I settled in front of the tv around nine and set the alarm on my phone for one in the morning. The alarm woke me, and I went upstairs to check on Morton. He was out cold, curled up on his pillow. I made myself a chicken sandwich, tossed it into my computer bag along with my laptop, and headed over to the Landing Strip.

The Landing Strip is across the river in West St. Paul, actually a different town than St. Paul, but driving there, you wouldn't know that unless you were a local. It just seems like one large city, although West St. Paul is in Dakota rather than Ramsey county; and therefore, the property taxes are roughly half of what I pay in the city.

The Landing Strip has been open for maybe fifteen years. It's in an industrial area in a one-story building that once housed a manufacturing business. From the outside, the place is pretty much on par with Tubby Gustafson's other clubs. LANDING STRIP in purple neon lights with 'DANCERS' in red neon letters that flash off and on. The front door is edged in red neon as well. I pulled into the parking lot with maybe twenty other cars. Since the building was unattached, if your car was in the lot, there was about a ninety-nine percent chance that you were in the Landing Strip. At close to two in the morning on a weeknight, it appeared to be a lot busier than the Lumberyard the night before.

I pulled on my face mask, grabbed my computer bag, and headed in through the neon-red entry. An older woman was seated in a glass-enclosed booth. She laid the novel she'd been reading, some romance thing, facedown and said, "We're about to close, sir. I believe the bar is no longer serving."

"That's why I'm here. I'll be working security on the premises until the cleaning crew arrives in the morning."

"No one informed me."

"Sorry to hear that. Is there a manager around?"

"Jerry, he's behind the bar. Big guy in a white shirt."

"Okay if I go in and talk to him?"

"Suit yourself," she said, picked up her novel, and returned to reading.

The place was maybe a third full. Still, a lot busier than the Lumberyard last night. The bar was up against the back wall. I counted six guys seated at the bar. They were sitting on bar stools facing the stage with their backs against the bar. Four guys were seated along the stage with stacks of dollar bills resting on the stage in front of them. Five tables had guys sitting at them. Everyone seemed to be facing the stage. Two women were up on the stage dancing.

There were two bartenders behind the bar. One was a woman, maybe fifty. The other was a large guy with a goatee and a long-sleeve white shirt. His sleeves were rolled up to his elbows, and he was busy washing glasses. I headed over to him.

"Afraid we're finished serving for the night," he said without looking up.

"Yeah, I'm supposed to be doing security here from close 'til the cleaning crew comes in."

"You Hazard?"

"Actually, it's Haskell, but yeah."

"Grab a seat. The ladies will be finished up in just a bit," he said and still hadn't looked at me.

I grabbed a stool at the far end of the bar.

The women finished dancing two songs later. I hadn't recognized any of the music. They got a round of applause and some whistles as they blew kisses, waved and strutted off stage. The moment they disappeared backstage, the place began to empty out. Five minutes after they left the stage, Jerry turned the lights up in the room in case anyone didn't get the message. Fifteen minutes later, the place was empty. The woman tending bar said goodbye to Jerry and left. The girls who'd been on stage walked out from behind the stage, dressed in jeans and t-shirts and carrying bags over their shoulders. Neither one asked for a drink; they just waved goodbye and headed out the door.

Ten minutes after that, Jerry began flicking a number of switches and said, "Okay, the place is yours. Have a quiet night." He left and locked the door behind him. So much for a tour of the place. I checked both restrooms to make sure they were empty. Looked around the place to make sure no one was hiding beneath a table or behind the bar. I flipped some switches behind the bar until I got the right one to turn up the lights. I settled in at a table, took out my laptop, and my chicken sandwich.

I turned on my laptop, and maybe a minute later, it said 'No Service.' I checked the wi-fi networks. There were six, but they were all secure, and you needed a password. Stupid me, I should have gotten the password from charming Jerry. I put the laptop away and devoted my attention to my chicken sandwich. Once I was finished, I did a quick walkthrough again. One door labeled private and another labeled office behind the stage were both locked. I couldn't find a radio or a tv, so I sat on a barstool drumming my fingers. A little after three, I set the alarm on my phone for 6:00 AM, lined up four chairs, one next to the other, stretched out, and closed my eyes.

Seventeen

It was a scraping noise that woke me. Well, that and the fact that having been stretched out on four uncomfortable wooden chairs, all slightly different sizes, my body now looked like a length of damaged plumbing. I rolled my shoulders and blinked my eyes open. There it was again, that scraping sound. I half sat up on my elbows and popped my head above the table.

She was standing on a chair, dressed in jeans and a blue hoody sweatshirt. She wore a baseball cap and a face mask. There was a sudden rattling sound, and it dawned on me that she was shaking a can of spray-paint.

"Hey, what the hell do you think you're doing?" I shouted, rising up off the chairs.

She dropped the can of spray-paint, attempted to jump off the chair, and promptly landed on the edge of a table and fell to the floor. The table seemed to wiggle for a moment before it landed on top of her.

I was standing over to her in an instant, and as she stretched her arms out to move the tabletop, I stepped on her hand. Not too hard, but with enough pressure to keep it in place.

"Ouch, hey, stop, you're hurting me," she said, looking up at me.

"What the hell do you think you're doing?

"Oh no, oh no. God, where did you come from? Get off my hand and get this table off me."

"What are you doing here? How in the hell did you get in?"

"I said, get off my hand, okay." I thought about that for a moment. "Please, it really hurts, and my knee is killing me. Please."

I slowly removed my foot, reached down and picked up the tabletop. It was at least an inch thick and solid wood. It apparently had been attached to the top of the cast iron pedestal with very small screws. It was heavy, and I leaned it against the wall before I helped her to her feet.

She was attractive with brown hair, brown eyes, and what looked like a very nice figure beneath the hoodie sweatshirt. She groaned as she stood and limped around in a circle for a few steps. "Oh, God, that really hurts. You didn't have to scare me like that," she said and limped around some more.

"Scare you? Are you kidding? You're lucky I don't have you in handcuffs, and I'm not calling Tubby Gus-tafson right now."

At the mention of Tubby's name, her eyes grew wide. "Oh please, don't call him. Please don't."

"Are you the one who painted all the graffiti at Nasty's the other night and Dolly's last night?"

"I, I don't know what you're talking about."

I glanced down at the can of black spray-paint that had rolled under a table. "Here's the deal, you better start telling me the truth, and fast, or I'm going to have to call Gustafson. And let me just warn you, he's not going to call the cops. If you're lucky, you'll end up in the hospital, but knowing Tubby, he'll probably kill you. If you think I'm fooling, just try me."

She seemed to think about that for a moment. "Could we maybe sit down and talk?"

"Yeah, okay. Just don't get any ideas like you're going to sweet talk me or you're going to write graffiti on these walls. I'm not kidding you. You're in some serious trouble. What the hell were you thinking?"

She groaned as she sat down and kept her right leg more or less extended. She pushed back her hood and took off the baseball cap. I pulled a chair up across from her, keeping some distance just in case.

"You think you could maybe get me some ice from behind the bar? My knee really hurts."

"We'll see. First of all, how in the hell did you get in here? Or, for that matter, how did you get in Nasty's and Dolly's?"

"I work here."

"Work here? What do you do?"

"What do you think I do? I dance. It's a circuit. Old man Gustafson has us dancing in a different place every night."

"So, you were working here tonight?"

She nodded and said, "Yeah, four to eight. Once I finished dancing, I just hid beneath the stage and waited until everyone left. At least this place still has some business, so I could make a couple of bucks tonight. With this damn pandemic, no one's going out. We have to pay seventy-five bucks each night to dance, and we have to pay them twenty-five percent of our tips. That worked great until COVID-19 came along."

"And it's not working now?"

She shook her head. "It's been a disaster. I've had to dip into my savings account. I'm up there shaking my ass for four hours, five days a week, and I'm losing money."

"So, that's why the graffiti?" I asked.

She shook her head. "No, I'm in my last semester of nursing school. We're actually working in hospitals across the city. They're really understaffed, and there's been so many of the staff infected. A number of staff have died, and they simply needed us to fill the gap. There was no one else. So they gave us our diplomas and sent us into battle."

"Yeah, I heard about it on the news. But what's with the graffiti?"

"Gustafson owns all these clubs, right?"

"Yeah, I know that. I've had a relationship with him for a number of years."

She jerked back and gave me a two-second look when I said relationship.

"No, not that kind of relationship. Don't even go there. What I meant was, I've had to deal with him in a number of situations. I'm a private investigator. That means, on any given day, I'm dealing with a level of society we would all just as soon not have to deal with."

"You have to know about his company Virus Protection Incorporated."

The blank look on my face must have given me away. "Virus Protection Incorporated?"

"It's a company Gustafson owns. A shell company actually. They don't manufacture; they distribute respirators and PPE, personal protective equipment, under the name Virus Protection Incorporated. The respirator masks are actually manufactured in Uzbekistan if you can believe that."

"Tubby Gustafson does business with a company in Uzbekistan?"

"He's their national distributor. Well, one of his shell companies is. But yeah, and he's making a ton of money. Doubled the price at the initial outbreak and raised it again just last month. As if that isn't bad enough, the masks don't work. They literally disintegrate while you're wearing them."

"Tubby Gustafson is involved in surgical masks?"

She nodded and said, "These are actually respirators, a step up from surgical masks. He also supplies gloves. About every third one tears as you're trying to put it on. The level two gowns he has leave you exposed in the back, the ties pull apart, and the wrist bands don't really work."

"But why would they buy them if they're so bad?"

"They're better than nothing. We were wearing trash bags before, and now these are all we can get."

"And you're a nurse, dancing here five days a week?"

"A nursing student. Dancing five days a week and nursing five hours a day, six days a week."

"And so you're spray-painting these clubs why?"

"Because everyone I've tried to contact isn't interested. I've tried the newspapers, radio, tv stations. They all think I'm making it up. They don't even bother to check to see if I'm telling the truth. They just dismiss me. Hey, I'm not working tomorrow. Do you mind if I grab a glass of wine? Want me to get you something?"

"Don't do that. They monitor the stuff behind the bar. They'll know you took some."

She snickered and said, "Believe me, they don't monitor. They just say that, so you won't take anything. You see those cameras up in the corners and the one on the stage," she said, pointing at the cameras with the green lights. "If those are working, how come they had to hire you to try to catch me? They're bogus, fakes. You can buy them online for about eight bucks. Gustafson has them in all his clubs. They don't record anything. They just have that green light that makes you think the things are working."

"They're fake security cameras? Is that even legal?" I asked.

"I don't think legality has ever been much of a concern with Mr. Gustafson."

"Mmm, probably right."

"You want a glass of wine or a beer or something?"

I shook my head, no.

She slowly stood, worked her right knee up and down a few times. "Oh, I guess I should introduce myself. My name is Jasmine," she said and held out her hand.

"Nice to meet you, Jasmine. Dev Haskell is my name."

"Dev Haskell? No kidding? Your name is written in one of the ladies' rooms. You're very highly rated."

"The ladies' room here?"

"No, one of the other clubs. I just can't remember which one. I'm gonna grab a wine. You sure you don't want something?"

"Thanks, but I better not."

I watched her step behind the bar and fill a wine glass from a box of white wine. She took a sip and bent down behind the bar. I was ready to jump if she tried to head for the door, but she stood up and walked back to me carrying her wine and a bag of ice. She placed the ice on her knee, took another sip of wine, and said, "So you were telling me you work for Mr. Gustafson."

"That's too strong a term. A lot of the investigations I deal with, he turns out to be involved in some way, shape, or form. He is not the guy you want to be on the wrong side of."

"Are you going to tell him about me?"

"There's not much to tell. Other than having a glass of wine, you haven't really done anything here."

She smiled at that and took a sip. "You know, I could get to like you."

"You should probably set your sights higher," I joked.

"So, are there security guys like you in all the other clubs now?"

"It's funny you ask that. I've suggested a couple of times that he do that, but he doesn't want to spend the money. I was at the Lumberyard last night, here tonight. He'll probably send me somewhere else tomorrow night."

"And you're getting paid, right?"

"Not exactly. He bitches at me a lot, probably won't pay me for any of the time I've spent, but there's always kind of an unwritten rule that, when I ask for a favor or information, he complains but ultimately he gives it to me. I'm making him sound like a bit of a character, and in a lot of ways, he definitely is, but don't cross him. The list is long of people who got on his bad side and have never been seen since."

"Well, I just want to expose him for ripping off and endangering health care and—"

"You hear that?" I said, just as I heard the sound again. Like someone slamming a car door. "Jasmine, get over there by that table. I lined up four chairs behind that table. Lay down on them. It sounds like someone might be coming in." I pointed at the table where I'd been sleeping twenty minutes ago.

"Are you—"

"Go, now, go," I said. I set her wineglass on the floor and headed for the front door. I was halfway there when the lock clicked, the door opened, and Fat Freddy Zimmerman waddled in.

"Wakey, wakey, Haskell you— Oh, Haskell, you're actually awake. What a surprise."

"Pretty tough to keep an eye on things if I'm asleep."

Fat Freddy glanced around the room, looking to see if everything appeared to be in order. He pointed toward the restrooms, and the muscular thug behind him wearing a faded Ramones t-shirt headed in that direction. "Humph, I was sure I'd find your worthless ass asleep, Haskell."

"Hardly. Say, you could do me a favor, though. I brought my laptop, and I forgot to ask Jerry for the password. Would you happen to know it? I can answer some emails and check the news as long as I'm sitting here."

"Dumb shit," Fat Freddy said.

"Hey, come on, Fredrick. It's not like it costs you any money. I just want to log on and—'"

He shot me a look at the sound of his name. "Were you listening, Haskell? That's the password. Dumb shit is the password. Two words, capital 'D' small 's.' Amazing the password is the same as your name. Anything happening here?"

"Not a thing. You checking all the clubs?"

"Maybe," he said, trying to act sly. The muscular thug came back, shaking his head and stood behind Freddy.

"Well, I told Mr. Gustafson he should have someone stationed at every place," I said.

"At no surprise, so far tonight, you've been proven wrong, once again. All right, clean-up crew should be here in a little more than three hours. Hey, is that your cop car out there in the lot?"

"Yeah, the Crown Vic? I got to thinking if anyone has any ideas about breaking into the clubs, that car might just give them a second thought."

"Humph, who knew you had a brain. All right, we've gotta run, so I'm outta here."

"Give my best to Mr. Gustafson," I said.

"His day is best when he doesn't hear anything from you, Haskell. Try not to mess this joint up," Fat Freddy said. He gave one more quick look around and headed for the door. I quickly followed, so when he closed it, I was right there and turned the lock. A moment later, I heard the car doors slam. The engine started, and the car screeched out of the parking lot.

I waited a long moment just to be sure, before I said, "Okay, Jasmine, it's safe to come out."

She peeked over the top of the table and mouthed the word 'gone.'

"Yeah, but let that serve as a lesson. They're checking everywhere, even the place I'm in. I don't know if you're aware of this, but the two places you spray-painted, your graffiti was completely painted over before they even opened up the next day. Tubby had a painting crew in there about forty-five minutes after the cleaners unlocked the place.

She got a disappointed look on her face as she rose from the chairs. "God, you just can't win."

"Don't give up. Just think of some other way," I said.

"Yeah, I guess, it's just so frustrating. Everyone risking their lives to help folks and people like Mr. Gustafson only care about themselves and the almighty dollar."

I reached into my wallet and handed her my business card. "Here, let's stay in touch. Obviously, I'm not going to mention our meeting to Gustafson, but you better be a little more careful. You dodged two bullets tonight, me because I'm a nice guy, and Fat Freddy Zimmerman because he's an idiot."

She took the card, leaned over and gave me a passionate kiss on the cheek. "You're living up to your rating in that stall in the ladies' room."

I locked the door behind her, and walked through the place to make sure Fat Freddy's accomplice hadn't left something behind. I glanced at the cameras up in the corners in the main room strolled behind the bar, filled a bowl with a mixture of peanuts and pretzels, and sat on a barstool nibbling and thinking.

Eighteen

I logged onto my laptop using the password 'Dumb shit.' I should have tried it before and thought there was a pretty good chance it would be the same password for all of Tubby's clubs. The cleaning crew arrived just a little after seven. I was seated at the bar watching a Netflix movie I'd seen before.

The two guys took two steps into the barroom, stopped, and gave me the eye.

"Hi, guys. I worked security here last night. Everything was nice and quiet. Good to see you. It means I can go home," I said and shut down my laptop. I put the laptop in my computer bag and headed for the door. They still hadn't said anything, and they hadn't moved from when they first came in. I smiled as I walked past and headed out to my car. I tossed my computer bag onto the passenger seat and pulled the note stuck under my windshield wiper.

I climbed in behind the wheel and opened the note. *'Dev, Thank you. You saved me. I owe you big time. Call me. Waiting to hear from you. Jasmine. '* Her phone number was written below. I placed the note in my pocket and headed home.

Morton was still asleep upstairs. Amazingly, the kitchen appeared undisturbed. I put the coffee on and turned on my laptop. I pulled out Jasmine's note and did a search on her phone number. Unfortunately, nothing came up.

I was pouring my third cup of coffee when Morton wandered into the kitchen. He stopped about three paces into the room and did his stretch, before he wandered over for his morning head scratch. Once that was completed, I let him out the kitchen door and filled his food and water dish. He was back in ten minutes later, finished his breakfast in about sixty seconds, and we headed down to the office.

We were the first ones there, and I was yawning, not for the first time, when I heard the stairs creaking. I dumped yesterday's remnants from Louie's coffee mug and had just filled the mug and set it on the picnic table when he opened the door.

He murmured something I couldn't understand and settled into his chair. He was maybe halfway through his mug before he asked, "Anything happen last night?"

I shook my head and said, "No, nothing. Fat Freddy and some thug popped in to check things out around four this morning, but other than that nothing."

"They checking to see if you were awake?"

"I think they were checking all the clubs, including the Landing Strip, where I was last night. I heard their car doors closing and met them at the front door. They more or less said they were checking out every club, but with Fat Freddy, who knows?"

"And your pal Gustafson doesn't have anyone in the other clubs?"

"As far as I know, he doesn't, and nothing Fat Freddy said has me thinking otherwise."

"Be interesting to see if Gustafson calls you ranting because another place was painted."

"Maybe word got out that the stuff was painted over before anyone had a chance to see it. Tubby probably has that painting crew on standby ready to go as soon as they get the call. Hopefully, that's enough to deter anyone from continuing. I could sure use a night in my own bed and—"

My phone rang. Barbie.

"Gustafson?" Louie asked.

I shook my head and picked up the phone, "Hey, good morning, Barbie. Anything happening on your end?"

"Nothing related to Ken, if that's what you're asking. You canceled his credit cards?"

"I did, and I would guess he became aware of that sometime yesterday. I canceled both of them just a few minutes after you sent me the information. Even if he can get new cards, it's going to be a week before they arrive.

Hopefully, that will put the pressure on him to call you. If you hear from him, let me know right away."

"I will. Did you hear anything about that LOBO thingy you were going to do?"

It took me a moment before I figured out what she was talking about. "Oh, you mean the BOLO, Be on the Look Out. No, I ended up leaving a message and haven't heard back. As soon as we're off the line, I'll place another call."

"Well, I had better ring off anyway. I'm doing a podcast today anyway, and I should get ready for that."

"Okay, Barbie. As soon as I hear something, I'll let you know. Talk to you later," I said, but she'd already hung up.

I placed a call to Devan Riley. The phone rang four times, and I was just getting ready to leave another message when Riley answered. "This is Devan Riley."

"Hi, Devan. This is Dev Haskell I called yesterday but—"

"Yeah, I got your message, Haskell. Who's handling this investigation?"

"The investigation? Well, I am. See my client—"

"Wait a minute. You're doing this investigation? This is a private investigation?"

"Umm, only until I have enough information to pass on to you guys. I don't know if you listened to all of my message, but a private collection has been stolen. I've been able to track the individual responsible through his credit card receipts from Los Angeles, California, all the way to Saint Paul. He's been in the metro area for five or six days now. Unfortunately, we don't know where. So I was thinking, a BOLO might be just the thing to find this collection worth somewhere between one-point-five million and two-point-five million dollars. The guy and—"

"What's the individual's name?"

"His given name is Arnold Rudolph Wazinski. He may be operating under the alias, Ken Carson. I have his social security number, bank accounts, and credit card numbers, although his credit cards have been recently canceled."

"And you said this was a private collection. What is it, artwork, classic cars, jewelry?"

"No, well, not exactly."

"So, what is it?"

"It's actually a collection of dolls."

"Dolls? What kind of dolls? Antiques or something?"

"Not quite. They're actually Barbie dolls. See my client—"

"Barbie dolls? You mean those things my girls had growing up? Blonde, well-endowed, that Barbie?"

"Yeah, that sounds about right."

"Where are you coming up with this shit?"

"Well, it represents a collection that has been assembled over the years, and as I said, the estimate is between—"

"Yeah, I heard you the first time. One-point-five to two-point-five million. I gotta tell you, Haskell. It sounds like a hell of a stretch to me. I'm sure we've got a box or two of those damn things up in the attic. They're all missing a leg or an arm or something. The wife won't get rid of the damn things, and I don't dare mention it to my daughters. A million and a half bucks worth of Barbies? You gotta be kidding me, Haskell. Every father in a five-state area would drive for hours to donate more Barbie dolls. They're probably worth more in the recycle market than anywhere else. Couldn't you make tires, asphalt, bicycle pedals, or something out of them?"

"These items have all been appraised and—"

"Yeah, and I'm sure that's reputable. Look, Haskell, here's an idea. Read the paper or watch the news and see the shit we're dealing with in today's world. Barbie dolls? You gotta be kidding me," he said and hung up.

"Prick!" I exclaimed and tossed my phone back on the desk.

"Not exactly what you were hoping for," Louie said.

"No, the guy went off on a tangent. I better call, Barbie," I said.

"Oh, Dev, I can't believe it. You already found him?" was how she answered.

I had talked to her not five minutes ago, and I could feel a headache already coming on. "Not exactly, Barbie. Actually, what I think would help to get this moving would be if you could send me copies of the dollar estimate of your collection. That will add some credibility to our cause and once they get that BOLO out there, we—"

"What do you mean copies of the estimate?"

"The estimate on the value of your Barbie collection. You said you had an estimate for between one point five and two point five million dollars. If I could get a copy of that to the police, that adds credence to our request for a BOLO."

"But that's my estimate."

"Your estimate? You mean it wasn't an authority on collectibles? It wasn't an appraiser? Maybe Christie's out in New York?"

"Dev, I'm an authority on Barbie. Let me rephrase that. I'm *the* authority on Barbie. I'm intimately familiar with my collection. I'm intimately familiar with Barbie. I'm opening a Barbie hospital, my Dream House. I'm going to make the world safer for Barbie. I plan to restore all sorts of Barbies. Therefore, I have established the value of my collection at between one point five million and two point five million dollars."

I felt as though I'd just been hit over the head. "I understand that, Barbie. But, is there someone you know who could provide a third party, unbiased estimate as to the value of the collection?"

"Probably, Dev. Of course, what we'll need to do first is get the collection back so that the items can be examined, and that's your job," she said and hung up.

Nineteen

I searched online for any activity related to Arnold Wazinski. At no surprise, after_canceling his credit cards, there wasn't any. Toward the end of the morning, a text message came through. I figured it was Barbie wondering why I hadn't found Wazinski yet. Thankfully, it was nurse Jasmine, part-time dancer, and I hoped, former spray-painter.

'Just wanted to thank you again for being so kind, listening to me, and protecting me from that dreadful fat hoodlum. He always walks into the ladies room, stands there, and tells you he made a mistake but never leaves. Would love to get together with you sometime.'

I thought about that for maybe sixty seconds and figured, what the hell. Why not? So I called her.

"Dev?"

"Hi Jasmine, just wanted to tell you thanks for the text message."

"Listen, I owe you, big time. I've been thinking about it, and if I ended up with that fatty guy—"

"Fat Freddy Zimmerman."

"Yeah, that's the one. If you had turned me over to him, I'd probably be floating face down in the Mississippi right about now."

"Yeah, not the nicest group of people. If I could give you any advice, it would be to get out of that business. Working for people like Tubby Gustafson, you're never going to come out on top."

"Like I told you earlier, the money that used to be there is gone. I have one semester left, and I never had to take out a loan for any of my schooling, only because dancing paid so well. But now, with the pandemic and no change in sight, it's just not worth my while anymore."

"You have an alternative plan?"

"All I have to do is pick up the phone, and the hospital will give me all the hours I can handle. I won't be making as much money, but it'll be nice to get out of the dance business."

"Are you dating anyone?"

"Why? Are you asking me out?"

"What if I was?"

"If you were asking me out, of course I'd say yes, provided we were somewhere we could social distance."

"You know, LaGrolla?"

"That Italian place down on Selby?"

"Yeah, I'll book a table there for seven on the patio if you want to join me."

"I would love it. God, I haven't been out to dinner in months."

"Okay, I'll plan on seeing you at seven. The table will be in my name if you get there early," I said, and we disconnected. Since I lived directly across the street from LaGrolla, I figured she wouldn't be the first one there.

I went onto Google and did a search for Virus Protection Inc. Other than an online site to order product, there was no information. The address was somewhere out in South Dakota, and that was a P.O. Box instead of a street address. I thought about that for a bit. Tubby, scamming the nation in a time of crisis. It figured. I made another phone call and left a message.

"Hi, Nancy. Long time no talk. A voice from the past, Dev Haskell. Please don't hang up. I have a contact you may be interested in talking to. You can reach me at this number. I look forward to hearing from you."

Nancy Ehrhart was a woman I had a fast, hot, three-week relationship with a decade ago. I'd tried to contact her a couple of times over the years but never got a response. She used to work for our local paper, but I heard she lost her job in one of their many layoffs over the last few years. Like the vast majority of the newspaper industry, they seemed to have a layoff every six months or so. Now I think there's just a skeleton staff, and the local joke is, if they were going to do a story about someplace on the Eastside of town, they'd have to get their GPS out to find the location.

I more or less wasted time over the course of the afternoon. A little after four, my phone rang. It was the one call I wasn't looking forward to.

"Good afternoon, Mr. Gustafson."

"What do you mean by that, Haskell? I understand you were actually awake last night when Frederick arrived."

Fat Freddy must have told him about seeing me at the Landing Strip. Thank God I was awake, and Jasmine was hiding. "Yes, sir, it was nice of him to stop in and make sure everything was okay. Hopefully, you didn't experience any graffiti incidents last night, sir."

"Thankfully, not. God help the idiots involved if I get hold of them," he growled. "I want to keep up our efforts tonight. I'll expect you to be at Scuttlebutt before close."

"Actually sir, I have a meeting this evening, and I don't think—"

"A meeting? At two in the damn morning? I think not, Haskell. You'll be there, on time, or there will be hell to pay. Do I make myself clear?"

"Mr. Gustafson, I just wonder if it wouldn't make more sense to—"

"Silencio, you half-wit," he shouted. "Haskell, the last thing you know anything about is making more sense. Honest to God almighty. If you had even half a brain… Oh, why do I even bother? You just plan on being there or else," he shouted, and the line suddenly went dead.

"Hello? Hello, Mr. Gustafson?" Great, my first night out in close to a hundred years, and Tubby Gustafson inserts himself into the situation and screws it up.

I debated calling Jasmine back, but then what? Reschedule for tomorrow night, just so Tubby could insert himself and have the pleasure of ruining two evenings? No, I decided. I would rise above it.

Morton and I headed home a little after five. I let him out into the backyard and hurried upstairs to shower. It was a hot, humid, midwestern afternoon, and I pulled on a reasonably clean shirt, a pair of jeans, and got Morton back inside. I grabbed the face mask hanging from my doorknob and wandered across the street to LaGrolla. There were a number of cars parked in front, and I could hear a buzz of conversation coming from the patio. I pulled the mask on and had to wait just inside while the hostess seated the couple ahead of me. She returned to the front podium a minute or two later, smiled, and said, "You have a reservation?"

"Yes, I do. Dev Haskell is the name."

She checked a list, found my name, and drew a line through it. "If you'll please follow me, sir."

We walked through an empty dining room, out a door and the air-conditioned comfort, and onto the patio. Each table, there were an even dozen, had an umbrella in the middle. They were all social distanced. The patio was actually two tiers, and I followed her up the steps to an empty table in the far corner.

"Here you are, sir. I'll alert your server, and she'll be over in just a moment." She flashed a smile and quickly headed back inside to the air-conditioned restaurant.

My server was a heavy-set woman wearing a face mask with the Italian flag across the front of it. She set a menu down in front of me and asked, "Will there be anyone else joining you this evening?"

"Yes, one other individual."

She nodded, set another menu at the place directly across from me, and said, "Something from the bar?"

"Yes, a Peroni beer."

She left, and I looked over the menu, checking out starters and the main courses. I could look over the wrought iron fence and see the second floor of my place right across the street. My beer arrived, and even though my stomach was growling, I decided it would be prudent to wait until Jasmine arrived before I ordered anything to eat.

Fortunately, I didn't have to wait long. Five minutes later, Jasmine stepped onto the patio, and the hostess pointed her in my direction. I waved, and Jasmine waved back as she hurried up the three steps to our table. She was wearing a short, low-cut summer dress and a white face mask.

"Hi, Dev, hope you haven't been waiting long," she said, as she lowered her face mask. She leaned over and gave me a kiss on the cheek.

"No, not a problem. I just got here myself. How'd your day go?"

"I remain the most boring woman in town. It's my day off, no dancing tonight. No hospital today. So I slept in and studied all day."

"You said you have a semester of school left?"

"Not exactly. They actually finished us up a semester early. Now I'm studying the things I learn every day, all on the job training. We're probably doing five to ten times more on any given day than what was standard up until the time of the pandemic. It's just the way it is."

"Sounds a little like the army. You do all sorts of training, and once you're thrown into combat, all that training more or less goes out the window and you're adjusting to a constantly changing situation."

She nodded and said, "You were in the army?"

"Yeah," I said and dodged the rest. "Hey, check out the menu. Our server will be here in a moment. There's a wine list. Obviously, I'm having a beer, but get whatever you want. You interested in a starter?"

"I could be talked into one. How about you?"

"I'm going to have the Funghi Misti, it's that garlic mushroom starter and the lasagna for dinner." As I spoke, my stomach suddenly growled.

"Oh, God, listen to that. We better get you fed."

We both ordered. A guy brought slices of home-made bread with olive oil and balsamic and set them on the table. I had two pieces of bread before Jasmine got her glass of wine, and the wine was at the table in about a minute and a half. At least my stomach didn't growl when we raised our glasses and toasted one another.

Twenty

We chatted about everything and nothing. Jasmine was born in St. Paul, one of four children, three girls and a boy. Her brother had done a tour in Afghanistan in 2011. He was wounded, and that played a big part in her decision to go into nursing. She had some funny stories about dancing in Tubby's clubs, but I had the feeling she was looking to get out of it, and maybe the decline in attendance and revenue was just the thing to push her out the door.

She'd met Tubby Gustafson twice. Both times had served as a reinforcement to the thought that she wanted to stay as far away as possible from him. She was adamant about her assessment of Tubby's company Virus Protection Inc and mentioned that a number of people at the hospital, the nurses' union, and organizations across the state had filed formal complaints as to the quality and the outrageous prices.

She did mention that neither her family nor anyone in the medical side of her life knew about her dancing, and once again, I had the distinct feeling she was close to being finished if she hadn't quit already.

Once our dinners arrived, I asked, "So, what do you think about your protest, the spray-painting?"

"Well," she said and shoveled a forkful of pasta into her mouth. She chewed for a moment and took a sip of wine, thinking. "If what you told me is true and everything was painted over before they even opened for business the following day, it didn't do much good. I guess the only thing that makes me happy was that it upset Mr. Gustafson. But I'm not sure he ever got the message."

"Don't let my story of his phone calls be a downer. He was upset, and Tubby likes to keep things close to the vest, so the fact he didn't make some outward gesture or comment doesn't mean much. He had his paint crew on standby. He had me booked; in fact, I have to be at Scuttlebutt tonight. And, don't forget, he had Fat Freddy Zimmerman checking on every club in the middle of the night. You definitely got his attention. That said, did it change his mind? No, in fact, if he figured out it was a protest against the poor quality of his product, it might have made him even more determined to continue. Dealing in actual facts is probably not his strong suit unless he's hit in his pocketbook."

"Yeah, and he's still making a ton of money selling a lousy product to people on the front line, and no one seems to care."

"Maybe spray-painting the inside of a strip club wasn't the best way to get the message out."

"Yeah, I get that, but do you have a better idea?"

"As a matter of fact, I just might."

She set her fork down and looked at me. "Dev, this is serious. People are dying. Do you listen to the news? Do you—" The couple at the table next to us glanced over as she began to raise her voice.

"Jasmine, calm down. Look, I got an idea. It may not work, but if it doesn't work with this person, there'll be someone else."

"What are you talking about?"

"You ever hear of an investigative journalist named Nancy Ehrhart?"

She shook her head.

"Okay, she used to work for our local paper. I kind of knew her a number of years ago and—"

"Define kind of knew her?"

"We went out a couple of times, and she came to her senses after about three weeks." Jasmine smiled at that. "Anyway, she was and still is an investigative journalist. The paper had to let her go because they were letting everyone go. She was nominated for a Pulitzer once, didn't win, but even getting a nomination is a big deal. Anyway, she's been freelancing for the past few years and I'm thinking we should contact her. You can give her your story, see if she would be interested."

"Mmm, I don't know. Why would she care?"

"Why? Because in the biggest health crisis we've seen in at least a century, with over a hundred and fifty thousand people dead, there's a guy, right here in town, who is scamming our first responders and forcing shoddy, overpriced protection gear on them. It's like selling bullets that don't fire to the army."

She took another bite of pasta and seemed to think for a long moment. "The problem I see is that I just know a little bit. I know the masks and the gowns are bad, but so what? I don't know anything about shipping or distribution or what other places are buying his stuff."

"You don't have to, Jasmine. She's the investigator. She'll find out about all that, and believe me, she will. You just have to get her interested."

"Did you talk to her?"

"I left a phone message."

She smiled at that and said, "Oh, but she didn't call back, right?"

"Yeah, but that's neither here nor there. You want her number, I'll give it to you. You call, and I guarantee she'll at least get back to you and listen to what you have to say."

"Yeah, I guess it's worth a try. You might as well give me her number," she said. She pulled out her phone, and I gave her Nancy Ehrhart's number. "Okay, guess we'll see what happens. I'll keep you posted."

"Might be a good idea if you don't mention my name," I said.

"Mmm, that bad?"

We finished dinner and skipped dessert. Jasmine said the meal was on her, but after a quick five-second conversation, I paid. We stepped outside onto the sidewalk, and she looked across the street at my house. "Oh, wow, that's a lovely place."

I stared at her for a moment, and she suddenly laughed.

"You want to come in and see the place?"

"That sounds like a good idea if you wouldn't mind. Maybe you have some white wine in the fridge?"

"I just might. Come on over." We waited for a car to pass before we crossed the street. By the time I got the door open, Morton was there. Jasmine stepped inside, and Morton immediately shoved his nose between her thighs.

"Morton, damn it, back off. Sorry about that," I said.

"Mmm, oh, that's very a cold nose. He must have learned that move from you," she said.

I gave her the five-minute tour, and we ended up back in the kitchen. Fortunately, I had an unopened bottle of Sauvignon Blanc in the refrigerator. It had been there long enough that I'd forgotten who brought it. I filled her glass, popped the top on a can of Summit IPA, and we toasted one another. One thing led to another, and my phone alarm woke me a half hour before I was supposed to be at Scuttlebutt.

Jasmine rolled over and, sounding not quite half-awake asked, "What time is it?"

"Oh, shit, I got a half-hour to get over to Scuttlebutt before they close. I gotta hurry."

She smiled, pulled me back into bed, and slid on top of me. "Not so fast, mister. I think it might be nice to send you off with a little thank you."

"Oh yeah, that's a nice thought, Jasmine, but I have to— well, actually yeah, now that you mention it. Mmm-mmm."

Scuttlebutt is located fifteen minutes away in the near north suburb of Maplewood. It has a parking lot on three sides. I finally arrived just a little after three. The lights were off, the place was locked, and no one answered the door when I pounded on it. Bottom line, I was screwed if Fat Freddy showed up. I was worried for about sixty seconds before I came up with a brainstorm.

I pulled across the street and parked next to the dumpster at a pizza place. I sat in my car for the better part of an hour and a half before a black Escalade drove into the Scuttlebutt parking lot and pulled in front of the door. Fat Freddy and his thug friend oozed out of the Escalade. Freddy looked around the parking lot for a moment before he unlocked the door and stepped inside.

I drove across the street, pulled behind the Escalade, and stopped no more than an inch from the back bumper. I climbed out of my Crown Vic and sat on the hood of my car. Not quite ten minutes later, Fat Freddy and his pal stepped out the door. They were both carrying a can of beer and didn't see me. Freddy locked the front door, took a sip, and said, "I can't wait to tell the old man he wasn't—"

"You guys pay for those beers, Frederick?"

Fat Freddy literally jumped, bobbled his beer can, and dropped it on the sidewalk. The can rolled toward the edge and dropped onto the parking lot, leaving a foaming trail in it's path.

"Haskell? What the hell? Aren't you supposed to be inside?"

"Yeah, I thought I'd change things up tonight. I wanted everyone to think I was a no-show. You know, just to see if that maybe encouraged whoever was spray-painting to show up. Unfortunately, no such luck, at least not yet."

"You're supposed to have your ass inside."

"You listening? That's why I wanted to try something different, Frederick. Someone sees my car, they'll think a cop is in there. I'm trying to catch whoever is doing this, but unfortunately, all I caught was you two."

"We didn't do anything wrong."

"Maybe. You should probably pick up that beer can. Someone sees it there in the morning they might put two and two together."

"Nothing to put together here," Freddy said, but he stepped over and picked up the beer can. He turned it upside down and poured the remnants into the parking lot. "Better move that cop car of yours so we can get going. We still got a lot of places to get to."

The thug tilted his head back, put the can to his lips, and drained what was left in about five seconds. I climbed in behind the wheel, turned the ignition, and quickly backed up about fifty feet.

Fat Freddy backed up, turned around, and as he drove past, he gave me the finger. I drove over along the side of the building, parked, and killed my lights, so Freddy would think that's where I'd been parked all along. He seemed to pause before he turned onto the street. He lowered his window to give me the finger once again before he sped off into the darkness. I set my phone alarm for 6:50. When my alarm went off, I parked in front, and the cleaning crew pulled up ten minutes later.

I rolled down my window as the couple got out of their van. "Just working security here tonight. Everything was nice and quiet. Freddy Zimmerman was here maybe two and a half hours ago checking things inside. You have a good day," I said and drove off.

Once home, I turned on the coffee and tiptoed up the stairs. Jasmine was out cold in bed, and Morton was curled up next to her. I debated moving him, but I wouldn't be able to do it without waking her, so I left the two of them in bed and went back downstairs.

Morton appeared maybe an hour later, and after a long scratch behind the ears, I let him outside. I heard the shower running twenty minutes after that, and Jasmine walked into the kitchen just before nine. She was dressed and had this funny look on her face.

"What?" I said.

"Did you, umm, do something with my thong?"

"Do something?"

"Yeah, I can't seem to find it. I know I was wearing it when we went upstairs."

I shook my head. "Morton, he steals thongs."

"God, he is just like you."

"Can I make you some breakfast?"

"Oh, thanks, but I should take off. I just called the hospital and told them I could do eight-hour shifts."

"What did they say?"

"I'll be starting at noon. Thanks for a lovely dinner last night, and I'll phone this newspaper lady friend of yours."

"Nancy Ehrhart."

"Yeah, I'll phone her this morning."

"Good luck, I hope it works in your favor."

"We'll see. It's certainly a better alternative than spray-painting. Oh, I phoned the big man."

"Tubby?'

"Yeah, I told him I have to work at the hospital, and so I have to give up dancing."

"What'd he say?"

"He just said, do what you have to do, and hung up."

"Charming," I said.

"Thanks again, Dev, for dinner and well, for the night."

"Thank you, Jasmine."

"I'm not sure how I'll be after working an eight-hour shift, so how 'bout I give you a call once I get into this new routine?"

"Yeah, of course. No pressure."

"Thanks," she said. She leaned up and gave me a kiss, picked up her purse, and headed toward the front door.

I opened the door for her and got a kiss on the cheek. I watched her cross the street, climb into her car, and drive off. She gave a little wave as she drove past, and I closed the door once her car disappeared.

Twenty-one

Louie was gone by the time Morton and I finally made it down to the office. The coffee pot was still on. There was barely a half-mug left in the pot. I turned it off and dumped the remnants down the sink. My phone rang an hour later. Barbie.

"Haskell Investigations," I answered.

"Dev," Barbie cried and started sobbing.

"Barbie? Barbie, what's wrong?"

"He's selling her? He's selling her, and he doesn't even list her at the proper price."

"Selling her? What are you talking about?"

"Barbie. He's selling Barbie, and I know it's him. I know it's Ken, and he's selling my Pink Splendor Barbie on eBay. You've got to stop him, Dev. She's mine, and she's not for sale. Oh, what am I going to do? Why is he doing this to me? Why, Dev? Why?"

"Barbie, calm down and give me a minute here. He's selling one of your dolls on eBay?"

"Not just any doll, Dev. He's selling the Pink Splendor Barbie. My Pink Splendor Barbie. There's only ten thousand of them in the entire world and—"

"How do you know that?"

"Don't you dare interrupt me, Dev Haskell. There were only ten thousand ever made. They were released in 1996. Oh God, I was barely five years old. 1996, Dev, and they were priced at nine hundred dollars. Can you believe it? Nine hundred dollars in 1996 that would be like a million dollars in today's world."

I thought it best not to correct her. She would have been eight years old, but why mention it? As for the million-dollar value, best not to go there.

"Pink Splendor Barbie has a sky-high blonde hairdo, a gorgeous pink gown with white lace. She's wearing gold lace bracelets, jeweled earrings, a beautiful necklace, and that worthless bastard Ken has her up for sale online!" She shouted those last few words.

"Did he list his name, Barbie? Where did you see this?"

"Where did I… Were you listening? I just told you. I saw it online. On eBay, as a matter of fact. You have to go over to eBay and stop them from selling this."

"Go over to eBay? It doesn't work like that, Barbie. eBay exists online. It's not an office or a building that you go to. Besides, how do you even know this is Arnold Wazinski selling this Sky-High Barbie?"

"Dev, I'm calling you for help, and you're not even listening. It's not Sky-High Barbie. It's Pink Splendor Barbie."

"Okay, okay, I got that, Pink Splendor Barbie," I said, writing it down on the back of an envelope.

"Yes, and she was the most expensive Barbie ever. Nine hundred dollars, Dev. Nine hundred." I jerked the phone away as she shrieked those last two words.

"And how do you know this is Arnold Wazinski selling this. Is his name attached?"

"Well, no, but this particular Pink Splendor Barbie is being sold for nine hundred dollars."

"Okay, and that was the original price twenty-five years ago, right?"

"Yes, but they're available on Amazon and eBay for around three hundred dollars. Any number of them are available at that price. My Pink Splendor Barbie is in the original box, and the box still has the nine-hundred-dollar price tag. Who else but Arnold Wazinski, the wannabe Ken Carson, would be stupid enough to try to sell this for the original price?"

"Mmm-mmm, I see your point. Do you happen to have that item up on your computer now?"

"Yes, I do. I'm looking at it right now, and I just know it's mine."

"Send me the link, Barbie. And I'll deal with this."

"What do you intend to do?"

"I intend to get ahold of Ken, email me the link."

"All right, you should get it in just a moment."

A half-minute later, an email from Barbie came through.

"Okay, I got your email. I'll deal with this from here."

"I need to know what's happening."

"Right now, nothing. But when something does happen, you'll be the first to know."

"Keep me posted, Dev. It's important I'm kept informed. This is my collection, after all. Oh, God, I can't wait to get my hands around Ken's neck."

After swearing and promising to cut off a major organ on Arnold Wazinski, aka Ken Carson, she eventually hung up. I clicked on the link. Sure enough, there was the image, pretty much as Barbie had described it. The Barbie doll with a mile-high blonde hairdo, no doubt plastic jewels, a sparkly gold top and a fancy pink gown with white lace. I wouldn't give ten bucks for the thing, but once again, I was clearly out of the demographic. I made a note of the item number and the seller's name; WAZ.A.R. Interesting, it wouldn't take a rocket scientist to link WAZ.A.R. to Arnold Rudolph Wazinski.

Barbie was correct. The doll was priced at nine hundred dollars cash. I scanned through the other images of Pink Splendor Barbie. There were an even dozen. They were priced from $299 to $335. Interestingly, all the other offers accepted credit cards and PayPal. WAZ.A.R. apparently only accepted cash. I sent him a message saying I was interested in purchasing and to please contact me so I could make a cash offer. I mentioned in my message that I was located in St. Paul, Minnesota.

Arnold Wazinski was confirming my suspicions of him. Between his neurotic Ken doll routine, all the plastic surgery, stealing Barbies doll collection, and ending up in the same city as Barbie, not to mention the over-priced offer, the guy had to be certifiable.

My phone rang. The call came across as unknown, and I debated about not answering. I'd been getting a lot of recorded calls lately for life and health insurance. Against my better judgment, I answered, "Haskell Investigations."

"Dev Haskell, please." The voice sounded somewhat familiar, but I couldn't place it.

"Speaking."

"Mr. Haskell, this is Lieutenant Devan Riley. We spoke on the phone yesterday."

"Yes, I remember."

"I, umm, spoke with Lieutenant Aaron LaZelle this morning."

"Oh?"

"Yes, he thought maybe it might be a good idea if we met and discussed your situation with this stolen collection."

"Wonderful, I'd love to meet. You tell me when and where and I'll be there."

"You free for lunch today?" Riley asked.

"You bet I am."

"You're up on Randolph Avenue, is that right?"

"Yes, that's my office."

"You familiar with Shamrocks, down on West Seventh and Randolph?"

"Very familiar. What time would you like to meet?"

"Maybe a little after one, we can miss the lunch crowd, such as it exists in today's world."

"I'll be there. Oh, hey, Lieutenant. I'm buying, okay?"

"How 'bout we split it? That way I won't get hit with accepting a bribe."

"Okay, deal. See you a little after one." We disconnected, and I phoned Aaron LaZelle. Amazingly, he actually answered his phone.

"Hi, Dev, no, I'm not giving you bail money if that's why you're calling."

"Very funny, not."

"What's up?"

"Just wondering if Devan Riley mentioned me to you in the last day or so."

"Riley, no, why? What's up?"

I went on to tell him about the stolen Barbie collection, my client Barbie, and last but not least, Arnold Rudolph Wazinski.

"Oh, that's fantastic. No, Devan didn't call me. But I heard the story. Didn't realize it was you who was involved. Apparently, he went home last night, happened to mention some version of this tale to his wife. She reads him the riot act, goes up into their attic, and finds these old Barbie dolls, and now she wants to take them to this woman with the doll fix-it-up place."

"Yeah, actually, she'd going to call it the Dream House."

"Fine, whatever. Here's the incentive for Devan. He's sleeping on the couch until this hospital thing is up and running. Just to add fuel to the fire, I guess she called their daughters this morning and gave them a more sanitized version of the story, but there you have it. God, I didn't know it was you on the other end. Is this the woman you took out to Vegas a few years back, and there was some craziness going on?"

"Yeah, Aaron, thanks for reminding me. She got hired by a casino, played the part of Barbie for a couple of years. Drifted out to Hollywood and made something like a half-dozen movies in five or six weeks if that gives you an idea about the type of flicks she was in."

"Yeah, say no more."

"She's back here in town, and actually, as crazy as it sounds, she wants to start this business fixing Barbie dolls. Riley's wife sounds like she would be the perfect customer. She'll pay to get the dolls put back together and give them as gifts to her adult daughters. This Barbie woman does a weekly podcast now. She told me, between Facebook, Twitter and the podcast, she's got something like two million followers. I gotta be honest. I was laughing about this at first, but the more I learn about what she wants to do, as crazy as it sounds, I'm thinking it may just be a potential gold mine."

"Well, I think Devan Riley will welcome the opportunity to assist if only to stay on the wife's good side. Is there really a million-dollar collection that's been stolen?"

"That's maybe a bit of a gray area— one point five to two point five million based on Barbie's estimate. But, in saying that, even though it's her collection, she is an authority. So, let's say it's only worth nine hundred grand, that's still a big chunk of change you're looking at."

"I guess my only question is, where do you find these people?"

Twenty-two

Shamrocks is one of the more popular bars and restaurants on my end of town. Once the pandemic hit, about the only place I'd been in was The Spot and never for very long. I was pretty keen on playing it safe. I pulled into the parking lot a little after one. In a different time, I would have had to park a block or two away, but that wasn't the case in the current world. I climbed out of the Crown Vic, locked it, and headed in the side door, pulling on a face mask as I went. There were seven people seated at three separate, socially distanced tables. A guy and a woman sat at the bar, a good five stools apart and obviously not together.

I didn't see Devan Riley anywhere, so I caught the eye of one of the staff and pointed to a table. "Okay if I grab one of these tables?"

She nodded and said, "Sure thing. Will there be anyone else joining you today?"

"Yes, another guy should be here shortly."

She grabbed two menus from a pile and set one in front of me and the other on the opposite side of the table. "Can I get you something to drink?"

"I think just a root beer for me."

Devan Riley stepped in through the front door maybe five minutes later. He was dressed in uniform. I waved as he looked in my direction and headed over to the table.

"Dev, nice to see you again. Thanks for making the time." Instead of extending his hand, he lifted his elbow toward me.

I did the same thing, we bumped elbows, and he sat down. The server arrived, and Devan ordered a decaf coffee.

Once she left, I said, "I really appreciate your phone call this morning, Devan. It looks like the guy who stole this collection is trying to sell some of it online." I went on to give him a quick version of the Pink Splendor Barbie for nine hundred bucks on eBay.

The server returned with Devan's decaf, and we ordered. Once she left, he said, "So, you sent him a message saying you were interested?"

"Yeah, I mentioned I would pay cash and told him I was located here in town. Hopefully, he'll think that's just a nice coincidence, and it will serve as an incentive to get back to me and get his hands on the cash. No idea where he's staying. I believe he doesn't have access to credit cards, at least for the time being. Even if he's staying with friends, he's got to be wearing out his welcome at some point."

"You have that vehicle information?"

I pulled out a number of sheets stapled together that I'd printed off. They had all my Arnold Wazinski information. Name, date of birth, credit cards, the license number on the truck, along with the photo images Barbie had sent me.

Riley quickly went through the first two pages. He stopped and stared at the photo images for a long moment before he looked up at me. "This guy paid for plastic surgery to end up looking like this?"

"Afraid so."

"He should get his money back. That's absolutely crazy."

"You should see my client. She's done the same thing to look like Barbie. Some of the enhancements I have to agree with, but, well, it's a little out there. I'm afraid to touch her for fear of breaking something." I went on to tell him about Barbie in Vegas and the crowds of adoring fans. Her working at the casino, the Barbie room, and her fascination with all things pink.

He shook his head and said, "Look, I love my wife, but she and the girls would be in with the Vegas fans. What can I say? I happen to like The Big Lebowski, and they think I'm nuts. It works both ways."

The server brought out our sandwiches. Riley just ordered a cheeseburger and fries, I got the bourbon bacon chicken sandwich. As she set Riley's plate down, she glanced at a page with an image of Wazinski. "Oh, wow, that's cool. Anyone ever tell that guy he looks like the Ken doll?"

Riley smiled and said, "I'll take another decaf when you have a chance."

"See, it's crazy," I said. We went on to discuss other subjects. Riley never mentioned sleeping on the couch, but he gave me his home number to pass on to Barbie. He left me with the distinct impression that, as long as he was going to help, it might be nice if Barbie gave his wife a call. He handed me his card, told me to email the Wazinski images to him, and promised to get the BOLO out that afternoon. I told him I would stay in touch and to please keep me updated should he learn anything or, God forbid, get a response on the BOLO.

As soon as I got back to the office, I sent Riley the images I had of Wazinski. I took Morton for a walk, and once we were back in the office, I checked my email. No response from Wazinski on my offer to pay $900 cash for the Pink Splendor Barbie. I crossed my fingers, hoping I wouldn't hear anything from Tubby Gustafson, and closed my eyes to take a brief nap. My phone woke me.

"Hello," I answered, still half-asleep.

The woman on the other end of the line chuckled and said, "Did I wake you?"

"Hi, Nancy, no, just juggling a number of things," I lied. Nancy Ehrhart, the investigative journalist. If she was calling, I took it to mean she'd spoken with Jasmine.

"I got a call from your friend, Jasmine," she said, confirming my suspicion. She emphasized Jasmine's name, but I didn't respond.

"Oh, good, I'm glad the two of you connected. You think there might be something there of interest?"

"Possibly. What can you tell me about this Virus Protection company?"

"All I know is what Jasmine told me. They sell masks, gloves, and I think gowns. They're apparently located in Uzbekistan; at least that's where the manufacturing is done. Virus Protection may be the name Gustafson cooked up for the US Market. My understanding is that he's their local Minnesota and presumably the national distributor in the US. Jasmine told me there have been complaints filed by nursing and medical organizations regarding the quality of the products. Beyond that, I'm pretty much in the dark."

"But you deal a lot with Gustafson. Don't you work for him?"

"Not by choice, and he is not my employer if that's what you're suggesting. He has his hands in a number of things and is always looking for the next one."

"Meaning what, exactly?"

"Just that he has a number of interests. He owns commercial buildings, a couple of restaurants, although cafe might be a better term. He has a number of nightclubs in the metro area, and he's got interests out in Las Vegas. He had an interest in a car dealership sometime back, but I don't know if that's current."

"So when you say you don't deal with him by choice, what exactly do you mean?"

"I have to deal with him. It's not by choice, but invariably, in any number of investigations, his name enters the picture. He's your classic successful criminal. He's involved in some form of illegal activity yet always manages to keep enough distance between himself and the actual crime, so he remains untouchable. This PPE situation would be classic Tubby Gustafson."

"Can you explain that?" she asked.

"His take on the PPE would be he's trying to help solve a national problem, make more equipment available to help people on the front lines of the pandemic. He would be unaware there is the occasional problem. Occasional being a term Tubby would probably use. If and when he does find out about it, his thinking will be along the lines of it was never his intent to provide poorly manufactured equipment, so the infections and deaths aren't his fault."

"But he is a criminal."

"Only half-correct, Nancy. He's a crime lord. I don't think there's much that goes on in this city without Tubby Gustafson knowing about it. I'm sure, if you look deep enough, you'll find some politicians turning a blind eye to import duties or tariffs or something. On the city, state, or federal level, at the end of the day, you know they're in it for themselves, and Tubby would like nothing better than to benefit from his campaign contributions. He donates to both parties."

"When did you get so cynical?"

"You suggesting I'm wrong?"

"You're a piece of work, Dev. I'm going to look into this. The timing couldn't be better, we're in the midst of another wave of infection, rates are climbing, and here's this character promoting faulty personal protective equipment. Mind if I touch base with you once in a while?"

"I look forward to it, Nancy. Call anytime."

"Thank you. I'll remember that," she said and hung up.

I sent Jasmine a text. *'Just heard from Nancy Ehrhart. Sounds like she's going to investigate Virus Protection Inc. Good Job. Dev.'*

I phoned Barbie. "Tell me you caught him and pushed him off a bridge or ran him over," was the first thing she said.

"Hi Barbie, fine thanks, how about you?"

"Enough with the making nice, Dev. Did you catch him?"

"No, but I made some good progress on the police front." I went on to tell her about my lunch with Devan Riley. "He took the information and said he would be putting out a BOLO this afternoon. So, with any luck, pretty soon, all the cops in a five-state area will be reading that, looking at the pictures, and keeping their eyes peeled for him."

"I can only hope I get to him first."

I mentioned that Riley's wife had some Barbies that maybe needed a tune-up and that she just might make a great first customer. Barbie promised to call her, and we chatted on for another minute or two before she hung up. Tubby Gustafson phoned me a little after four and ruined what was left of my day. "I'll want you down at Dolly's before they close," he said.

"Dolly's? I'm thinking we've probably shut down this spray-paint person, sir. There hasn't been an incident in the past couple of nights. I don't believe Frederick has run across anything. Everything has been quiet wherever I've been stationed. Hopefully, whoever this individual is, the urge to desecrate one of your establishments disappeared as soon as they realized it was a bad idea."

"Haskell, I've once again provided you with the opportunity to do something positive, and as per always, you're looking for a way out. Well, it's not going to happen. Dolly's, be there, or you'll answer to me and just a warning, you won't like what I'll have to say." With that, he hung up.

Apparently, my idea of congratulating Jasmine on surviving her first eight-hour shift at the hospital would have to wait. I debated heading over to The Spot but, in the end, decided that the better idea would be to go home. Amazingly, I did just that.

I let Morton out the backdoor, and coaxed him back in with a biscuit. I discovered what I think was a rice dish in a bowl hidden in the back of my refrigerator. I heated it up in the microwave, ate it, inhaled an ice cream bar for dessert, and settled in front of the tv to watch a movie. Apparently, I dozed off because the alarm on my phone woke me. Morton had already headed up to bed, so I tossed my laptop in my computer bag, climbed in the Crown Vic, and headed out to Dolly's.

Dolly's is located in the town of Rosemount, a community maybe twenty minutes south of St. Paul. The place is in a hundred-year-old two-story, red-brick building set on a corner of the downtown area. The parking in front is angled rather than parallel. Like all of Tubby's other establishments, a blue neon sign that said Dolly's was over the door. The standard red letters that said 'Dancers' flashed off and on. After being otherwise occupied and arriving late at Scuttlebutt the night before, I pulled up in front of Dolly's at 1:30, a full half-hour before closing. There were a half-dozen cars parked on the street, and Dolly's appeared to be the only place around that was open.

I grabbed my computer bag, climbed out of the Crown Vic, locked the car, and heard the music pounding from inside of Dolly's.

Twenty-three

When I entered, there were maybe twenty people inside. No one but me wore a mask. In fact, I couldn't see anything that even resembled a mask. The room was long, with a bar running the length of the room and a stage with a brass pole at the far end of the bar. The stage was empty, but only because the two women, a blonde and a redhead, wearing sparkling platform heels and smiles, were dancing back and forth on the top of the bar.

Both of the women were carrying what looked like a whiskey bottle with a metal free-pour spout, and when someone would slip money into their garter belt, they would pour whiskey into his open mouth. A number of the guys wore similar jerseys, and a couple of baseball hats seemed to match the jerseys. I guessed it was a softball team that had shown up for the entertainment.

I walked over to the end of the bar and one of the bartenders, there were two, eventually came over. "What can I get you? Sorry, but this is gonna be last call."

"Nothing for me. I'm working security here tonight after you close."

He nodded and said, "Oh, yeah. We got the call. What's going on? We've never had that before?"

"Nothing, other than playing it safe after the spray-painting at Nasty's the other night."

"These guys'll be out of here in about fifteen minutes. Might as well grab a chair and watch the show."

I pulled out a chair in a far back corner and sat down. Fifteen minutes came and went, and things still seemed to be going strong. After maybe forty minutes, the ladies were helped off the bar to whistles and applause as they headed backstage. The music stopped, the lights came on, and slowly but surely, the softball team began to head out the door.

It took another ten minutes before the last two guys said their goodbyes. The older bartender followed them to the door, smiling, and quickly locked the door behind them. He walked over to me and said, "You're the security guy they sent?" He said it in a way that suggested security would be the last thing I provided.

"Yeah, Dev Haskell's my name. Would you mind giving me a quick tour before you take off?"

"Follow me. This'll just take a moment." We walked down the length of the bar. "That there's the stage," he said, stating the obvious. "Dressing room is behind the stage. We got a back door, but it's an emergency exit. You open it and—"

"Let me guess, the cops and fire department answer the call and I'll have to pay for the pleasure."

"You got it. The cans are right over there," he said, nodding at two doors. One of the doors was labeled 'Pointers,' the other labeled 'Sitters,' with an appropriate silhouette image of a dog pointing and one sitting. "I can put some coffee on for you if you'd like. Don't even think about helping yourself to the bar stock. We keep track of it, and we got the camera's watching everything." He indicated the cameras in the four corners and the one above the bar. They all had a green light and looked just like the ones I'd seen in the other clubs. "Any questions?"

"Yeah, I brought my laptop. What's your password?"

"Dumb shit. Two words, capitol 'D,' small 's'."

"Okay, thanks, that'll be easy to remember," I said, wondering if any of the staff realized all of Tubby's clubs apparently had the same password.

He stepped behind the bar, filled a cocktail shaker with ice, poured in some vodka, followed by what looked like a little lime juice and some triple sec. He took two stem glasses out of the freezer, filled the glasses with the drink, and added a twist of orange. It suddenly dawned on my thick skull that he'd just made two Cosmopolitans.

As he set the glasses on coasters emblazoned with 'Dolly's' the two dancers stepped out from behind the stage. One was dressed in jeans and a U of M t-shirt, and the other had on navy-blue shorts and a white top. They looked like two moms on their way to the grocery store, except that I'd seen them just fifteen minutes earlier, strutting and prancing naked along the top of the bar. All the while pouring whiskey into the open mouths of an adoring softball team.

Both women stood on the brass bar rail, leaned forward, and gave the bartender a kiss. "Thanks, Carl," the blonde said and took a sip. The redhead just shrugged and wrinkled her nose before taking a gulp.

I went back to my table, pulled out my laptop, and put in the password. Other than the occasional laugh from the women, I couldn't hear anything they said. Carl, the bartender, topped up their glasses with what was left in the shaker before he proceeded to begin washing glasses. The women left maybe twenty minutes after they'd first appeared, and I had the feeling that the cosmopolitan at the end of their dance shift was a regular deal.

The younger bartender finished stacking stools along the bar before he left, and Carl called goodbye ten minutes after that and hurried out the door. I checked the time on my laptop. It was 3:10.

I waited for Fat Freddy to show, but he never did, and that got me wondering if maybe someone from Scuttlebutt had called and told him I never showed. Or maybe Freddy was simply checking on me every night just to see if he would be able to catch me doing something wrong.

I never did feel the need to stretch out and sleep. Right around 7:15, the lock in the front door snapped open. Two guys stepped into Dolly's and stopped. They looked like a father and son team. I guessed the son was maybe sixteen, and the dad was close to my age.

"Hi, fellas. My name is Dev Haskell. I was working security here after Carl closed up last night. Nice and quiet, not so much as a peep. You guys coming in are the only activity I've had."

"Security?" the dad said and shot a questioning look.

"Yeah. Mr. Gustafson has me in a different club every night."

"This because of the spray-painting?"

"Yes, it is. Although, you're one of the few people on a cleaning crew to mention it. How'd you hear about it? As far as I know, the couple of times it happened, it was covered over before the place opened for business. I don't think they missed so much as a minute's worth of business."

"We know someone on the paint crew. I think they painted two clubs. Got paid double time, so that was worth it for them."

"Good thing it worked out for someone. Every place I've been doing security in, it's been nothing but quiet. Well, I'll get out of your way. Have a good day," I said and headed home.

Morton was asleep on his pillow when I went upstairs. I pulled off my jeans and t-shirt, placed my phone on the bedside table, and stretched out on my bed. I'd been asleep for the grand total of about seven minutes before my phone rang. "Mmm, lo," was how I answered.

"Hello, Dev. Are you there? Dev?" Barbie said.

I cleared my throat and said, "Barbie, what's up?"

"That's what I want to know. What have you heard?"

"What have I heard, you mean from Arnold?"

"Who else? I'm not interested in whoever your latest victim in bed is."

I was now fully awake. "Thanks for that, Barbie. No, I haven't heard from Arnold. As soon as I do, I'll let you know. In fact, I'll send him another message right now. Maybe that will prompt him."

"And you'll call me as soon as you hear?"

"I promise. Let me send this second request to him now."

"All right, I'll be waiting by the phone."

"Before you go, did you call that Riley woman? The cops' wife with the dolls?"

"Yes, Denise Riley, lovely woman. We chatted last night. I'm going to meet with her at 5:00 today. She actually has three Barbies, plus Skipper and Ken."

"How wonderful I'll send a message to Mr. Wazinski right now. Thanks for the call," I said, disconnected, and fell back to sleep.

Morton woke me maybe forty-five minutes later and wouldn't take no for an answer. I followed him downstairs, let him out into the back yard, and filled his food and water dish. I was asleep in front of my laptop after sending another eBay message to Arnold Wazinski when Morton's barking woke me.

I let him in and dragged myself back upstairs to the shower.

Twenty-four

ouie was on his laptop at his picnic table when we stepped into the office. Morton headed over to his pillow and settled in. Louie watched me as I settled in my desk chair.

"You look more dead than alive," he said.

"Oh, man, between working these night shifts for Tubby and dealing with Barbie, it's all starting to catch up with me. I'm just dragging. I almost fell asleep just driving over here."

"That doesn't sound good. Why not just lean back and close your eyes? You got anything you have to deal with that can't wait?"

"Actually, no, I don't."

"Well that's perfect. Turn your phone off and close your eyes."

"You going to be here for a while?" I asked.

"I plan to be here for the rest of the day. Sack out. If anything comes up, I'll wake you."

"Thanks," I said. I turned my phone off and set it on my desk. I pushed my chair around, put my feet up on the windowsill, and closed my eyes.

When I woke, Louie was still working on his laptop. There was a Styrofoam container stamped with the name Rooster's BBQ resting on my desk. I opened the container, and the heavenly scent of a Rooster's BBQ pork sandwich wafted over me.

"Feeling better?" Louie asked. "You've been snoring your brains out for the last four and a half hours."

"Four and a half? What the hell time is it?"

"It's almost three. Morton and I walked up to Rooster's. They tossed in a bone for him. The guy behind the counter wondered if you'd maybe been arrested."

"Arrested?"

"Hey, past history, man. Don't forget to turn your phone back on."

I took a bite of my pulled pork BBQ and turned on my phone. Two missed calls, both from Barbie, obviously stressing out about my message to Wazinski. Since I had nothing to report, there was no point in calling her back. I turned on my laptop, took another bite of my sandwich, and there it was, an email reply from WAZ.A.R. I smiled, took another bite, and clicked on the message.

'Thank you for your response. I've had a number of offers, but since yours was first, I'll sell this gorgeous Pink Splendor Barbie to you. Payment must be in cash. If this is agreeable, contact me in the next two hours, or I will be forced to contact the next person on this very long list.'

Despite what the message said, based on the tone and the price he had on the doll, I was pretty sure I was the only person who had contacted him. The email had been sent almost three hours ago. I typed my reply and clicked on send.

'Sorry for the delay. I had a Dr's appointment and I stopped at the bank to get the cash. I hope you didn't contact the next person on the list. Let me know where to meet you, and I'll respond immediately. Thank you.'

I hadn't finished the next bite of my sandwich when my laptop alerted me to an email arriving. I clicked on it.

'I haven't heard back from the next person, so if you can meet me in front of the state capitol in the visitors' parking lot, that would be best for me. I'll plan to be there at 5 pm. Please acknowledge receipt of this email and agreement to meet. Thank you.'

I emailed back. *'Perfect, I look forward to seeing you. I'll be wearing blue jeans, a black t-shirt, and a St Paul Saints baseball cap. Thank you in advance. This is a special anniversary gift for my wife. See you at 5:00.'*

I went onto Google images, clicked on the image of a hundred-dollar bill, and printed off nine color copies. The copies were slightly larger than the real thing, so I cut them down more or less to size. I stuffed them in a blank envelope and called Barbie.

"Anything?" was how she answered.

"As a matter of fact, yes. I'm meeting with Arnold Wazinski in just a little more than an hour."

"And he's going to return my collection?"

"He will once I'm finished with him. As far as he knows, I'm meeting him with nine hundred dollars cash to buy that pink Barbie."

"Pink Splendor Barbie."

"Oh yeah, how could I forget. Anyway, I'm meeting him. Once he proves to me he has the doll, I'll tell him I know what he's done, and he needs to turn the collection over to me. With any luck, I'll have everything back to you tonight."

"Oh, thank God. This is such good news, Dev. I can't tell you how happy this makes me. Oh, my, I can feel the stress of the past two weeks beginning to fade away. Thank you, thank you so much. I'll have to find a special way to repay you."

"Let's just get everything back to you first, and after that we'll see what happens. I would strongly advise that you do not, in any way, associate with this guy, Barbie. Either professionally or personally. Once we get the collection back, he's going to be desperate and is liable to promise you anything."

"Well, thanks for the warning, but don't worry. Getting back with Ken is the absolute last thing I want to do. I had so many things planned for him, but he's destroyed it all. Good riddance is all I can say. I'd still like to cut off a souvenir, just to remind him every morning," she said.

"Let's just focus on getting your collection back first. I'll call you later tonight."

"I'll be waiting by the phone," she said and disconnected.

"Sounds as though things might be looking up," Louie said as he turned around in his chair to face me.

"Yeah, in an incredibly crazy way. I think I've got a pretty good shot of getting Barbie out of my daily life, and I'm going to take it." I went on to fill Louie in with all that had happened.

"And you think this guy is going to show?"

"I think he's desperate for cash and thinks he can get nine hundred bucks from me. He's meeting me in a public place, so there's very little chance of me attempting to rip him off. As far as he knows, I'm just a guy buying a gift for my wife. He's made up some nonsense about other buyers waiting in line, which suggests he's probably pretty desperate. The key will be, once I get this doll, I'll have to pressure him to get the rest of the collection."

"Just how do you intend to do that?"

"Ask nicely for starters. If that doesn't work, I'll subdue him and call the cops. If he still won't talk, I'll hand him over to Barbie. She's already threatened to castrate the guy."

"Sounds charming. Keep me posted," Louie said, and watched me as I pulled my set of handcuffs from the middle desk drawer.

I pulled the bottom desk drawer open and took out the lockbox. I input the combination, opened the box, and pulled out my Glock 43. It's a nine-millimeter with a six-round magazine. My sticky holster rested just beneath the gun, and I pulled it out.

I checked the magazine just to make sure it was loaded. It was. I pushed the Glock into the sticky holster and shoved the holster into the front of my belt. I draped the handcuffs over my belt, untucked my t-shirt, and covered the cuffs and the Glock.

"Looks like you're expecting trouble. You sure you want to do this? Why not just call that Riley fella with the police and have them deal with this nutcase?"

"I don't expect there to be any trouble, Louie. But I want to stay on the safe side just to be sure. Besides, if I contact the police, what's this idiot going to think when a squad car pulls up?"

Louie chuckled and said, "You ever wonder what's he going to think when you drive up in that sinister looking black Crown Victoria of yours?"

That actually hadn't crossed my mind. "I better park in the abandoned Sears lot and walk a half-block over to the parking area in front of the capitol. I just plan to be Mr. Nice on this whole deal and keep my fingers crossed nothing goes wrong."

Twenty-five

The Minnesota state capitol is just a ten-minute drive from my office. I left a full forty minutes before I had to be there and made the trip in nine. I parked a block away in the abandoned Sears store parking lot and walked across Rice Street. I was about to cut through the Department of Transportation building and walk out onto the capitol mall when I happened to glance up the street and saw a white box truck parked along the curb.

I had plenty of time and walked toward the truck. As I approached, I saw the California plates with the orange colored tag in the upper right corner that read 2020 and the tag in the upper left corner that read AUG. I kept walking and gave a quick glance inside the cab as I passed. It was empty.

I hurried to the back of the truck. A black heavy steel step ran across the back of the truck just below the door that rolled up into the top of the box. There was a handle attached to either side of the door frame so you could pull yourself up and into the box. The lever to open the door was locked to the frame, with a shiny brass padlock.

The dual rear wheels appeared worn. I checked the cab. The doors were locked. The gray upholstered seats looked worn and appeared cracked and torn around the edges. Three or four McDonalds bags were crumpled on the floor of the passenger seat. There was no place to sleep in the cab unless you stretched out in the passenger seat.

I did a quick glance up and down the street but didn't see anyone watching me. I placed a call to Devan Riley and, after four rings, ended up leaving a message. "Yeah, Devan, Dev Haskell here. I located the truck with the Barbie collection. It's parked along Rice Street on the west side of the Department of Transportation Building." I walked to the front of the truck. "The truck is a white box truck with California plates, license number," I read off the number.

"I'm meeting this Arnold Rudolph Wazinski guy in about twenty minutes in the parking lot in front of the capitol. Ostensibly to pay nine hundred bucks for one of the stolen dolls that he had listed on eBay. Please give me a call when you get this. It is now twenty minutes before five. Thanks."

I looked up and down the street again but didn't see anyone. I debated flattening one set of duals on the rear of the truck, but if I did that and managed to get the keys from Wazinski, I wouldn't be able to go anywhere. Against my better judgement, I made a decision and placed the call.

"Oh, please tell me you found him," Barbie said by way of a greeting.

"Maybe. Where are you now?"

"Actually, I'm in St. Paul on my way to meet Denise Riley. And just what did you mean by maybe? Do you want me to stop by your office when I'm finished?"

"Here's the deal. I'm meeting Wazinski at 5:00 to pay nine hundred dollars for that Pink Splendor Barbie and I—"

"What! Dev, I told you that's way too much money. Current pricing is two-ninety-nine to—"

"Hey, can I finish here? I know all about that, and I have no intention of paying. But I need to get ahold of Wazinski. Now, I've found the truck. But I have to go meet him. He's going to be watching me from a distance to make sure everything is all right. If I can get hold of him, I can not only get the Pink Splendor Barbie, but I can get the keys to the truck, and hopefully, your collection will still be inside."

"Where are you? I need to be a part of this."

"I've got a plan for that, Barbie. Now listen. I'm—"

"Dev, this is my collection, my life. Do not tell me what—"

"Barbie, if you don't shut up, I'm going to hang up this phone. Now shut up."

"But I—"

"Last chance," I half-yelled. A woman walking along the sidewalk looked at me, shook her head, and kept moving. It was suddenly very quiet on the other end of the phone.

"Here's what I want you to do. The truck is parked on Rice Street across from the old Sears store. Do you know where that is?"

"Yes, of course, I do."

"Okay. I want you to pull alongside the truck and park so you're blocking him in, and he can't go anywhere. I'm going to meet him in the parking lot in front of the capitol in a few minutes, so I have to hurry. I'll get the truck keys from him, and we'll have your collection."

"But what about him? You're not planning to let Ken get away, are you?"

"Let's stay focused on the collection for right now and worry about him later. Just pull alongside the truck and park. Okay?"

"Alright, already. I'm heading there now."

"Thank you. I'm heading to the parking lot," I said and hung up.

I walked around the Department of Transportation building and onto the Capitol Mall. The Mall was a large green area with a manicured lawn, trees, benches, statutes, and my favorite, the cannon that fired the first American shot in the second world war. The USS Ward, manned by Naval Reservists from St. Paul, fired at a Japanese midget sub sneaking into Pearl Harbor an hour before the December 7th attack. The first shot missed, but they hit the conning tower on the sub with a second shot and sunk it. The gun is on the Mall. I walked past it, heading for the parking lot.

Along the way, I spotted three different guys sitting on benches. Two of them were too far away to get a good look at. The one guy I did walk past, nodded at me, smiled, and didn't look anything like the photo I had of Wazinski. I walked twenty feet further and stood at the top of the parking lot.

The parking lot is 'U' shaped and doesn't have more than thirty parking places. At the moment, it was maybe half-full. I studied the cars in the lot. They all appeared to be empty. I heard some footsteps behind me and turned to look. A woman headed toward me with a black shoulder bag. There was no way it could be Wazinski in disguise. For one thing, she was in heels and making pretty good time, and she was maybe five one with long blonde hair and a nice figure. She nodded and smiled as she walked past.

I watched her head toward a white SUV. She pressed a fob to unlock the driver's door when she was about three feet from the vehicle. She gave a quick glance to see if I had moved before she opened the car door. Once she saw I was still back on the sidewalk, she opened the driver's door, hopped inside, and quickly locked the door.

A guy suddenly appeared on the far side of the park-ing lot carrying a brown paper grocery bag by the han-dles. He was dressed in black jeans, a blue shirt with the sleeves rolled up, and he wore a black baseball cap with a gold 'P' for the Pittsburgh Pirates. He had a black face mask covering most of his face, but there was something about the cheekbones and the wrinkle-free skin that made me pretty sure this was my guy. He walked toward a car and at the last moment did a half-turn and headed directly toward me.

"You wouldn't happen to be the fella interested in a Pink Splendor Barbie, would you?" he asked as he drew closer.

"You wouldn't happen to be the person who had the Pink Splendor Barbie on eBay, would you?" I answered in response and smiled.

He laughed and gave a little wave. "Pleasure to meet you," he said. "Well, here she is, in all her glory and in the original box," he said and pulled the handles apart, exposing the pink cardboard box. The box was dented on the top, but the original nine-hundred-dollar price tag was still there. The front of the box had an image of Barbie in her pink gown. The words 'Pink Splendor' were written in an elegant gold script, and below that in much smaller letters 'Barbie.'

"Oh, terrific, my wife is going to love this. She's a real Barbie fanatic, and we finally have the wherewithal for her to pursue her obsession. She is going to be thrilled."

"Oh, so your wife is a collector?"

"Yeah, but she's really just getting started. We're in the process of adding a showroom to the back of the house where she can display her collection and still have plenty of room for the collection to grow. The room will be temperature and humidity controlled with special lighting to protect not only the dolls but the original packaging as well."

"Sounds like a wonderful idea. I might be able to help her, both of you actually, in acquiring a number of hard to get items. You want to be careful of forgeries and newly released items coming out of China. Sorry to say, but it's the price we pay for dealing in quality originals."

"We would be very interested. My name is Dev Haskell, and I don't believe I caught your name."

"I'm Ken. Ken Carson."

"Really, Ken Carson. Like the doll?"

He smiled, lowered his face mask, and said, "Exactly like the doll."

"Oh my goodness. I don't believe it. Oh, Ken, that's so wonderful, absolutely marvelous. Would you mind if I took a photo? Please, oh, this will make it so special for my wife. Amazing, simply amazing," I said, pulling out my phone.

Ken stepped back, pulled his mask off, removed his Pittsburgh Pirates cap, and struck a pose. There wasn't so much as a wrinkle on his face, anywhere. His eyes appeared to be squinting, and his hair was dark on the sides and closely trimmed. I could clearly see the strands of long blonde hair implants across the top of his skull. They looked like seedlings planted along the edge of a pond. I clicked the camera once, twice, and was going to wait for a vehicle that just entered the lot to pull into a parking place before taking the third picture when it dawned on me that the vehicle was pink and suddenly accelerating. The driver had an evil look on her face, and her blonde hair was flowing in the wind as she picked up speed.

Ken Carson turned around at the same time I looked over the top of my phone. He suddenly screamed, "Oh my God!" and pushed me down as he ran past, heading up the sidewalk on the Capitol Mall. Barbie bounced over the parking lot curb and sped along the sidewalk in hot pursuit. I was still on all fours as she shot past me, knocking me back down on the ground. My head hit the concrete curb, and I saw stars for a brief moment.

When I looked up, Ken was running left and right as Barbie fishtailed back and forth across the sidewalk. She slammed the brakes on her pink Mercedes. It skidded across the sidewalk, leaving a muddy tire trail as it tore up the manicured lawn. She jumped out from behind the wheel and started chasing Ken with what looked like a tennis racket. I staggered to my feet and attempted to run and catch up, but I was so dizzy I had to stop. I took a couple of deep breaths in an effort to stop my head from spinning before I walked in the general direction of the two of them.

I looked up just in time to see Ken duck as Barbie spun around after missing a swing at his head with the tennis racket. He pushed her down from behind, vaulted over Barbie and leapt over the door and into the driver's seat of her pink Mercedes. He shifted into drive and took off across the park, fishtailing and tearing up the lawn as he went. Barbie screamed something profane and threw her tennis racket at him. The racket bounced harmlessly off the trunk.

He skidded to a stop on the far side of the Mall, bounced over the curb, then sped up the street past the capitol, waving as he disappeared.

Barbie had picked up her tennis racket and was furiously swinging back and forth as she headed toward me, red-faced. She stopped along the way, reached down, and picked up the paper grocery bag. She looked inside and let out a scream.

"What in the hell do you think you're doing? You trying to get us all killed?" I shouted.

"I just wanted to kill that worthless piece of shit, Ken."

"Well, way to go. It's gonna be a cold day in hell before we see him again. God, I was all ready to have him take me to his truck and— His truck, come on. Let's go," I said and started to hurry over to Rice Street where Ken had parked.

"But what about my car?" Barbie screamed.

"I'm sure you'll think of something," I said and picked up my pace.

Twenty-six

My head was beginning to throb. I ran my hand over the back of my head and felt a large lump growing, compliments of Barbie. I checked my hand. Fortunately, there wasn't any blood.

"Dev, could you just wait a minute? I think I sprained my ankle or something," Barbie called.

I kept moving, maybe even picking up speed. I needed to calm down before I talked to her, or I was liable to say something I'd regret the moment it crossed my lips. I hurried around the Department of Transportation building and fortunately saw the truck maybe twenty feet down the street. Ken had apparently just left it there when he fled the scene. With any luck, Barbie's collection would still be inside.

I waited alongside the truck for three or four minutes until Barbie arrived. As she rounded the corner, she began to fake a limp, which became more pronounced the closer she got. "Oh, I think I may have really done some damage to my ankle fighting off Ken. It's just killing me."

I ignored her comment and said, "Does this truck look familiar?"

"Huh?"

"The truck, Barbie. Does this look like the truck Ken or Arnold, or whatever we're calling him now, loaded your collection in?"

"Mmm-mmm, now that you mention it. Yeah, I mean, I think it was a white truck."

"And, if you look, this has California plates. The same plates I saw on the security tape from the station out in Woodbury. This is it. He drove it here."

"Oh hurry and open it up, Dev. I need to see if the collection is in there. It has to be. It just has to be. I don't know where else he could keep it." She ran to the back of the truck, her ankle suddenly healed, and pulled on the door handle. "Oh, damn it must be locked."

"Yeah, that's because of that brass padlock. See how it goes through the handle and that hatch welded to the floor of the truck," I said, stating the obvious and thinking, 'incredible.'

"Well, what are you going to do?"

"I'm going across the street to that parking lot and my car. I've got a bolt cutter in the trunk of my car, and I'll be back in just a minute. You are going to stay right here and watch the truck."

"A bolt cutter? Will that work on a padlock?"

"Trust me, Barbie. It will." I waited for a bus to pass before hurrying across the street. I grabbed the bolt cutter out of my trunk and hurried back to Barbie standing guard. I cut the shackle on the lock, twisted the brass body, and pulled the remainder of the shackle through the handle. It sounds complicated, but it wasn't. I lifted the handle and raised the door on the truck box up into the ceiling. As the door rose, it echoed through the empty box. There was nothing but the naked upper portion of a dark-haired doll near the front of the truck and an empty pizza box.

"Damn it. I was afraid of this," I said.

Barbie took in a deep breath and held it as she stood there wide-eyed. Suddenly, her attempt to run over Ken had even greater ramifications. He was gone, taking Barbie's Mercedes convertible with him. We were left empty-handed with no idea where Ken or the doll collection were.

Barbie let out a long groan. "No, no, no, it can't be. I'm ruined. He's ruined me."

I put my arm around her shoulder. "We're going to get them back, both your car and the collection. I promise," I said.

She climbed up onto the black step, took hold of the handle on the side of the door frame, and pulled herself up into the truck box. She walked to the front and picked up the dark-haired upper half of the doll.

"Oh, Skipper," she said, almost crying and sounding like it was a family member. She pressed what was left of the doll against her left breast. She stepped out of the truck box, lowered herself to the street, and carefully placed the portion of the doll into the paper grocery bag with Pink Splendor Barbie.

"Well, let's get out of here. I'll give you a ride home. I think you better call 911 and report your car stolen and maybe call Denise Riley and explain why you're not going to be there. When you talk to her, mention that you'd like to have her husband find your car. Remember he's a cop."

"I think I know that, Dev."

She carefully placed the bag with Pink Splendor Barbie on the backseat of my Crown Victoria and climbed in the front. Once she was buckled up, I headed over the bridge across I-94 and onto the entrance ramp for 35-E. I turned onto Highway 36 five minutes later and headed toward Oak Park Heights.

She called 911 to report her car stolen and say that she was safe before she called Denise Riley. That conversation went on for the remainder of the drive. Barbie detailing the damage done to her original Pink Splendor Barbie box, as well as the partial recovery of the dark-haired doll, Skipper. They were still talking twenty minutes later when I pulled in front of Barbie's townhouse and put the car in park.

Barbie continued talking for another couple of minutes before she gave me a quick wave and headed out of the car, still carrying on her conversation. As she walked up to the door, I watched, wondering how she was going to get inside, since she didn't have her set of keys.

Amazingly, she had planned for just such an emergency. She reached beneath the welcome mat, pulled out a key, and unlocked the front door. She gave me a brief wave without looking back, stepped inside, and closed the door. All the while, still on the phone.

Twenty-seven

I closed my eyes for a moment, took a deep breath, and drove to The Spot. Louie was on his usual stool, reading the newspaper. Other than Mike bartending with a mask and blue latex gloves, no one else was in the place. The national news was on the TV, but the sound was off. Michael Jackson singing 'Beat It' was playing on the jukebox.

"Hi, Mike. I'll have a beer and better give Louie a refill," I said as I headed down towards Louie. At the sound of my voice, Louie lowered the paper and watched as I approached.

"What'd you do with Morton?" he asked. I noticed the unopened bag of pork rinds sitting beneath the want ads on the bar.

I shook my head and said, "Fortunately for him, I brought him home." I went on to give Louie the details on my effort to recover Barbie's collection and her failed attempt to run over Arnold Wazinski.

"So, this guy ends up stealing her car?"

"Yeah, after trying to run him over, she climbed out and attempted to assault him with a tennis racquet. Not her brightest move."

Louie drained his glass as Mike approached with a fresh drink and my beer. I tossed a twenty on the bar and reached for my beer. Just as I took a sip, my phone rang, Nancy Ehrhart. I took a second sip and answered. "Haskell Investigations."

"Hello, Dev. Hope I'm not interrupting."

"Hi Nancy, you're not interrupting at all. I'm just reviewing a file here," I said as Elton John suddenly started to play on the jukebox, and I hurried out the side door.

"Yeah, sure you are. That's what it sounds like. Listen, I spoke with Jasmine this afternoon, and I have a couple of questions. I'm guessing you're at The Spot. You going to be there for another fifteen or twenty minutes?"

"Yeah, sure, you plan on swinging by?"

"I'm already on my way," she said and disconnected.

"Someone crazy enough to want to meet you tonight?" Louie asked when I stepped back inside.

"Nancy Ehrhart, the investigative reporter. She spoke to Jasmine earlier. I'm guessing she's got some questions about Tubby Gustafson and Virus Protection, his company that supplies the PPE."

"What are you going to tell her?"

"Not much. I know virtually nothing about the company, so about all I can do is give her some background on Tubby and his businesses. Hopefully, she'll take it as a warning and be careful. He's not the kind of guy you want upset with you."

"Wouldn't she know that already?"

"Never hurts to give a second warning where Tubby is concerned."

Nancy walked through the door maybe ten minutes later. She looked like a million bucks in a short black dress. Her hair was draped over her right shoulder. She pulled off her sunglasses as she stepped through the door, glanced around the empty bar, and eventually focused on me.

"Oh, here's Nancy. I'm going to talk with her in a booth, Louie. Shouldn't take too long."

"Enjoy," Louie said, not taking his eyes off her as she strutted toward us.

"Hi Nancy, great to see you again Let's sit in one of the booths, and we can talk uninterrupted. Can I get you something to drink?"

She looked past me and focused in on Mike. "I'll have a glass of Sauvignon Blanc," she said.

"Have a seat, and I'll bring it over to you. You okay, Dev?"

"Yeah, I'm good, Mike," I said and indicated my beer with only a couple of sips missing.

Nancy slid into a booth, and I sat across from her. "Nancy, it's great to see you. You look wonderful, really, you do."

"Thanks, Dev. You don't seem to have changed," she said, sounding like she didn't mean it as a compliment. "So, this is the center of your social life?" She made a face and indicated the empty barroom.

"Not exactly. My office is just across the street, so it's convenient to meet people here occasionally. The guy reading the paper at the bar is my officemate. After the end of a long day, it's nice to slip in for just one."

"Slip in for just one? When did you change?"

"So, you spoke with Jasmine?" I asked, moving on.

"Yes, actually a couple of times. Interesting situation and I've been able to corroborate what she's told me with other people on the front line of this pandemic. Unfortunately, none of what they've had to say has been good, and that's where you seem to come in. Your name has come up more than once."

"My name? What have I done wrong?"

"Surprisingly, nothing I've been able to discover thus far. But two of my connections with the police department mentioned you as a credible source of information when it comes to learning about Mr. Gustafson and his operation."

Mike suddenly appeared with Nancy's glass of wine and a bowl of pretzels. He set both down in front of her. He pushed the bowl a little closer to her, signaling they were for Nancy and not me.

"Oh, thanks," she said, taking a couple of pretzels and not offering me any.

"I'll be happy to help in any way I can," I said. "I need to stress I knew nothing about Tubby's involvement with Virus Protection until Jasmine mentioned it. My sense is it's still pretty much a well-kept secret, which would suggest to me that Tubby is aware of the faulty material problems. That said, from what I know of him, and since he's not directly affected, he wouldn't demand the problems be corrected. Instead, he would point out the problems and insist that there be a price reduction because he'll have to deal with people complaining."

"How did he make all his money?"

"No single way. Over the years, he's created an empire in a number of businesses, bars, strip clubs, prostitution, illegal drugs, the sorts of things you would expect a gangster to be involved in. That said, he either owns or is the largest shareholder in a number of developments, both commercial and residential. He's got enough money that he's able to donate to both political parties. It wouldn't be unusual for him to contribute to individuals running for mayor, governor, the state legislature, or congressional seats. He'd contribute to both candidates just to cover himself and be in the good graces of whoever wins.

"He knows all sorts of 'the right' people. It would be the rare bird in the political world who would distance themselves from him. First, that would require a backbone, and second, if they did that, he would be quite capable of working to help whoever was running against them. He'll do a favor for people if it's worth it to him. He is all about Tubby, and the rest of us will always come in a distant third if at all."

"How does he get away with it?" Nancy asked and took a sip.

"Money, influence. You don't have to like him, but you will have to deal with him in some way, shape, or form if you work for the city, county, or state. If the money thing doesn't work, maybe your car will get stolen or set on fire. Suddenly, a city inspector shows up out of the blue and wants to inspect your home, or maybe your internet keeps going out."

"He can do all that?"

"He has people who do that."

"Tell me about his home. He works from home, correct?"

I nodded. "Yeah, he works from home. His place is gorgeous and monitored twenty-four hours a day, seven days a week. The entire exterior is covered by surveillance cameras with people watching a bunch of video screens all day, every day.

"He's got armed thugs guarding the place. He has at least two women, maybe more, who attend to his every need. Massages, manicures, pedicures, umm entertainment, if that translates."

"And you've seen this?"

"Oh, yeah. He has no intention of interrupting whatever he's doing to talk to me. Ever since the beginning of the pandemic, when I've been summoned to Tubby's, I have to speak to him on a computer screen, and he's in some other room. He carries on with whatever activity he's involved in. It's almost as if he's trying to gross me out, embarrass me. So far, I've been able to deal with it."

"Who are these people that work for him?"

"I'm not sure about the women attending to his needs, but if I found out they were in the country illegally, it wouldn't surprise me. The men are pretty much a bunch of thugs and people on the take. A guy named Fat Freddy Zimmerman is more or less his second in command. He has a rotating group of thugs doing everything from driving Tubby around to picking up protection payments, to threatening someone, or worse."

"And he gets away with all this?" Nancy asked, drinking the last of her glass of wine.

"Tubby gets away with all this because he's always distanced himself. It's never him personally delivering the threat. Anyone who appears in front of him, including me, is searched at least twice, once with an electronic wand and also hand searched as well. He has a platoon of attorneys and accountants at the ready to deal with anyone who even thinks of filing a complaint or charges."

Mike suddenly appeared with another glass of chilled white wine.

"Oh, thank you, but I don't think I ordered this," Nancy said.

"That's right, you didn't, but I felt it was the least I could do if you have to sit here and listen to this guy." He smiled, set the wine down, and pushed the bowl of pretzels a little closer to her.

"Oh, you're very nice," she said. Once he left, she took a hearty sip of wine and said, "You've given me a lot to think about."

"Well, just in case you get any second thoughts, a word to the wise. Be very careful when you're dealing with Tubby Gustafson. If you could somehow approach through the nurses' union or some independent organization, that would probably be the safest. After all the negative stuff I've told you, let me add he's not stupid. He values public opinion and will do anything to remain on the good side of that. He'll weigh the odds in any scenario and take the path most beneficial to him. That's always a given."

"Plenty to think about," she said and took another hearty sip from her wine glass.

"You interested in grabbing some dinner, Nancy? I know a place with a lovely patio and great food. We could carry on from there if you'd like."

She smiled and said, "This wouldn't, by any chance, happen to be the place right across the street from your house, would it? You could order a bottle of wine and a couple of after-dinner drinks and the next thing I know I'll be waking up in your bed."

"I hadn't thought of that, but we could certainly do it if you wanted."

She flashed a smile and drained her glass. "Gee, sorry, Dev, but no. If you must know, I've got a date with a guy who's just a doll." She chuckled for a minute. "Maybe some other time. As a matter of fact, I should get moving. You mind if we maybe stay in touch?"

"Not at all. If I can be of any help, just let me know."

She slid out of the booth, leaned over, gave me a peck on the cheek, and said, "Say, what is the barman's name? I want to tell him thanks."

"Oh, that's Mike. He's a nice guy."

"Got it. See you around. Thanks again," she said and headed over to the bar. She said something to Mike, he laughed, and she headed out the door. Once she was gone, Mike came out from behind the bar and over to the booth. I'd just finished my beer.

"Twelve bucks for her wine, Dev, and I'm supposed to make sure you stay here until she gets away. Said she was afraid you might try and follow her." He laughed but didn't move.

Twenty-eight

O nce Mike let me out of the booth, I walked over to Louie. We chatted for a few more minutes, before I headed home. I couldn't get the image of Nancy in that sexy short black dress out of my mind. I let Morton out into the backyard and sent Jasmine a short text message. *'Met with Nancy Ehrhart this afternoon and gave her some general information on Tubby Gustafson. Give me a call tomorrow, so I know you're OK. Dev'*

I tossed Morton a dog biscuit once he came back inside, and it suddenly dawned on me that I hadn't heard from Tubby Gustafson about pulling all night security at one of his clubs. I settled in front of the tv to watch a movie. It took me a half-hour to find one I was halfway interested in, but after twenty minutes, it was so bad I turned it off, and went upstairs to bed. I woke before my alarm, showered, shaved, and headed downstairs. Morton eventually joined me some time later, and after receiving his morning scratch behind the ears, I let him outside.

We were down in the office an hour later. I was on my second cup of coffee when I watched Louie pull up and park behind my car. He edged forward until he hit my rear bumper jerking my car forward, before he pulled back no more than six inches and parked.

I filled his coffee mug and set it on the picnic table as he made his way up the stairs. I heard him groan just before he opened the door. He'd been settled in his chair and slurping coffee for the better part of five minutes before he said anything.

"That hot number from last night call you later?"

"Nancy? I think I'd probably be the last person she'd call, well unless she wanted to call me names. No, I didn't hear from her. I suggested we might go to dinner and she said she had a date with a doll. Those were her exact words if you can believe it, a date with a doll."

Louie chuckled and said, "Maybe it was the kind of doll you have to blow up."

My phone rang before I could respond. The call was identified as St. Paul Police Department. I answered, hoping I sounded serious, "Haskell Investigations."

"Hi, Dev. Devan Riley here. Got your message late last night. Sounds like you had an interesting time out in front of the capitol. That box truck with the California plates is being towed to the impound lot as we speak."

"Did your wife give you an update? She and Barbie were on the phone when I dropped Barbie off at home."

"Oh, yeah. Denise gave me an update on the stolen vehicle. We've got a BOLO out there on it. Denise is meeting that Barbie woman this morning. She lives in Stillwater, I think."

"Actually, Oak Park Heights. Yeah, she was pretty upset when we found the truck and it turned out to be empty."

"So I heard. Any idea where this character may have gone?"

"Absolutely no idea. With the truck empty, it suggests to me he's landed somewhere and unloaded all the Barbie dolls. Funny thing is, he's gotta be living pretty much out of a suitcase. He's got boxes of stuff in Barbie's basement but hasn't made any effort to contact her. He has to be hurting for cash right now unless maybe he sold some or all of that collection."

"Well, if he did that, Denise would have him on a death list. She's gone completely over the top on getting her dolls repaired and giving them to the girls. She's literally obsessed."

"Yeah, and Barbie is her own worst enemy on dealing with this guy. I was hoping to recover her collection last night, but she screwed that up, and now we're back to square one."

"You learn anything, please let me know."

"You still sleeping on the couch?" I asked.

"Fortunately not," he said but didn't go into any further detail. We disconnected, and I wondered where Arnold Wazinski, AKA Ken Carson, was getting his money. I'd canceled his credit cards and drained a good portion of his bank account, paying off the card balances.

He had to eat. He had to sleep somewhere. How was he surviving?

Twenty-nine

I scanned the apartment building across the way with my binoculars for the better part of thirty minutes and didn't see anyone. Louie left for a client interview over at the Detox Center, and I took Morton for a walk. We had just returned to the office, and Morton was settling onto his pillow with a rawhide chew when my phone rang.

I glanced at the screen and answered. "Hey, Jasmine, how's the nursing world?"

"Oh, Dev, a lot of work, but I'm loving it."

"You staying safe?"

"Yeah, same problems as before, faulty PPE, but we're getting by. Testing numbers are up, but there's still a time lag between when you're tested and when the results come back. At least four to eight days, depending. That's a lot of people who can get infected in the meantime."

"They still got you working nights?"

"Yeah, eight-hour shifts, ten till six in the morning, six days a week. That's not a complaint. I've wanted to do this my entire life, and now I can. The staff at the hospital are so great about teaching us. Any questions, and I just have to ask, and if they have time, they don't just tell me, they show me what to do."

"You done dancing?"

"Oh, yeah. I simply don't have the time, and maybe more importantly, I don't want to. I'd still like to pursue bringing attention to the condition of some of the PPE we receive. I've started an online site where people here can report faulty PPE. I keep track and submit the information to the purchasing department. I also submit a daily total to the nurses' union, and they've started gathering information from other facilities. Your email said you met with Nancy yesterday?"

"Yeah, we talked about the problems you and other locations are facing with PPE. I gave her some general information about Tubby Gustafson. Basically told her to be careful."

"Yeah, she asked me about him, but other than my initial interview and another three-minute meeting, I never really had to deal with him."

I began going through my email account, deleting messages as we spoke. "I haven't gotten a request to do nighttime security at one of the clubs for the last couple of days. Hopefully, that's gone off Tubby's radar. You said you spoke to Nancy a couple of times?"

She chuckled. "Yeah, she can actually be pretty funny."

A side of Nancy I couldn't recall. "She seems to be pursuing Gustafson's Virus Protection company."

"Yeah, when she's not trying to line up a date with this Ken character," Jasmine said.

I suddenly stopped and said, "I'm sorry, something cut out on my phone for a second. Did you say Ken character?"

"Yeah, I guess she found him on some *dating* site." She emphasized the word dating suggesting there was a lot more to it than meeting for coffee.

"I'm not quite following."

"Dev, come on. It works for women too. You know, services rendered, pay in advance by the hour. Set up an appointment and no strings attached. You don't have to deal with the guy in the morning. He attends to whatever your specific needs or desires happen to be. You don't have to pretend to be charming, don't have to cook. You do exactly what you want, and you don't have to put up with a phone call the following day. Well, unless you want to schedule another appointment."

"She did mention she had a date with a doll last night."

"Yeah, that was the guy. I guess he's had some plastic surgery done that kind of makes him look like the Ken doll. You know, Barbie's guy. He even goes by the name Ken Carson."

"And she pays him?"

"Yeah, I don't know how much, but she paid him. My understanding is he's pretty busy. I think she had to schedule this a few days in advance."

"How'd she meet this guy?"

"Dev, get into the twenty-first century. It's online. She connected with him on some dating site called NastyNeighbor. I've never been on it, but I'm kind of thinking about it. Be nice, you know, to relieve the work stress occasionally. Besides, how crazy would it be to spend a night with Ken?" she said and laughed. She quickly followed up with, "But if you wanted to get together again, I'd much prefer that. It's just that with my new work schedule, I'm still in the process of adjusting to working nights."

"You just let me know when you're adjusted, and maybe we'll go out for breakfast."

"I'd like that, Dev."

"You got it. Back to Nancy for a second. This Ken guy is local?"

"Yeah, local and apparently popular. Like I said, she had to make an appointment a couple of days in advance. When I was dancing, we would get offers, but you could never be too sure about the guy, and besides, meeting someone in one of Tubby Gustafson's clubs didn't seem like the best start to an enduring relationship."

"Maybe like this Ken guy, they weren't looking for the relationship aspect."

"I'd say that was always the case, a hundred percent of the time, and even with tuition and rent, I never was that stressed that I had to do it. I didn't mind dancing, but that was as far as I went."

"And NastyNeighbor is the website?"

She giggled and said, "Yeah, why? You thinking of scheduling some time with Ken?"

"I just find it interesting. Listen, let's stay in touch and let me know when you'd like breakfast."

"I will, Dev. You let me know if you get a date with Ken."

"You'll be the first person I tell, Jasmine."

I hung up and googled NastyNeighbor. I had to register a fake name and email address and fill out a profile before I could actually go on the site. Even after all that they just sent me a one-time password. It took the better part of a half-hour before I went through the process and eventually got the password. Once on the site, I stated I was a woman looking for a man and quickly typed in the name Ken Carson.

Seven profiles came up. No image was attached to the profile listing until I clicked on the address, after clicking three images would appear, along with some general information. Ken Carson, actually Arnold Wazinski, was the fourth profile I clicked on.

Thirty

The first two images of 'Ken Carson' were taken from a distance on what looked like an ocean beach. I figured the odds were pretty good that the photos were from California and had been taken by Barbie. One photo looked like the image I'd seen earlier, Ken holding a surfboard, a Styrofoam surfboard. Only now, the image appeared to have been photoshopped. Ken's eyes didn't look like slits, and the blonde hair implants had been retouched to eliminate the appearance of implants looking like so many rows of corn on the top of his head. Now it just looked like a full head of hair.

Another photo, again taken at a distance, had him leaning against a lifeguard stand on the beach. He was wearing a red strappy t-shirt with a whistle around his neck. I had the feeling there was an awfully good chance Ken probably couldn't swim.

The third photo was the best, and I suppose it could have been taken as recently as yesterday. Ken, in black jeans, a light blue shirt with the sleeves rolled up to the elbow and holding a Pittsburgh Pirates hat. He was leaning against the trunk of a pink Mercedes convertible with the top down and the black leather interior exposed. Unfortunately, his legs were covering up the license plate, so I couldn't copy the number down and send it to Devan Riley.

Ken's description was a short three sentences.

'I've been blessed to live the part of a Barbie doll. I've learned a lot and would love the opportunity to provide you with an unforgettable experience. Just think, your first love, Ken. Click on the link to make your appointment NOW!'

I clicked on the link, and an email address suddenly appeared; KenCarson@hottimes.com

I had to think that, from a business perspective, as crazy as it sounded, it wasn't all that bad. At two appointments a day, if he could survive that schedule, he'd be knocking down at least six grand a month, tax-free. There seemed to be a weird allure to the whole thing. A one-time get-together with Ken. Probably a young girl's first love and envious of Barbie, she could now pull herself up onto the same level. Who would have guessed?

I picked up my phone and called Nancy Ehrhart. Just as I thought I was about to be dumped into her voicemail, she answered. "Yeah, Dev, what's up?"

"Hi Nancy, just checking in. I wanted to thank you for taking the time to meet with me yesterday. It was great to see you after all this time."

"Yeah, I appreciate the update on your friend Tubby Gustafson. Nothing I didn't really know before but thank you for the verification. One can never be too cautious."

"Exactly. If there's a way I can be of any help just give me a call."

"Oh, yeah. I'll be sure to do that," she said, sounding like she didn't mean a word.

I waited an awfully long moment before I said, "So how did things go with that doll person last night?"

"Delightfully entertaining."

"I see, you mind if I ask you a question?"

"Hey, I appreciate your information and advice yesterday, Dev. I think I've thanked you more than once, for putting me in touch with Jasmine. But, if you're looking to rekindle our disastrous affair from a decade ago, please don't take offense, or do. I don't really care, but I have absolutely no interest in going beyond a purely business relationship with you. Does that make things clear enough?"

"Yeah, and I'm fine with that, actually. In fact, I couldn't agree more. But I do have a question. It's regarding a case I'm working on. Since I've helped you, I'm wondering if you might be able to help me."

"What case is this?"

"It's regarding the theft of a collection that's estimated at somewhere between one-point-five and two-point-five million dollars. My client has reason to believe that a former business partner stole the collection, and as recently as yesterday, we thought we might have had a chance to get it back. Unfortunately, that turned out not to be the case."

"Be happy to help you if I can. I'm not aware of anything like that. Was this artwork or jewelry? No wait, Dev, if you're involved, was this some massive wine collection or maybe all the original photographs of <u>Playboy</u> foldouts, each one autographed by Hugh Hefner?" she said and laughed.

"Not exactly, the collection I'm trying to locate is one of, if not the world's largest, collection of Barbie Dolls and Barbie paraphernalia."

There was a long pause before she said anything. "I, umm, can safely say I haven't thought of, nor heard of, a Barbie collection being stolen."

"You have any recent interaction with anyone related to some aspect of Barbie?"

Again the painfully long pause. "I'm not sure what you're referring to."

"I've been tracking an individual named Arnold Rudolph Wazinski."

"Sorry, never heard of him," she said.

"He's working under the alias of Ken Carson. He's invested substantial funds in reconstructive surgery, attempting to appear like the Barbie doll's boyfriend, Ken. And, I believe he's online, offering a once in a lifetime, extremely personal experience to women. My understanding is it's one of those 'pay by the hour' experience."

"Who the hell blabbed about this?"

Her question led me to believe she'd told a number of people. "Nobody blabbed, Nancy. It's just that I've been working this case with the missing Barbie collection and your comment last night about having a date with a doll clicked inside my thick skull about three in the morning, and I just had to check."

"God, he even showed up in a pink Mercedes convertible, exactly like the car my Barbie had," she said and half-laughed.

"I got news for you. He stole the car from my client yesterday."

"What?"

"Yeah, it's a long story and actually might make for an interesting article for you. I'd gladly fill you in if you want to meet for dinner. I'll buy, absolutely no strings attached. You choose the place."

She seemed to think about that for a moment, eventually she said, "You know where Emmett's is?"

"I do. What time works for you?"

"Say seven?"

"I can do that. I'll call and make a reservation."

Thirty-one

I was at Emmett's fifteen minutes early. Nancy arrived fifteen minutes late, which gave me plenty of time to finish my beer and order another.

"Hi Dev," she said, settling in across the table from me. No kiss, no 'sorry I'm late.' "Been here long?" she asked without really looking at me. She checked her cellphone, set it on the table, and picked up the menu.

"Just got here myself," I lied and nodded at the full beer in front of me.

She ordered a glass of wine using a French accent and and said, "So, you mentioned your attempt to recover the Barbie collection was unsuccessful."

"Yeah, unfortunately, I'd say there was a better than fifty-fifty shot at getting hold of it, but Barbie got physically involved, and that pretty much botched the whole affair."

"And she scheduled an appointment to meet him?"

"No, actually nothing like that. I found him on eBay." I went on to give her the general details, including Barbie trying to run over Ken and her failed attack with the tennis racket. "He ducks her swing, pushes her down, and hops in the pink convertible she conveniently left running, and he took off.”

She literally laughed out loud. “Oh, that is so perfect on so many different levels. I will write something about that.”

“Well, I gave you the short version, so when you want to get to it, let me know and I’ll fill you in.”

She took a sip from her wine glass and seemed to relax a little. “So, you’re thinking my involvement the other evening may have been with this same individual?”

“Actually, I’m pretty sure. A lot of plastic surgery. Not just his face, but his stomach, his chest, biceps, triceps, his butt, his—”

“Sounds like the same guy,” she said, cutting me off. “It was pretty much a do not touch night from my side. On the other hand, he was rather adept at following directions. And the best part was, once he’d completed his job, I just told him to leave, and he did.”

“Mind if I show you a couple of photos?”

“If you must. Your listing of the various surgical adjustments seems to have eliminated some of the exotic aspects. Let me see what you got.”

I pulled out my cell, brought up the Ken photos, and passed the phone over to Nancy.

“Oh yeah, no question. This is him. I have to be honest. The hair implants were a real downer. And his rule was, hands off, as far as I was concerned. I could look, but I couldn’t touch his hair.”

“Really?”

"Oh yeah, he was adamant about that. Check this out, I took a picture," she said and picked up her cellphone. She clicked through a couple of screens and suddenly grinned. "Oh yeah, here he is," she said and held the screen over the table. It was Ken all right, the hair implants, the slit eyes. His wrinkle-free face just happened to be framed by Nancy's knees.

"Oh, yeah, interesting," I said and quickly changed the subject. "Did he happen to mention where he was living?"

"No, but to be honest, it never came up. I, umm, had paid for an hour, and so I wasn't interested in wasting time."

I nodded like that made sense, which, yeah, in a way, I guess it did. We ordered, chatted some more, and our meals arrived. "So your investigation into Virus Protection and the faulty PPE equipment, how's that going?"

"It's going. What can I tell you? The initial information that Jasmine had has been proven correct. I guess the one thing I'm learning is that it's not just a couple of facilities here locally, but the problem seems to be all over the country. Gustafson isn't some small-time distributor. He's big. In a normal time, the reviews would be so bad that he'd probably be out of business. But in today's world, people are figuring even with a thirty percent rate of flawed PPE, that's better than ordering stuff they can't get."

"So, he's getting away with it?"

"In a manner of speaking. All it will take is another organization able to fulfill orders, and he'll end up out of business. The national attempt to deal with this has been such a failure that Gustafson and his ilk are just one small cog in the wheel that makes up the story."

"Anything I can do to help you?" I asked.

She studied me for a long moment and finally said, "No, Dev, but thank you for asking. Actually, I'd love it if you kept me posted on how this situation with Ken and Barbie works out. It's crazy, but in a way, it's the kind of tale that could represent all of us. A picture of the insanity that our lives seem to have taken on."

"Well, yeah, it's certainly crazy. I'm just going to have to find this guy somehow and try to get that collection back to Barbie."

"Yeah, that and her idea of this doll hospital, the Dream House. By the way, I like that. It sounds like a success from adversity type of thing. I'm thinking this could be, not just an article, but maybe even a series. How they met, her collection, all the Vegas nonsense."

"Don't forget the triple X in Hollywood."

"Yes, perfect, and from it all, she ends up establishing a hospital to repair wounded dolls and allow women a few moments to travel back to a much simpler time."

I shot her a look and said, "Really?"

"Oh, Dev, you've no idea."

Thirty-two

I paid the bill and learned that Nancy's three glasses of wine were twelve dollars each. I walked her to her car in the parking lot. We shook hands before she quickly hopped in and locked her door. I was parked in the street, and my phone rang just as I climbed into my car.

"Hi Jasmine, how are the new hours working?"

"Still trying to adjust, but they're getting better. I, umm, have tomorrow off. I was wondering if we maybe could meet up."

"I think that's a great idea. You set a time, and I'll adjust to your schedule. You're the one working nights."

"Mmm, that would be nice. Tell me if this sounds too crazy. I'm done at six. That's six in the morning. I could come over to your place, and we could have a romantic breakfast. I'll even bring breakfast."

I didn't even have to think. "Yeah, that sounds perfect. You sure you don't want me to cook? I'll make whatever you want."

"Oh, that's sweet, but let me just pick something up. There's a nice little place right next to the hospital, and I can order and pick up as soon as I'm off work."

"Sounds great. I'll see you tomorrow morning. I'll have the coffee on."

"Make it decaf," she said.

I drove home to pick up Morton, and we headed down to The Spot to find Louie. We didn't have to look very hard. He was the only person seated at the bar. He was on his usual stool, hiding behind his newspaper when we walked in. Morton picked up speed as we entered and almost pulled my arm off as we made our way toward the far end of the bar.

"Well, Morton. So nice to see you again," Louie said as he leaned down with a handful of pork rinds. "Have you been keeping Dev out of trouble?"

"Believe me, I can't find any trouble to get into," I said.

"Another boring day, huh."

"Yeah, although I got a call from Jasmine. She works until six in the morning and she's agreed to come over for breakfast."

"Whoa, that sounds like a pleasant change."

"Yeah, so I'm not sure when I'll be in tomorrow, if at all."

"Can't say as I blame you. Say, not to change the subject, but I think you may have aroused someone's interest. There was a car going up and down the street every fifteen minutes this afternoon. I could be mistaken, but it sure looked like your pal Gustafson. Black Cadillac Escalade. Two guys in the front. The guy in the passenger seat looked a lot like that Fat Freddy character. With the tinted windows, I couldn't be sure, but whoever it was in the passenger seat, the guy was huge."

"Sounds like them. And what? They were just driving past?"

"If they went by once, they went by at least a half-dozen times over the course of an hour. At one point, they pulled up the block and parked for maybe ten minutes. I'm guessing they were waiting for you to show up."

"I wonder what they want."

"Based on what you've told me in the past, the timing would be perfect for them to ruin your breakfast date tomorrow."

"It's interesting. I met Nancy Ehrhart for dinner. She's continuing to investigate Tubby's Virus Protection business. Apparently, he's doing business nationally, so it's a lot bigger than I originally thought. The guy's probably making a ton of dough selling faulty PPE to hospitals."

"Wouldn't you think that, at some point, with everything going on, he'd develop a conscious somewhere along the way?" Louie said and took the final sip from his drink.

Mike looked away from the twenty-year-old hockey tournament playing on the tv just long enough so I could catch his attention, signal for a beer and another drink for Louie. He set them down in front of us a minute later.

I pulled two fives out of my wallet and tossed them on the bar. "Keep the change, Mike."

"Thanks, Dev. Just give a yell when you need a re-fill. I already know who's going to win the game." He indicated the tv with a nod of his head and walked back down to the far end of the bar.

Louie and I clicked glasses, and after a sip, Louie said, "You learn anything more about this Ken character being out there on the dating sites?"

"Yeah, I'm about ninety-nine percent sure it's our guy. I'm not sure how much he's charging, but if Nancy is to be believed, there is a waiting list. She showed me a photo she took. It sure looked like the plastic surgery guy, and he showed up driving a pink Mercedes. It has to be the same one stolen from Barbie yesterday."

"You come up with some way to catch him?"

"I intend to discuss that over breakfast tomorrow morning with Jasmine."

We chatted for a little while longer, and after Louie gave Morton another handful of pork rinds, we headed out the door. It was dusk, not completely dark, but it would be in twenty minutes. We stopped at the grocery store, and I picked up two caramel rolls and a dozen eggs just in case Jasmine forgot to pick up breakfast. I got a bottle of Prosecco since I knew Jasmine liked the stuff.

By the time we headed home, it was getting pretty dark and everyone was driving with their lights on. As I went down the street, I noticed the black Cadillac Escalade parked in front of my house. Fortunately, as we approached, a bus was coming from the opposite direction and blocked anyone sitting in the Escalade from seeing us. I just kept going, checking in the rearview mirror to see if the car moved. Thankfully, it didn't. We drove around town for another hour, and when we went by the house again, the Escalade was gone.

I quickly turned into the driveway, parked in the garage, and hurried in the back door. I left the lights off in the house and looked out the window but didn't see the Escalade anywhere. I was sure it had to be Fat Freddy and maybe Tubby in the car. Funny they wouldn't just call and tell me to get over to the mansion. I put my phone on airplane mode, went upstairs to bed, and laid awake in the dark.

Thirty-three

I peeked out the window a little after midnight. The street was empty. I made my way down to the kitchen in the dark and turned on the light over the stove. I set the kitchen counter for two, filled the coffee maker, turned off the light, and went back upstairs. I set my alarm for five-thirty and went back to sleep.

I woke a couple minutes before my alarm went off. After checking the street outside, I shaved, grabbed a quick shower, and headed downstairs. The coffee had just finished perking when I heard footsteps on the front porch. Jasmine was carrying two Styrofoam trays. I let her in, got a big kiss, and took the trays from her.

"What'd you bring for breakfast?" I asked as we headed back to the kitchen.

"I hope you like blueberry pancakes."

"I love them. I didn't know if you'd be able to get any pastry, so I picked up a couple of caramel rolls. Hope you don't mind," I said as we headed into the kitchen.

"Oh, perfect. I'm absolutely starving." Before I could say anything, she'd grabbed one of the caramel rolls and took a large bite. "Mmm-mmm, just what the doctor ordered."

I pulled the bottle of Prosecco out of the refrigerator, filled two champagne flutes, and handed one to Jasmine. She took a sip, followed by another bite of the caramel roll. She grabbed me with her right hand, held the Prosecco in her left, and led me out of the kitchen and upstairs. "Breakfast can wait," she said as she led me into the bedroom.

Morton was curled up on his pillow. He half-opened one eye, gave a quick glance, and went back to sleep. He woke me about an hour and a half later. I pulled on some jeans and let him out the back door.

I was on my laptop when Jasmine walked into the kitchen. She was wearing the t-shirt I'd worn yesterday and a smile.

"Oh, ready for some breakfast?"

"God, I can't believe I fell asleep. I was thinking about our early morning reacquaintance all during my shift last night. I just never expected to fall asleep afterward."

"No complaint from me. How about some decaf coffee, and you can finish that caramel roll while I microwave the blueberry pancakes?"

"Mmm-mmm again, sounds like just what the doctor ordered."

"Coming right up. Hey, isn't this the culmination of your first full-time work week? We need to celebrate. Congratulations," I said and poured Jasmine a coffee. I arranged the pancakes on two plates. Even after sitting in the Styrofoam box for the past two-and-a-half hours, they smelled delicious. I microwaved both plates, and we settled in at the kitchen counter for breakfast.

"You have plans for the rest of your day?" I asked as I stabbed the last bit of pancake with my fork.

Jasmine was only half-finished, and at the moment, she was in the process of cutting another petite little forkful. "I want to go back to bed right around noon just to try and stay on my new sleep schedule. Otherwise I'll be screwed up for the next three or four days."

"You're welcome to sleep here if you want. I'd love to have lunch and dinner with you."

"Oh, that's so nice, but I think I should go home. Believe me, Dev, I've had exactly what I wanted for breakfast."

"You really like blueberry pancakes?"

She gave me a look, laughed, and shook her head. "I didn't exactly mean breakfast."

"Can I ask you a somewhat serious question?"

"Is this something bad? Is there someone else?"

"Yeah, but not what you're thinking. I'm working this case with the Barbie Doll lady…" I went on to bring her more or less up to date, told her about the Pink Splendor Barbie fiasco. Barbie attempting to run down Ken and him stealing her car in the process. "So, what I was hoping to do was maybe use you as a fake customer. I was thinking you could email him and set up a date.

When he shows up, I'll be there waiting and just grab him. You don't have to be anywhere around."

"What are you going to do? Kill him?"

"No, in fact, I don't think I'm even going to get the police involved. I just want to get this woman's collection of Barbies back to her, oh, and her car. I might suggest it would be a bad idea to contact her ever again. But after that he'd be free to go."

She placed another petite forkful in her mouth, seemed to think for a moment, before she nodded and said, "Yeah, I suppose I could do that. Couple of thoughts. If he's scheduling these outings twice a day, I could schedule in the daytime instead of the night. Oh, and one more thing, I would want to use your address rather than mine. Just in case there's some screw up, I don't want him knowing where I live. Does that sound fair?"

"That would be great. I'll owe you big time, Jasmine."

"Yes, you will, and I intend to be paid in advance, right after breakfast." This time she took a large forkful of blueberry pancake and shoveled it into her mouth.

I took a long shower and tiptoed back into the bedroom. Jasmine was sound asleep in bed and snoring softly. I quietly got dressed and went downstairs. I sent Louie an email telling him I was working from home. I scanned eBay but couldn't find any Barbie items for sale from WAZ.A.R., which suggested either we'd scared him off of eBay, he was using a completely different name, or there was the outside chance that he had found a buyer for the entire collection. I still wondered where he was staying and where he was keeping the collection.

Thirty-four

I heard the shower running upstairs a little before three. Jasmine came into the kitchen dressed in her slacks and blouse.

"Hey, you're up. You have a good sleep?"

"Mmm-mmm, I didn't mean to sleep that long, but I guess I earned it, and the Prosecco helped. I can maybe have a short sleep later tonight and hopefully stay on some semblance of my schedule. Oh, your canine version of you, Morton, hid my thong somewhere."

"Sorry about that. I'll see if I can find it," I said, knowing it was already chewed up. I quickly changed the subject. "Any chance you can get on the day shift?"

"Not at this time, but to be honest, there is so much to learn, and I'm so happy to have the opportunity, I wouldn't want to change. I really like the people I'm working with, and they could not be nicer."

"So, it's still going okay."

"Yeah, all things considered. I mean, I don't think there's been a day I haven't cried for these poor people, but there's no time to dwell on it, and with so much to do you just have to get on to the next thing, whatever that is."

I suddenly had a lump in my throat and flashed back to the Medevacs in Iraq.

"Dev?"

"Oh, sorry, I just want to let you know, I'm really proud of what you're doing."

"Right now, about all I'm capable of doing is hopefully following directions."

"You're helping to save lives, Jasmine. Don't think any differently."

"Hey, I'm about to head home. You want me to make that date with the Barbie doll guy?"

"Yeah, if you wouldn't mind. Here, let's check it out." I got onto the NastyNeighbor website and clicked on Ken's link. The three pictures of him came up, and Jasmine studied each one.

"Oh wow, gotta say he looks like what you'd expect Ken to look like. And this is all plastic surgery?"

"Yeah, but he's clearly photoshopped those pictures. He's hidden some of the obvious signs of over a hundred grand worth of plastic surgery. A lot of which he didn't pay for. He'd be in some serious trouble on the past due bills, although he may be past the statute of limitations on the things by now."

She scrolled down to Ken's little note, *I've been blessed to live the part of a Barbie doll. I've learned a lot and would love the opportunity to provide you with an unforgettable experience. Just think, your first love, Ken. Click on the link to make your appointment NOW!'*

She clicked on the link, and his email address appeared, KenCarson@hottimes.com.

"Okay, first problem I see, Dev is if I contact him on your laptop, it may leave a trail, or even your email address, depending on how techy he is."

"So, you want to do this when you get home?"

She shook her head and said, "No. I'll just send him a text message." She pulled out her phone and copied his email address. Her fingers flew across the screen as she typed a message. "How about this?" she said and handed me her phone.

'Ken, dreaming about getting together with you. Talk about fulfilling something on my bucket list! Would a daytime get together work for you? Please let me know as soon as possible. So excited.'

"Yeah, that's great, Jasmine. As long as you're comfortable with it, go ahead and send it."

She pushed send, and a moment later, her phone made a swishing sound signaling the message had been sent. "Okay, I'll let you know as soon as I hear anything. Now, Dev, just so you understand, if he wants an address, I'm planning on giving him your address. Is that okay?"

I thought for a moment and said, "I got a better idea. When he contacts you, tell him you want to get a hotel room to make the event extra special. Let him choose the hotel and tell him you'll pay. If he still asks for your address, give him mine, but let me know before you send it to him. I want to make sure I keep a low profile, and he doesn't see me in the driveway or out on the front porch."

"Okay. Well, I'd better take off. Oh, just in case he wants a credit card, you want to give me yours?"

I thought about that, figured he would probably want it, and gave her the number.

"Thank you for an absolutely wonderful morning," she said and gave me a kiss.

"Yeah, delicious breakfast. I love blueberry pancakes."

"I wasn't talking about the pancakes, Dev."

"Call me later," I said as I walked her to the door. I did a quick check out the window before I opened the door. I didn't see anything that looked like a black Cadillac Escalade. I got another kiss on the front porch and waved as she blew me a kiss before she climbed into her car and drove off.

I cleaned up the kitchen, put Morton in the car, and we drove down to the office. Louie was out, and I turned off the empty coffee pot. I decided to hopefully eliminate a potential problem on the horizon, took out my phone, and dialed Tubby Gustafson's number.

A voice, not Tubby's, answered on the third ring.

"What is it, Haskell?"

"I'm calling for Mr. Gustafson, please."

"What's this about?"

"That's between Mr. Gustafson and myself."

"You want to talk to him or not?"

"It concerns money," I said, thinking that was bound to get Tubby's attention.

"Hold for a minute."

It was more like five minutes before Tubby came on the line. "I'm busy, Haskell. What is it?"

"Thanks for taking my call, Mr. Gustafson. I wasn't sure where you wanted me to send my invoice and thought I'd better check with you, so it's done correctly. I know how you hate—"

"Invoice? What the hell are you talking about?"

"My invoice for pulling all-night security in a number of your locations, sir."

"My locations?"

"Yes, sir. The Lumberyard, The Landing Strip, and Dolly's. It seems with the help of my working the night shift, the graffiti attacks have stopped in your clubs. I'm glad I was able to help, and now I'd like to send you my invoice, sir."

"Let me get this straight, Haskell. I introduce you to an aspect of your business you never considered. I let you practice at my operations, at no charge I might add, and now you want to invoice me for being the kind-hearted, generous individual I am."

It would have been funny except that Tubby really believed what he was saying.

"Well sir, those were three middle of the night shifts that I was more than willing to do, but I think it only fair that I'm paid for my time. Have you had any additional incidents since I worked, sir?"

"Clearly not the point, Haskell. I swear to God. I once again offer to help, and you can't wait to make a mess of the whole affair. It's beyond amazing."

"Shall I just send the invoice to your home address, sir?"

"I'll tell you where you can send that invoice," he said and hung up.

Thirty-five

y phone rang a minute or two after Tubby hung up. I figured it was him calling back to give me the right address to send the invoice to… not! "Haskell Investigations," I said, staring out the window at two attractive women jogging up the street.

"Have you heard anything from Ken?" Barbie asked.

Suddenly, a call from Tubby wasn't looking too bad. "Oh, hi Barbie, how's it going?"

"Answer my question. Have you heard from him?"

"No, I haven't. I'm in the process of working on something that will hopefully put me in touch with him. But, it's liable to take a day or two."

"What is it? I need to be involved."

"No, you don't, Barbie. Let's just let this work its—
"

"Did you hear what I just said, Dev?"

"Yes, I did. But with all due respect, your involvement is going to delay any response from him. Or, if he does respond, it's not going to be what you want to hear. So let me just see how this works and—"

"What exactly are you planning?"

"Barbie, I'm not going to tell you. So stop asking."

"You're working for me, Dev Haskell."

"I tell you what. How 'bout I quit, and you get someone else to find your collection?"

There was a long pause before she said, "I really need to be kept informed," and hung up.

It actually felt like a weight had been lifted from my shoulders. Now all I had to do was wait until Jasmine called with the timing on her appointment with Ken. Louie pulled to the curb maybe fifteen minutes later. I was scanning the apartment across the street with my binoculars. I watched as he parked behind my Crown Vic. He climbed out of his car, gave a longing glance in the direction of The Spot, before he headed across the street and into our building. After a moment, the stairs began to creak as he made his way up to the second floor.

Morton stared at the door as the creaking grew louder. When the door opened, a red-faced Louie stood there for a moment and exhaled as if he'd just lifted some massive weight. He gave a simple nod as he headed behind his picnic table and settled into his desk chair. It was a couple of minutes before he said, "So how'd your day go?"

"Good, I told Tubby I was going to send him an invoice."

"There's a first," Louie said.

"And, I told Barbie she could find someone else if she insisted on being involved in trying to get her collection back from that numbskull Ken or Arnold or whatever name he's going by."

"Numbskull seems to be fairly accurate. I spent the better part of my afternoon waiting in the courtroom for my case to be called."

"Everything go okay?"

"About what I expected. License suspension, a fine, and my client is mandated to attend meetings."

"How long is the suspension?"

"Six months."

"He going to be able to do that?"

"He'll have to. He really doesn't have much of a choice. I, however, do have a choice. You interested in stopping for one at The Spot?"

"Yeah, I'm more or less in a holding pattern on a couple of things. I tell you what. Let me get that invoice typed up and in the mail to Tubby, take Morton for a short walk, and we'll be over."

"Works for me," Louie said and headed out the door a few minutes later.

I typed up Tubby's invoice, billed him three-hundred and fifty bucks for each night. I gave him a preferred client discount of a hundred-bucks a night. I listed 'travel time' at no charge and typed up an envelope. I clipped on Morton's leash, and we headed out the door. The mailbox was just at the corner, and I tossed in Tubby's invoice.

Morton checked out three fire hydrants, just about every front gate, half the trees, and a pair of squirrels that ran up an oak tree. It took fifteen minutes, but we finally made it into The Spot. Whereupon Morton charged down the length of the bar toward Louie sitting on his usual stool. I signaled Mike for a beer and a fresh drink for Louie.

"Well, Morton. Are you trying to get away from Dev? I can't say I blame you. He's tough work, and it's constant. Better have some pork rinds to help you get your sanity back," Louie said. He emptied the better part of the bag into his hand and reached down. Morton inhaled everything and sniffed around the barroom floor in an effort to find any wayward crumbs.

Mike delivered our drinks, and I handed him a twenty.

Louie took a healthy sip of his first drink and said, "You never gave me an update on Barbie's reaction when you told her she could find someone else."

"Well, yeah, I told her that so she wouldn't insist on getting involved. She's pissed off at this guy, and I don't blame her. She has every right to be mad. The problem is, she becomes her own worst enemy. That disaster in front of the capitol was just the latest example."

"You think she learned from that?"

"I think about all she learned was that, next time she should stay in the car and just run him over. Once he's

on the ground with broken legs and probably uncon-
scious, she can get out of the car with her stupid tennis
racket and beat him to her heart's content."

"Yeah, sound advice, Dev," Louie said. He drained
his glass, set it off to the side, and pulled the fresh drink
closer to him. "You type up that invoice for Tubby?"

"I did, and after I typed it up I put it in the mailbox.
With any luck, he'll get it in forty-eight hours. I told him
I was going to send it. Of course, that set him off. Hopefully, it will discourage him from having me spend any
more nights in one of his clubs."

"One can only hope," Louie said and sipped his
fresh drink. "It will be interesting to see what he does
when he receives it."

"When I told him I was sending it, he started yelling
at me, said it had been an opportunity to learn something
about the industry."

"Meaning the security business?"

"Yeah, I guess so. Sitting in an empty strip club until
seven in the morning is not what I want to do with my
life."

"Not when there are criminals out there like this Ken
character Barbie's dealing with."

"Yeah, well, that would have been taken care of by
now if she hadn't inserted herself. Plus, she'd still have
her car."

"How is she getting around?"

"I have no idea, and I have no desire to find out. I
just want to get her collection back to her and move on

with my life." My phone rang, and I glanced at the number. "Oh, what do you know. Talk about moving on. Hi, Jasmine."

"Dev, I just got a text message from that Ken guy."

"Really? What did he say?"

"He wants to meet tomorrow morning."

"Tomorrow morning, that was fast. I thought it would be at least a couple of days," I said.

"Well, apparently not, and he picked out a hotel."

"Really? Which one?" I was thinking maybe the Holiday Inn downtown or the Marriott if he wanted to go a little higher class.

"He said the Hotel Confidential, downtown."

"Oh really," I said, trying not to sound too surprised. I knew of the place, but I'd never even darkened the doorway. There was always a guy in a top hat and a gray coat with tails standing out in front. He opened the door for you when you entered and expected a five-dollar tip for his effort. If it wasn't the most expensive place in town, it had to be the second most expensive.

"You know the place, Dev?"

"Only by reputation. It's pricy. Why don't you call and see if you can make a reservation? Did he give you a time?"

"Yeah, ten tomorrow morning. I made a one-hour appointment with him."

"Perfect, hang on for just a minute." I pressed my phone against my leg and said, "Hey, Louie, it looks like I'm going to have to work tonight. Would you mind looking after Morton? I should be back in the office around noon tomorrow."

Louie looked down at Morton, sitting at his feet. "Your prayers have been answered, Morton. You get the night off. Yeah, sure, Dev, not a problem."

"Thanks, man, I owe you. You still there, Jasmine?"

"Yeah, what's up?"

"Go ahead and make the reservation for tonight. I'll pay. Hang on. Let me give you my credit card number."

"You gave it to me earlier, Dev. I had to pay Ken in advance. I'll ask the hotel if they have a late checkout. As long as I'm going to book this for tonight, you think you might be interested in, umm, getting together?"

"Amazing, even over the phone, you can read my mind, Jasmine."

"Let me make the reservation, and I'll get back to you in a couple of minutes."

"You and Jasmine?" Louie asked when I hung up. He'd just emptied the pork rind bag into his hand and leaned down to Morton. As Morton lapped up the last of the pork rinds, his wagging tail kept slapping against my leg.

"It's a set-up to get this Ken character. He's made an appointment with her for tomorrow morning. I'll be waiting in the hotel room when he knocks on the door and hopefully be able to bring this whole thing to a close. God, with any luck, I just might be able to have Barbie out of my hair by the end of the day."

"Here's to success," Louie said and raised his glass. We toasted, and I drained my beer.

"Let me run home and get Morton's food," I said.

"Relax, I've still got some from the last time he spent the night."

"You sure?"

"Well, I didn't eat it, so it should still be there. Go on. Enjoy the night and good luck. Hey, Mike," Louie called, "we're gonna need another bag of pork rinds here."

Thirty-six

It was now just a little after eight. Jasmine had called me back a couple of hours earlier with the room number. I pulled into the parking ramp next to the hotel. I took my suitcase out of the Crown Vic, rode the elevator down to the main level, and walked over to the hotel.

The Hotel Confidential occupied a five-story limestone building that was built a hundred and fifty years ago. It was originally a factory of some sort but had since added electricity, running water, a swimming pool, and a bar, not to mention hotel rooms. I pulled the small suitcase behind me and smiled at the guy in the top hat when he held the door for me.

The lobby was paneled, and the reception counter featured heavily carved wood with a white marble top. Large, gilt-framed oil paintings that looked like they were a hundred and fifty years old hung on the walls. The woman behind the reception counter smiled at me as I walked past, maybe suggesting that guys making their way to a room where a woman was waiting was an everyday occurrence, which maybe it was.

The door on the elevator opened as soon as I pressed the up button. I stepped in, pressed five, and the door closed. A sign on the fifth floor directed me to the right. Jasmine's room was 508.

The hallway on the fifth floor was relatively short. It had mahogany paneling maybe four feet high and light blue walls above that. Like the lobby, antique-looking gilt-framed oil paintings hung on the wall. All the light fixtures along the ceiling were brass. Room 508 was the fourth door down the hall.

I knocked, and a moment later, Jasmine opened the door. "Well Dev, any trouble finding the place?" she asked, and smiled. She was dressed in tight black slacks and what looked like a white silk blouse with the top three buttons undone. A small gold crucifix dangled enticingly just above her deep cleavage. She didn't appear to be wearing a bra.

"Nice digs you've got," I said, stepping into the room. There were two good sized rooms, well three if you counted the bathroom. The floors were oak in a parquet pattern with large, thick, oriental rugs. The main room had light grey walls, a fireplace with a coffee table in front of it, and antique couches large enough for two on either side of the coffee table. A cushioned chair with a matching footstool was in one corner, and an antique desk sat in the other. A tv was mounted on the wall above the desk. An antique sideboard with a tray, glasses, and a phone was against the back wall. Next to the sideboard was a small refrigerator.

"Come on. Let me show you the party room," she said, and I followed her into the bedroom. A queen-sized four-poster bed was centered in the room. The covers were carefully folded back, and what looked like two chocolate-covered mints rested on each pillow. Matching nightstands with brass lamps were on both sides of the bed. An upholstered bench was at the foot of the bed, and just opposite the bench, a marble-topped antique chest of drawers had a tv sitting on top of it. An upholstered chair was in the corner next to the chest of drawers. Once again, a thick oriental rug covered the floor."

"Nice digs. What's all this costing me?" I cringed as I waited for her answer.

"At the moment, nothing, big spender. Your credit card was declined. I had to use mine."

"Oh, sorry about that."

"Yeah, well, you can pay me tomorrow, in cash," she said.

In an effort to change the subject, I set my suitcase on the bench at the foot of the bed, unzipped it, and pulled out two bottles of pink Prosecco and a bottle of Jameson.

"Dev, you know I don't drink whiskey," she said.

"Good, that will work out perfectly, because I'm not really wild about Prosecco, and certainly not pink Prosecco."

I grabbed all three bottles and brought them into the front room. I placed one of the Proseccos in the refrigerator, tore the foil off the top of the other bottle, pointed it toward the fireplace, and began to work the cork loose until it finally shot into the fireplace. Jasmine laughed, grabbed a glass, and held it out.

I filled her glass almost to the top and poured maybe a half-inch of Jameson into a glass for me. We took up positions on the two antique couches. I kicked off my shoes and stretched out, placing my feet on the coffee table. I was barely settled in when she gave me a look, and I set my feet back on the floor.

"Much better, thank you," she said and took a big sip of Prosecco. We chatted for a good while over two more glasses of Prosecco about how nice the place was. Jasmine actually used the word 'romantic.' We avoided the real reason of why we were there, setting up Ken and recovering Barbie's collection. Finally, Jasmine held out her empty glass and said, "We should talk about what happens tomorrow."

I refilled her glass, making note of the fact there was maybe half a glass of Prosecco left in the bottle, and I hadn't been drinking the stuff. "Yeah, so tomorrow. I'm thinking you should leave no later than 9:00. I don't expect any trouble, but I want to play it safe. I plan to talk to this guy, and hopefully, he'll see the wisdom in turning over the Barbie collection and Barbie's car. If he does that, he's free to go."

"And if he doesn't?" she asked and took a hearty gulp.

"If he doesn't? It's pretty simple. I'll call my contact in the police department. This Ken character will be arrested, and he'll end up with a lot more problems to deal with."

Thirty-seven

It was close to midnight when we headed toward the bedroom. Jasmine's blouse was unbuttoned, and her slacks were on the floor next to the coffee table. She was wearing a black thong and carrying what was left of the second bottle of Prosecco. She was feeling no pain as she attempted to refill her glass, sloshing Prosecco onto the thick Oriental rug.

She set the almost empty second bottle on the nightstand in front of her and gulped down what was in her glass. She seemed to weave back and forth for a few seconds, let off a loud burp, and more or less collapsed into the bed. She attempted unsuccessfully to focus and said, "I'm just going to close my eyes for a little minute."

I stepped over to the far side of the bed, started to pull off my shirt, and said, "Jasmine, honey, don't go to sleep now. Remember, you promised we were going to— Hey, Jasmine? Jasmine?"

She responded with a loud snore. I hurried back to her side of the bed and gently shook her shoulder. "No, Tommy, not now," she mumbled and slapped my hand away, never opening her eyes.

"Jasmine, hey, Jasmine, honey."

She let off a throaty groan, reached over, and pulled a pillow over her head. So much for the romantic night. I stood next to her for a long moment waiting for the 'little minute' to end, but it never happened. I walked back over to my side of the bed, picked up the remote, and turned on the tv. I found a movie channel and started clicking through my choices. Nothing was really catching my interest, and to top it off, there was the snoring, which, despite the pillow over her head, had increased in volume. I put the lights on dim and went back out to the main room, settled into the cushioned chair, and stretched out on the footstool. I clicked on the tv and landed on The Big Lebowski.

My phone vibrating in my pocket woke me. It was close to 2:00 in the morning. I could still hear Jasmine's snoring coming from the bedroom, and Nancy was calling.

"Hello, Nancy?"

"Dev!" she shouted. "Dev, I'm being followed. They're following me, Dev. They're following me."

"Nancy, calm down. Who's following you? Where are you?"

"I don't know who they are, but they're following me. It's a big black car, and there are two men in the front. I can't see anyone else, but there are at least two of them."

"Where are you?"

"I'm in the warehouse district. I snuck into Gustafson's warehouse, where he ships out all the Virus Protection equipment."

"Tubby's got a warehouse?"

"They're following me, Dev. I think they've got a gun."

"Where are you now?"

"I'm just turning onto the interstate heading south on 35E. They're right behind me, Dev. Right behind me."

"I'm heading your way. I'm going to call the cops now."

"Hurry, Dev, you've got to hurry."

"You just keep driving I'll catch up to you. Do not stop. Do you know your license number?" I said, slipping into my shoes.

"No, no, I don't."

I grabbed a card to let me back in the room and hurried out the door. "What kind of car are you driving?"

"A white SUV, a Chevrolet."

"I'm on my way. You just keep heading south," I said as I stepped onto the elevator and lost our phone connection. I tried to call her a half-dozen different times but couldn't get an answer.

I tossed my phone on the passenger seat and sped down to the parking ramp exit. I passed someone in a sleeping bag next to an elevator. The gate was down, and I inserted my credit card and waited for what seemed like an hour before the gate rose. I sped up the street to the freeway entrance at least ten minutes behind Nancy.

I accelerated down the entrance and floored the Crown Vic, moving into the far left lane and pushing the car to eighty, ninety, and finally ninety-five miles per hour. Fortunately, at this hour there was very little traffic and absolutely no one in my lane. I raced along the freeway, crossed the bridge over the Mississippi, and kept going.

I saw taillights up ahead and pushed the car to nearly a hundred miles per hour. It seemed to be holding together, and I quickly gained on the taillights. It turned out to be a Toyota of some sort, and I shot past as if it were standing still. I called Nancy's number again and hit the speaker option.

"Dev?" she answered.

"I'm coming down the freeway, just passed the airport exit. Where are you?"

"Wait, here's a sign. Hang on. I'm just a mile before Pilot Knob. They're still behind me."

"Take the exit, Nancy. If you get to a red light, run it. Don't stop. I'm just a couple miles back and gaining."

"These guys mean business, Dev. Okay, I'm going up the exit."

"Just keep going," I said and shot past the 'Pilot Knob 2 Miles' sign a moment later. The speed limit for the circular exit was twenty-five miles per hour. I braked hard and slowed down to thirty-five as I screeched around and up the exit to Pilot Knob Road. I could see two sets of taillights up ahead, and I floored it again, picking up speed as the road straightened out. The stoplight ahead was yellow for just a few seconds before it turned red. I couldn't see any cars, crossed my fingers, and shot through the intersection, doing about sixty-five and climbing.

I was gaining, and the rear set of taillights suddenly pulled into the oncoming lane and picked up speed, pulling alongside the white SUV that had to be Nancy. The brake lights on the white SUV suddenly went on as the car fishtailed from side to side. One of the taillights went out, and the SUV pulled to the side of the road.

The other set of taillights appeared to accelerate off into the distance. I pulled behind the SUV and hurried out of my car. The taillight on the left side of the car was smashed, and the car was dented and marred by what looked like black paint. I hurried toward the driver's door. Passing what looked like three bullet holes on the driver's side, one in the rear window and two more in the middle window. I didn't see anyone behind the wheel until I looked in the driver's window and there was Nancy, lying face down and leaning into the front passenger seat. She was wearing jeans and a black t-shirt.

"Nancy, Nancy," I yelled, all the while pulling on the locked car door. She suddenly half-turned and stared at me for a long moment before she sat up and unlocked the door.

I opened the door, and she half-jumped out of the seat and rushed into my arms. "Oh, Dev, thank you, thank you, thank you, for being here. They were going to kill me. I've never, ever, been so happy to see someone in my entire life."

"You have any idea who it was?" I asked.

She shook her head. "No, not really, other than I'm sure they worked for Gustafson. One guy was really fat. He was the one with the gun. When he rolled down the window and stuck his head out, I could see his chins flapping in the breeze. I slammed on the brakes just as he started shooting, and they sped past. The driver, I don't know. I just caught a half-second glimpse. He wasn't fat, maybe more muscular."

"Did he have dark hair?"

She shook her head. "I couldn't tell. It all happened so fast. They must have followed me for about twenty minutes. I don't know how they found me. Who were they, Dev?"

I was thinking back to my night at the Landing Strip. The same night I met Jasmine, when Fat Freddy Zimmerman and that muscular thug interrupted us. They had come in thinking they were going to catch me sleeping.

"Yeah, I think I know one of them, the fat guy you mentioned. He's more or less Tubby Gustafson's errand boy or second in command. I happen to think he's an idiot, but for some reason, Tubby likes him."

"What's his name?"

"Frederick Zimmerman, everyone on the street calls him Fat Freddy Zimmerman. Like I said, he's an idiot."

"Yeah, well, thankfully, he's a lousy shot, too."

"Speaking of which, let's not press our luck. If they drive back this way, we'll be sitting ducks. Think your car will be able to make it back into town?"

"Yeah. I know I smashed into them when I hit the brakes. Didn't mean to, but I think it probably messed up that fatty guy's aim."

"Yeah, it took out your taillight. You're probably gonna need a new rear panel, but you're not shot. Why don't you follow me back to town."

"I don't want to go to my place. They might be waiting for me there."

"Do they know who you are?"

"If they don't know, they will soon enough. I'm going to finish my article tomorrow. Following me all that time, they were able to get my license number. It doesn't take a rocket scientist to figure a way to get my name from that."

I had a half-second thought of my pal in the state DMV office. "Well, follow me. I'm staying in a hotel. Actually, I'm working a case. You can stay there at least until the sun comes up and we can figure something out."

"Oh, Dev, I'm so sorry. Did I goof up your case?"

"Nancy, you've got three bullet holes in your car, and I was sleeping in a chair in front of the tv. You didn't goof up anything. Come on back with me. It's the last place in the world they'll think to look for you."

"Okay, yeah, that sounds like a pretty good idea. I think I've had enough excitement for one day."

Thirty-eight

I drove back to town at the posted speed limit with Nancy behind me the entire way. We pulled into the parking ramp next to the Hotel Confidential. It was after 3:00 in the morning. At this hour, not only was the guy in the top hat not around, but the door to the hotel was locked. Fortunately, I'd grabbed the card for the room. I pulled it out of my wallet and inserted it into the slot in the door. A green light flashed, and the door clicked open.

The lights in the lobby were dimmed, and with the small lights illuminating the oil paintings in the gilt frames, they stood out even more. "Quite the place, isn't it?" I said as we walked through the empty lobby to the elevator. For the first time, I noticed she had what looked like three or four accounting ledger books crammed in the purse slung over her shoulder.

"Yeah, it's lovely. Have you tried out their pool? It's really nice, and there's a great little sauna there too." I must have given her a look because she said, "I've only been here a couple of times."

"Working?" I guessed in a tone that suggested anything but.

She shook her head and said, "No, strictly pleasure. Pure pleasure."

We stepped onto the elevator and rose up to the fifth floor. "We're in 508," I said as the elevator door opened. Nancy stepped off the elevator and headed down the hall as if she knew exactly where she was going.

When I opened the door to the room, I said, "Wait here for a second and let me just check on my partner in crime."

"Someone's in here with you?"

"I'll explain it to you in just a minute," I said and peeked into the bedroom. Jasmine was nowhere to be seen. I pulled the bed covers back just to see if she might be hidden, but she wasn't there. The pillow where she'd been was smeared with melted chocolate. I looked under the bed, but the space was empty. I was about to think she'd gone home but decided to check the bathroom.

There she was, asleep on the floor, curled up around the toilet, still wearing her black thong and white silk blouse. Based on the large pink stain down the front of her blouse, it didn't take much of a guess as to what she'd been doing in here.

I bent down and gently shook her shoulder. "Jasmine, hey Jasmine. Wake up, and let's get you back into bed."

"Mmm-mmm," she groaned. "Leave me alone. I just want to sleep here."

"Come on. You'll feel better in bed."

"My head is killing me, and my stomach doesn't feel so good."

"I know. I'm going to get you some aspirin, and once you're back in bed, you'll start to feel better."

"Promise?"

"Yeah, I promise. Come on," I said and helped her onto her feet.

She stood for a moment, looking pasty and weaving slightly. Talk about the bloom being off the rose. Mascara surrounded her eyes. Her lips looked pale. Melted chocolate was smeared on her right cheek. Her hair was an absolute mess, and there was the large pink stain that appeared to cover the entire front of her blouse. The better part of a bottle of Prosecco, I figured.

She took hold of my arm, and I slowly led her toward the bed. Nancy stood in the doorway, staring with her mouth open. About halfway to the bed, Jasmine suddenly made a couple of loud swallowing noises, quickly turned, and charged back into the bathroom. The noise that erupted left nothing to the imagination. It was followed by a groan and coughing and still more noise that let you know exactly what was going on.

I walked back out to the front room. "So, do you have some safe place to go where these guys won't be able to find you?"

"Dev? What the hell was that all about? Was that Jasmine?" Nancy asked.

"Oh yeah, I forgot you two met."

"Met? She was the one who put me onto Gustafson's PPE scam. What is she doing here?"

"Better take a seat, and I'll tell you," I replied and pointed to the couches in front of the fireplace. Jasmine's slacks were still on the floor next to the coffee table. "Umm, can I interest you in a glass of Jameson?"

With that, the sound of Jasmine erupting again in the bathroom echoed out into the front room.

"I think I should probably stay away from the Jameson just now."

"Her poison was pink Prosecco. She went through two bottles of the stuff."

She made a face and said, "Thanks, but no thanks."

"Okay," I said, settling down on the couch opposite her. "So, do you remember my story about the Pink Splendor Barbie?"

"Gee, let me think. Do you mean where you set up a meeting with that Ken character and were going to recover this Barbie person's doll collection? Only she showed up and tried to run him over, that story?"

"Yeah, your one-night stand guy, Ken."

She shot me a look and said, "Jasmine is involved with him, too?"

"No, at least not really." I went on to tell her how I had Jasmine set up the meeting for later that morning with Ken. "Now, hopefully, she'll be able to drive herself home, and when Ken shows up, he'll just have me to deal with."

"He's actually coming here? To this room?"

"That's what I'm planning on. He picked the hotel and the time, 10:00 in the morning."

"You think he'll cooperate?"

"If I can get him in this room, I can't see any other choice for him. Either he cooperates, or I call the police. If he tries to run, I'll threaten to break his fake nose or kick him in his fake ass. Either way, he'll be screwed."

"I'm sensing a great story here."

"When all is said and done, he's all yours. You've, umm, already met him. When this is all over, you should meet Barbie, too. She's a little out there, but she means well. Like you said at dinner the other night, her Dream House will allow women to travel back to a simpler time."

"You should probably check on your friend in the bathroom," Nancy said. "Let me call room service and get some aspirin up here."

"They're probably closed until later this morning," I said.

"No, they're open twenty-four hours a day. I'll give them a call. You better check on your friend, Jasmine, see if she can get back into bed. She'll need some decent sleep if you want to get her out of here before Ken arrives," Nancy said and raised her eyebrows.

"Yeah, okay, you're probably right. Listen, if you want to settle into that chair in the corner, it's actually pretty comfortable."

"Thanks, Dev. Let me get those aspirins up here," she said and picked up the phone on the antique sideboard.

I cautiously approached the bathroom. Jasmine was kneeling on the floor with her head hanging over the toilet.

"Hey, how you doing, Jasmine?"

"Oh, God, Dev. I was afraid I was going to die, and now I'm afraid I won't. I don't think there's anything left in me to come up."

"Hell of a way to make your goal weight."

"Oh please, don't ever mention P-I-N-K," she spelled out the word, "Prosecco to me again, ever."

"I promise I won't. You think you can make it back to bed? You're going to have to head home in a couple of hours."

"Oh God, I'm not sure I'll be able to drive. My head is pounding, and I feel like it's ready to explode."

"I've got room service bringing up some aspirin. Let's get you back into bed so you can at least get a little rest. I think it will really help. Come on. I'll give you a hand getting up."

I took hold of her arm and eased her onto her feet. She glanced at me, took a deep breath, and nodded. Her face was pasty, and the right cheek was still smeared with melted chocolate. I slowly led her into the bedroom. She climbed into the bed, seemingly oblivious to her unbuttoned silk blouse. I was pretty sure the Prosecco stain had ruined the blouse. I tossed the chocolate stained pillow onto the floor and pulled the covers up over her shoulders.

"Thank you. I'm really sorry," she said while keeping her eyes closed.

"Don't worry about it. I'll bring you some aspirin as soon as they arrive," I said and headed back to the front room. Nancy was in the cushioned chair, breathing deeply, and appeared to be sound asleep.

I sat on one of the antique couches and waited for room service to bring the aspirin. Finally, there was a gentle knock on the door maybe a half-hour later. I opened the door, and a kid who couldn't be older than 18 stood there, holding a small plate with four aspirin on it. He looked like he'd probably been sound asleep five minutes ago.

"Oh, thank you, much appreciated," I said and took the plate from him.

He smiled and stood there, no doubt waiting for his tip. I couldn't blame him. I handed the plate back to him, pulled out my wallet, and handed him the last bill I had. It was a twenty.

"Thank you," he said, sounding like it was the usual amount for a tip at Hotel Confidential. He handed the plate back to me and hurried off down the hall. I brought the aspirin into Jasmine, filled her Prosecco glass with water, and got her to take all four aspirin.

I left the bedroom light on dim and went out to the front room. I set the alarm on my phone for eight, attempted to get comfortable on the couch, and eventually drifted off to sleep.

Thirty-nine

Nancy half shouted as she shook me. "Dev, Dev, you need to wake up. Dev, it's after 9:00. Dev, wake the hell up," she half-shouted as she shook me.

"What? What time is it?"

"It's after nine. Your Ken is supposed to be here in less than an hour and—"

"Less than an hour?" I picked up my phone from the coffee table and checked the time. Sure enough, it was after 9:00. "What in the hell? I set my damn alarm on this thing," I said, checking the setting. The alarm was set for 8:00, all right, but it was 8:00 PM.

"Oh, God, I've got to get Jasmine out of here. Jasmine, Jasmine, wake up," I shouted, jumping off the couch and running into the bedroom.

She was in bed with the blanket pulled over her head. It looked as though she hadn't so much as rolled over in the past four hours. "Jasmine, let's go." I said, raising the blinds on the window. Man, but that sun was bright. "Up and at 'em."

She stirred a little from beneath the bed covers, before she settled back down. I pulled the covers all the way down to below her knees and said, "Let's go, Jasmine. You've got to get out of here. Ken is going to show up in just a couple of minutes."

She groaned as I headed out of the room, grabbed her slacks off the floor by the coffee table, and hustled back into the bedroom. Jasmine had pulled the covers back up and dragged the pillow over her head.

"Jasmine, come on, damn it. You gotta get out of here." I pulled the covers down, wrestled with her for a moment as she held the pillow over her head. I tossed the pillow onto the far side of the bed.

"Ahhh, stop it, stop it, stop it," she said and curled into a fetal position on the bed.

"Oh, no. Come on. Sit up. Let's get these slacks on you," I said and pulled her halfway up on the edge of the bed.

"All right, all right. I get it. Just give me a minute, will you? God, take it easy and let me wake up."

"There isn't time for that," I said, grabbing one of her legs and pulling the slacks over her foot. I grabbed the other leg and did the same thing, pulling her slacks up only to realize when I reached her knees that I'd put the slacks on backward and inside out.

"God, I don't believe it," I said and pulled the slacks off her legs.

Jasmine's eyes suddenly opened, and she said, "No way, Dev. I am *so* not in the mood right now."

"What are you talking about? I'm trying to get you dressed so you can get out of here before Ken arrives. Come on. We're running out of time."

"Give me those," she said, grabbing the slacks from me. "God, you've got them backward and inside out. What were you thinking?" She took her time but gradually got them over both her feet.

"Okay, where are your shoes?" I said.

"I don't know. You go find them. I gotta pee."

"Me? I just want you to—"

"Let me just remind you, Mister. You're the one who got me so drunk last night I can't see straight. I was sick all night because you bought the cheap stuff. And now, I have to use the bathroom, so find my shoes for me."

With that, she stood and slowly made her way to the bathroom. I took it as progress and hurried out to the front room. Nancy was seated on one of the couches applying lipstick. She had a little round mirror positioned on the table and a half-dozen makeup brushes and containers scattered around.

"I can't believe this. Have you seen a pair of shoes somewhere around this place?" I asked.

She remained focused on the mirror and pointed with her lipstick tube toward the small refrigerator. I looked, and sure enough, Jasmine's heels were neatly positioned right next to it. I picked them up and hurried back into the bedroom.

"Jasmine," I said and went to open the bathroom door, but she'd locked it.

"Occupied. You'll just have to wait your turn," she said.

"We need to get you out of here before Ken arrives. We're running out of time, Jasmine. You need to hurry."

"Sorry, I'm going to be a couple more minutes, and there's nothing I can do about it."

"Really, you wait until—"

"Dev, give me a couple of minutes, will you? And I'm going to need a ride. I'm not able to drive."

"Not able to drive? No, Jasmine, that's not going to work. I've got to deal with Ken and—"

"Well you just better wait for me in the other room because all you're doing is making this take longer."

"Jasmine, I—"

"Go in the other room, Dev, and wait," she shouted.

"Okay, okay, I'm going, but hurry up."

"Get the hell out," she yelled as I headed back into the front room.

There was a slight scent of a nice perfume in the room, and Nancy was just putting the makeup and brushes back into her purse. Four accounting ledgers were piled at the end of the coffee table. She grabbed the ledgers and began to stuff them into her purse.

"Dev, you're going to have to get her out of here. Look, I'll stay here. I, umm, met him once before. I'll just talk to him and keep him busy. Besides, I can get some inside information on his business for the article.

If he's as self-obsessed as I think he is, he may be thrilled to give me the information. Take her home, make sure she's okay, and get back as soon as you can, it should only take you twenty minutes. I'll let you in, and he's all yours."

"I don't know, Nancy. I just need to get her to her car."

"Dev, she was up sick all night. She's horribly hungover. She hasn't slept for more than a couple of hours. She's liable to fall asleep behind the wheel or get in an accident. I know you well enough that, if that happens, you're going to blame yourself. Just get her home, so she's safe. This Ken idiot will probably be ten minutes late anyway. You've got plenty of time."

"You think so?"

"Dev, believe me, I know. Besides, I owe you big time after last night. This is the least I can do. I'll keep him here chatting."

"Yeah, I guess you're right. Okay, yeah, thanks, Nancy. I'll be back just as soon as I can."

"Don't worry. He'll be in good hands."

Jasmine stepped out of the bathroom five minutes later. She did not look good.

"Hey, I've got your shoes right here, Jasmine," I said as she slowly entered the front room. "Let me button up that blouse for you," I said.

"What's this stain on my blouse from? Did you spill on me last night?"

"No, you did that," I said as I tried to quickly button up her blouse.

"Me?" she said as she looked over my shoulder and said, "Nancy?"

"Hi, Jasmine, how are you feeling, honey?"

"Let's just say I've been better."

"Dev is going to give you a lift home. If you're not feeling well, you shouldn't be behind the wheel."

"Is that okay, Dev? You don't mind?" Jasmine asked.

"No, no, it's just fine, but we better get going." I handed Jasmine her heels, red stilettos. She bent over to slip one on and almost fell on the Oriental rug. She grabbed hold of the corner of the sideboard at the last second to stop her fall.

She got her foot into the heel, attempted to stand and slowly shook her head. "No, this will be a disaster just waiting to happen. Can you carry these for me, Dev? And don't forget my purse," she said and brushed her uncombed hair away from her face and her bloodshot eyes. At least she'd scrubbed the melted chocolate from her right cheek.

I took the shoes and escorted her to the door. "Let's touch base later, Jasmine," Nancy called.

Jasmine slowly nodded as she stepped into the hallway.

"I'll be back in fifteen minutes, Nancy. Thanks for your help," I said.

"So not a problem. Like I said, I owe you, Dev."

Forty

There were three people at the reception counter in the lobby. A hotel employee in a grey suit with her hair pulled back in a bun and a casually dressed couple in clothes out of my price range. All three smiled as we walked past. Jasmine looked like she'd slept in her clothes, which was true as far as the pink stained blouse was concerned. I nodded at them as we passed, but they didn't acknowledge it because they were all focused on barefoot, messed up looking Jasmine, and the pair of red stiletto heels and the purse I was carrying.

I left her in front of the hotel next to the guy in the top hat and tails. I hurried into the parking ramp to get my car. I pulled into the short circular drive in front of the hotel and hurried out of the car to help her into the backseat. She laid down on the seat and closed her eyes. I noticed I'd buttoned her blouse wrong, not that it made any difference at this point.

The guy in the top hat hadn't moved and was still standing on the red carpet just next to the entrance. "You some undercover cop?" he asked as I helped her into the backseat of my Crown Vic.

"Something like that," I said and hurried back behind the wheel. I pulled into the street, drove a half-block, and had to wait at the stoplight. When the light finally changed, the car in front of me didn't move, and I leaned on the horn.

"Oh God, please don't do that, Dev," Jasmine groaned from the back seat.

The car ahead finally moved, and I waited for two cars to pass me before speeding past the woman barely moving ahead of me. As I glanced over, she gave me the finger. I turned onto the interstate and picked up speed. I took the third exit, Randolph Ave.

I had to wait for the light to change before I could turn, went half a block and stopped at the light on Lexington. It was another three minutes while I frantically drummed my fingers on the steering wheel. Finally, the light changed, and I rolled forward five feet and waited for the jerk to make his left hand turn on the red light. Now it was my turn to give someone the finger.

I drove two blocks and turned onto Edgecumbe Ave. It's a winding street with a grassy boulevard and trees in the middle of the street. The homes are two and three-story mansions, and the property taxes are at least a couple of grand a month. The street had been patched over for the past fifteen years, and you'd think if you were paying those kind of property taxes and mortgages that at least the street would be decent. But that seemed to be the case with the majority of the city's streets in recent years.

Jasmine groaned a couple of times with all the bumps and potholes. I slowed down almost to the speed limit. After I hit the second pothole, she sat up and shouted, "Pull over, Dev. Pull over."

"Don't worry, Jasmine. Just a couple more miles and we'll—"

"Pull over. I'm going to get sick."

"Really? Maybe if you just—"

"Dev, I'm not kidding," she groaned and let off a sound that had me screeching to the curb. She opened the door, more dry heaving noise as she tumbled out on all fours in front of some three-story white mansion with big white pillars across the front. A dark blue Porsche 911, gleaming under about a dozen coats of wax, was parked in the driveway.

Jasmine remained on her knees for a while. Every time I was just about ready to ask if she was okay, her body would lurch forward, and she would make the corresponding noise. Fortunately, nothing came up. Two kids, maybe twelve or thirteen riding their bikes, stopped at the corner and watched her for a couple of minutes before they took off. I looked at the digital clock on my dashboard, 10:12. I was tempted to call Nancy, but then what?

Jasmine eventually climbed back into the car and remained seated as opposed to stretched out. "Okay, please don't drive fast anymore, Dev. I can't deal with it this morning."

I made a mental note to never, ever, buy another bottle of Prosecco and pulled away from the curb. The rest of the drive was uneventful except for the fact that some guy on a bicycle actually passed me, of course Jasmine had shouted at me twice to slow down.

I pulled in front of her apartment building and parked. "You okay to make it inside?" I asked leaning over the back seat. Hard to believe, but she looked even worse than when I put her in the back seat at the hotel.

"I think I can. Things are kind of spinning, so if I don't fall, I—"

"I'd better give you a hand," I said and hurried around the car and opened her door.

She gingerly climbed out of the car, closed her eyes for a brief moment, and took a deep breath. "Okay, I'm ready."

"Let me grab your purse and shoes," I said and reached into the front seat. I carried them in my left hand and gave her my right arm to hang onto. We slowly walked up to the front door. I thanked God there was only one step.

"Give me my purse so I can get my keys." She rummaged around in her purse for a bit before finally pulling her keys out. She unlocked the door and said, "Okay, thanks, Dev. I can make it from here."

"You sure?"

"Yeah, I'm just on the first floor. Umm, sorry if I maybe screwed things up. I didn't mean to."

"You sure you can make it in okay?"

"Yeah, I'm feeling much better after that last bout. I'd kiss you, but I'm thinking you probably don't want me near you right now. I'm just going to take a hot bath and climb into bed. I've got to work tonight."

"Well, call me. Your car is still down in the parking ramp."

"Oh, yeah. God, it just doesn't end."

"Go inside and get to bed," I said and handed her the shoes and the purse.

She stepped inside, gave a wave without looking back, and disappeared through the security door. I ran back to my car, sped down the street, and had to stop at the first traffic light and wait. I hit three more lights before I turned the corner and could see the Hotel Confidential up ahead. Of course, I had to wait at one more light before I turned into the parking ramp and took the first parking place I saw. It was labeled 'Compact Cars ONLY' on the wall, but I pulled my Crown Vic in and parked next to a Mercedes convertible. A two-seater as a matter of fact with a black interior. However, this one wasn't pink. It was painted flat black, and judging from the paint job, painted fairly recently with a can of spray paint. I looked at the California plates and scratched the trunk with my fingernail, revealing a sparkling pink undercoat. Idiot Ken was still in the hotel. I opened my passenger door, pulled my pistol from the glove compartment, and shoved it in the front of my belt.

Forty-one

The guy in the top hat was busy helping a young couple out of a shiny black Lincoln with limo license plates. Probably a wedding couple, I thought as I ran past and let myself into the hotel. I literally ran across the lobby, turning heads as I went, and pushed the up button on the elevator. I waited, waited some more, and finally dashed over to the staircase and hurried all the way up to the fifth floor.

I took a couple of seconds to catch my breath before I pulled the keycard from my wallet and inserted it into the slot. The light flashed green, I pushed the door open, and stepped into an empty front room. I noticed my bottle of Jameson on the coffee table and two glasses, one of which had lipstick. A cellphone was on the coffee table next to the bottle, and what looked like Nancy's black t-shirt was on the Oriental rug in just about the same spot as Jasmine's slacks had been.

I quickly stepped into the bedroom. Nancy's jeans lay on the floor, followed by her bra, and her a thong clearly marking the trail to the four-poster bed. I could hear the shower running, and I opened the bathroom door. The room was full of steam, and I called "Nancy?"

"Ken, honey?"

"No, it's me, Dev."

"You must have missed him. He just left," she said.

I hurried out of the room and ran down the hall. I pushed the down button on the elevator, and the doors immediately opened. I descended without stopping and stepped into the lobby, looking around.

There he was, apparently autographing what looked like a newspaper as two women stood ogling and grinning. He wore a blue short-sleeve shirt with a leopard skin print pattern. The shirt was unbuttoned almost down to his navel. His powder-blue short shorts were held up with a gold belt. A powder-blue scarf was tied around his neck, and his powder-blue loafers completed the ensemble. I wanted to punch him in the nose just on general principles.

"Hey, Ken," I shouted.

As he looked over at me, his eyes suddenly grew wide, he tossed the newspaper up in the air and took off running toward a set of double doors. Both women screamed, and as I ran past, one of them shouted, "I'm calling the police."

Ken ran through the set of double doors, down a wide hallway, and through another set of double doors. I was gaining on him, in no small part because he kept looking over his shoulder to see where I was.

The second set of doors led out to the swimming pool. A number of round tables with umbrellas were positioned around a rather large area, and lounge chairs were lined up around a diamond-shaped pool with rounded corners. The pool had a mosaic monogram at the bottom. Two women in bikinis were lying on lounge chairs on the far side of the pool, taking in the sun. They were the only ones at the pool, well until Ken and I ran in.

"Stop, Ken, stop. I just want to talk to you."

"I didn't know she was married. She told me she was a journalist," he shouted, as he turned to look over his shoulder. That's when he tripped over a hose coiled up at the edge of the pool and sailed into the water.

I slowed down and walked to the edge of the pool. Ken had gone into the deep end and was splashing around. The two women on the opposite side of the pool were now sitting up. They held their bikini tops in place with one hand and focused on Ken. He continued splashing and went under for a moment before he popped back up.

"I just want to talk to you, Ken. And I'm not married to—"

"I don't think he can swim," one of the women shouted as Ken went under again, this time sinking deeper. His flailing about only served to move him further away from the wall and toward the center of the pool.

"Hey, did you hear me? That guy looks like he's really drowning," the woman said. Neither one of them gave an indication they were going to jump in.

Based on what I could see, they were right. I pulled my wallet and cellphone from my pockets and tossed them on a chair. I turned around, pulled the pistol from my belt and placed it beneath my wallet, draped my shirt over everything, and kicked off my shoes. I watched him for another moment hoping he'd surface before I said, "Damn it, Ken," and jumped in.

It took two strokes, and I was almost on top of him. He was still flailing around beneath the surface. I reached down, pulled, and came up with a handful of hair implants. I reached down again, grabbed onto the blue scarf tied around his neck, and pulled him to the surface. He was still struggling and coughing up water, although now he was above the surface. I wrapped an arm around his chest, and we made our way to the closest side of the pool.

He seemed to calm down somewhat once he could grab onto the tiled side of the pool. I hoisted myself up and out, reached down, and pulled him out. He laid on his stomach, in a large puddle, coughing and sputtering. I sat down on the lounge chair next to him and watched.

After a good five minutes, he sat up and said, "I didn't know she was married, honest. She told me—"

"Listen, Ken, I'm not married to her, and she's not a girlfriend, so relax. It's not a problem."

"Hey, wait a damn minute. I recognize you. You set me up so Barbie could try to kill me. She tried to run me down," he said and glancing around frantically.

"Okay, first of all, relax. She's not here. Now, time out, I didn't set you up. I bought the Pink Splendor Barbie from you."

"It was fake cash. Not even good counterfeits."

"You mean that fake money for the stolen collectors doll that you were going to sell me. Yeah, you're right. Look. I don't want to arrest you. I just have to get Barbie's collection back to her, and you're free to go. Oh, yeah and I'll need her car, too."

"I don't know what you got going with her but let me give you a warning. Despite what she looks like, she's nothing like Barbie. She's one mean—"

"Ken, I just need to get the collection back, and you're free to go. Otherwise, I'm gonna have to call the cops, and you are going to end up all over the newspapers. Barbie will no doubt get a lawyer, and you'll be facing a bunch of charges and some pretty serious prison time."

"What am I going to do?" he exclaimed and suddenly looked like he was ready to cry.

"Why don't we go back to the room, and you can dry off. We can work out some kind of arrangement, and I want you can take me to the Barbie collection. Sound like a plan?"

"Do I have a choice?"

"Yeah, I can call the cops, and you can take your chances there."

"That's not much of a choice."

"It's the best you're going to get. Let's go back to the room."

As we left the pool area, I noticed the handful of blonde hair implants floating up toward the shallow end and thought it best not to say anything. The two bikini-clad women were back lying down, soaking up the sun rays as if nothing had happened. Ken's powder-blue shoes were squeaking across the marble floor in the lobby as we made our way to the elevator. The woman behind the receptionist desk smiled as we passed as if two guys fully clothed and dripping wet from the pool was an everyday occurrence.

I noticed the bald spot about the size of the palm of my hand on Ken's head as we stepped onto the elevator. Neither one of us said anything on our ride up to the fifth floor. I unlocked the door with the keycard and stepped in. Nancy was sitting on one of the couches, going over the accounting ledgers. "Oh, so you two were able to meet. Good. Hi, Ken, back for more?" she said and smiled.

"Bathroom is in there. Go ahead and dry off," I said. As Ken headed toward the bathroom, I directed my attention to Nancy and said, "What are you still doing here?"

"Short term memory, Dev? After those guys tried to murder me last night, I thought it might actually be just a little too dangerous for me to go home. Those two idiots might have missed last night, but I don't feel like pressing my luck a second time. By the way, I'm the one who worked to keep Ken entertained, so he'd still be around whenever you decided to come back."

"You going to stay here?"

"No. I'm just going over Gustafson's books. I got them out of the Virus Protection office last night. Could have gotten a lot more if those two hadn't shown up."

"So you broke into his office?"

"No, Dev, I told him I was going to write an article exposing him, and he suggested I might want to look at his financial records. Yes, of course, I broke in."

"Not the guy to fool with, Nancy. I'd offer to let you stay at my place, but he's been watching me for some reason. His crew has been driving past my office. They were parked in front of my house the other night. I fear it would be almost as bad as you going back to your place."

She shook her head. "I'm not sure what I'm going to do."

I thought for a minute and said, "You know, I might have an idea, and it could help both of us at the same time."

"What is it? God, I can only imagine."

Forty-two

Ken stepped out of the bedroom, patting himself down with a towel. He looked at Nancy seated on the couch and said, "Don't even talk to me. I should have known the moment you answered the door there was more involved than a simple second round."

"I don't recall hearing any complaints from you, Mister Sixty Seconds."

"Right now, that's the least of your problems, Ken. Take a seat on the couch."

He gave me a look but sat down on the couch opposite Nancy. He bent down and pulled the powder-blue loafers off his feet. As he bent over, Nancy's eyes grew wide, and her mouth hung open as she focused on the bald spot on the top of Ken's head.

I held my index finger to my lips and shook my head, signaling her not to say anything.

"Here's my idea, Ken. Take it or leave it. You don't like it, that's your choice, and I'll just call the cops."

"Oh, so I don't really get a choice."

"Actually, you do. You can go back to California, or you can go to jail. You take me to Barbie's collection.

You can pack your personal items, and I'll drive you to the airport where you'll buy a ticket to L.A. If you don't want to do that, it's fine with me, and I'll call the cops. One way or the other, I'm going to get Barbie's collection. You just have to decide where you'd prefer to spend the next couple of years."

"Okay, okay. I'll take you to the collection. I'm not all that wild about this town anyway."

"Good choice. Nancy, you follow us. While I'm taking Ken to the airport, you can guard the collection. I'll pick up Barbie, rent a truck, and we'll load up the collection. I'll fill you in on the rest of the details later. Okay?"

Nancy nodded.

"Good, let's get going. Ken, why don't you give me your car keys?"

"Oh, I'm okay to drive."

"You won't be with the broken nose you'll have if you don't hand over your car keys in about two seconds."

Ken's eyes seemed to grow wide, but no part of his wrinkle-free face moved. He dug into a wet pocket on his shorts, pulled out Barbie's keys, and handed them to me. All right, let's get out of here. I stepped into the bedroom, pulled my suitcase off the bench at the foot of the bed, and wheeled it out to the front room. I tightened the cap on what was left of my bottle Jameson, shot a frown at Nancy, and tossed the bottle into the suitcase.

We took the elevator down to the lobby and stopped at the desk to check out. I signed the bill with Jasmine's credit card number on it, seven hundred and fifty bucks for a one-night stay. The girl at the receptionist counter kept staring at Ken.

"Excuse me, but you look like someone I know."

Ken grinned.

"Yeah, and don't waste your time. Believe me, he wasn't that good," Nancy said.

"Okay, we're out of here," I said, and we headed out the door. I tossed my suitcase in the back of the Crown Vic and nodded at Ken to climb into Barbie's spray-painted convertible. Once he was in and buckled up, I hopped in behind the wheel of Barbie's car.

"I'm only going to say this once, Ken. You try anything, and I'll run you over without a second thought. Got it?"

He nodded and stared straight ahead. We drove out of the parking ramp and I pulled to the curb. We waited two minutes before Nancy drove out of the ramp. She stopped behind me, Ken gave me directions to the storage unit over on the Eastside, and we pulled into traffic with Nancy behind us.

We drove along East Seventh Street to White Bear Avenue and headed north. My phone rang a couple of minutes later.

"Nancy?"

"Dev, there's a guy on a motorcycle behind me. I think he's got a gun."

"What?"

"I said I think he's got a gun. He might be one of the guys who tried to kill me last night."

"We'll see. I'm taking a right at the next corner," I said and put on my blinker. We turned onto a quiet little industrial street. I watched in the rearview mirror as Nancy followed me around the corner. A second or two later, the motorcycle turned onto the street.

"Yeah, he's following. Okay, I'm going to slow down. I want you to race past me, and I'll pull right behind you. You keep going. I'll deal with this guy."

Nancy suddenly sped past me. I accelerated just as the motorcycle changed gears, and his front wheel rose as he started to speed up. I floored it and cut in front of him. He was maybe three feet from my bumper when I slammed on the brakes. Ken quickly unbuckled and slid down beneath the seat as we skidded to a stop. The motorcycle smashed into the rear of Barbie's car, and the guy sailed up and over the car. He let off a loud "Uff," as he bounced off the hood and slid down to the ground. Fortunately, he was wearing a helmet. Unfortunately, it bounced off the hood, leaving a big round dent. I turned the car off and jumped out.

The guy was sitting in the middle of the street, slowly shaking his head from side to side. I placed my foot on his shoulder, pushed him onto the street, and pulled the pistol from his belt. It wasn't until he was lying in the street that I recognized the Ramones t-shirt. The same muscular guy who'd been with Fat Freddy that night at the Landing Strip when Freddy tried to catch me sleeping.

"You okay?" I asked.

He slowly nodded and said, "Yeah, I think so."

"What the hell are you doing following us? How'd you even know where we were?"

"We, we got a tracking device on that broads car."

"A tracking device? What the hell for?"

"Mr. Gustafson wanted to scare her. Something about a story she's writing. Guess she works for the newspaper or something."

"Scare her? You guys tried to kill her last night."

He looked up at me and shook his head. "No, no, we just wanted to scare her off. That's why Fat Freddy shot at the back windows. We weren't going to kill her."

"And just now?"

"I wouldn't kill her, honest. I wouldn't. Hey, could you give me my gun back?"

"I don't think so."

"Come on, dude. It's just loaded with blanks."

I pressed the release button, and the magazine dropped out. He was right. They appeared to be all blanks. I dropped them one by one on the street and tossed the magazine a few feet away.

"See, I wasn't lying. So, can I have my gun back, please?"

"No, you can't. I tell you what. You know who I am?"

"You're that hassle guy."

"Haskell, Dev Haskell. You give me a call, and I'll think about giving it back to you. Oh, and I wouldn't mention this to Tubby or Fat Freddy. They're liable to take it the wrong way."

"Oh, man."

"Later, Dude," I said. I glanced at the motorcycle lying on its side in the street. The front tire rim was bent at about a ninety-degree angle. He wouldn't be going anywhere on that.

I hopped back into Barbie's car. Ken was curled up on the floor. He looked up at me as I settled in behind the wheel and turned on the ignition. "Is he dead?"

"No, it's his lucky day. I let him live."

"Oh, man. Hey, Mister, can you just take me to the airport? I want to get back to someplace sane like L.A. This town is crazy. Umm, no offense."

My cell phone rang. "Yeah, Nancy."

"You okay?"

"We're fine. Where are you?"

"About two blocks down the street."

"We'll be there in just a minute."

Nancy had pulled up in front of a three-story brick building. There was a parking lot with maybe a dozen perpendicular parking spaces in front of the building. Three cars were parked in the lot. I pulled behind Nancy's SUV.

"Wait here, Ken. This should only take a minute. Oh, and you can get up off the floor now."

"I just want to go to the airport," Ken said and made no effort to get up off the floor.

I climbed out as Nancy opened her driver's door. "Not to worry, the front wheel on his bike is damaged, so he's not going anywhere."

"How did he know where we were?"

"He said there's a tracking device on your car," I said, getting down on my knees and looking underneath the rear of her SUV. I ran a hand along the back of the bumper, felt something, and pulled it out. A Spark Nano 7 tracking device, maybe three inches long and an inch and a half wide. "Here you go," I said. A UPS truck pulled into the parking lot, and the driver hopped out, carrying a white plastic envelope as he hurried into the building.

"That's the tracker?"

"Yeah, they're magnetic, run on a battery and are good for fifteen to twenty-four hours. Hang on a second." I hurried over to the UPS truck and attached the tracker to the inside of the rear wheel well.

"Okay, that shouldn't be a problem. Let's get going. Ken wants to get back to the sanity of L.A."

Nancy gave me a look.

"Yeah, I know. Follow us," I said and hurried back to Barbie's car. Ken was still seated on the floor. "All set, Ken. Next stop the Barbie collection."

"And you promise to take me to the airport?" he asked from the floor.

Forty-three

The ten-minute drive was uneventful. Ken remained on the floor until we pulled into the storage area. Once we were inside the fenced compound, he sat up and gave me directions past five rows of storage units. "Turn left on the next lane and halfway down, number 1312, it's on the righthand side," he said.

The units were identical, long cinderblock, single-story structures, with green metal garage doors. The unit numbers were painted in red and looked like they had been stenciled. I pulled alongside 1312, and Nancy parked behind me.

Ken hurried out of the car and said, "The key is on the car keys, the one with the red plastic cover."

I slipped the key into the lock and turned it. Ken reached down and pulled the door up. The area was small, maybe eight feet wide by ten feet. Box after box was stacked inside in piles four and five feet high.

Over on the righthand side was a yellow air mattress, the kind kids would use in a pool or on a lake. A rumpled blanket was on top of the air mattress and what looked like a cushion from a chair. One side of the cushion was slit, and yellow foam was hanging out. An open suitcase lay on the floor next to the air mattress. Wrinkled shirts, jeans and boxer shorts were draped over stacks of boxes. A number of empty paper bags and cups from McDonalds, Burger King, Wendy's, and White Castle were scattered across the floor.

Ken hurried over to his suitcase and began tossing clothes inside. "I can be ready to go in five minutes," he said.

"Are you okay to cool your heels here?" I asked Nancy.

"Yeah, I'll just pull the door closed. Don't take too long."

"I'll drop him at the airport and have Barbie rent a truck. We'll load it up, and I'm thinking you could stay with her until I get Tubby Gustafson calmed down. You sure you want to publish that article on him?"

She nodded and said, "Now more than ever, after he tried to kill me."

"Well, the guy had blanks in the gun today."

"Oh great, and I suppose the three bullet holes in my car last night was just to get my attention."

"Let me see what I can do. Anyway, if you can stand Barbie, you'll probably be safe there. Fat Freddy will be tracking that UPS truck all over town."

"Just get sixty-second Ken on a plane and get back here."

"Hey, Ken, you about ready to go?"

He bent down, quickly zipped his suitcase closed, and shouted, "All set."

I had to force the trunk open on the Barbie's car after the motorcycle slammed into it. When I opened the trunk, the original pink color from inside seemed to glare out at me. Ken was already in the passenger seat and buckled up. I started the car, and he gave Nancy a wave as we drove off.

Twenty minutes later, I pulled in front of the Delta door at the MSP air terminal. I hopped out and opened the trunk. Ken reached in, pulled his suitcase out, and hurried into the terminal. "Nice meeting you, Arnold," I called after him. He didn't acknowledge that he herd me and seemed to pick up his pace.

I pulled out my phone and called Barbie.

"Please tell me you have some good news for a change."

"I do. I've got your car and your collection."

"What? You do? Where are you?"

"I'm on my way to pick you up. I've got someone guarding the collection. I want you to rent a truck. We'll load up the collection and get it back to your place, where it will be safe." I purposely didn't mention Nancy.

"Oh, thank God. How soon can you get here?"

"Maybe a half-hour, you just be ready to go when I get there."

"I'll be waiting outside," she said and disconnected.

Forty-four

I made it out to Oak Park Heights in twenty minutes and turned onto Barbie's street. As soon as I turned, I could see her standing out in her driveway. She was dressed in black slacks and a pink halter top, accentuating her surgically enhanced attributes. She had a blue purse that looked like it would have matched the powder-blue loafers idiot Ken had been wearing.

Her mouth seemed to open wider, and her eyes grew larger the closer I drove.

"Oh, my God. This can't be my car. What the hell happened? And, and what is this dent in the hood?" She softly ran her hand over the dent from the helmet as if it was a baby's butt. "Oh, my God. Did Ken do this? He will die if he did," she said as an evil look came over her face.

"Get in, and I'll tell you all about it. You got insurance?"

"On the car? Yes, of course."

"Okay good, relax. Look, we got it back, and we're about to go get your collection."

"I know, but, oh, I'm going to kill him."

"Get in. We've got to rent a truck and pack up that collection."

I drove back into town as Barbie stewed in the passenger seat. She rented the truck, and we drove out to the storage unit. I drove the truck, and Barbie followed me in her car. Nancy was sitting in her car when we pulled up. I did the introductions, and Nancy immediately started taking pictures of Barbie with her cellphone. Barbie appeared only too happy to pose once she learned Nancy wanted to write an article about the hospital and the stolen collection.

It took a couple of hours, but we loaded up the entire collection and even had some room left in the truck. We drove back to Barbie's townhouse and emptied the truck in about forty-five minutes. Barbie poured a glass of wine for her and Nancy, and I had a can of Summit IPA. Nancy gave Barbie some general information about her thoughts for the article, and Barbie hurried out to the garage to search for a particular doll.

"You okay with staying here for a couple of nights until I get Tubby Gustafson calmed down?" I asked Nancy.

"More than okay, it will give me some real insight into her collection, the Dream House hospital, and Barbie as well."

"Don't forget that numbskull, Ken. By the way, did you and Ken really—"

"Found her," Barbie said, stepping back into the kitchen. She was carrying four pink boxes. Each held a blonde-haired Barbie in a blue police uniform with a badge over her left breast and a name tag that read Barbie on her right side. She had a light blue tie, a hat with a visor, and what looked like it would have been a fourteen-inch waist.

"Gee, lovely. Hey, sorry Barbie, but I've got to run. I'll take the truck back. Let's all touch base tomorrow. Okay?"

"Thank you for recovering my collection. I'm going to podcast about this tomorrow morning. I don't think I'll mention Ken. That will upset too many of my followers."

"Probably a good idea. Talk to you tomorrow," I said and headed out the door. I drove around the block, pulled to the curb, and phoned Louie.

"Where in the hell are you? Everything okay?" was how he answered.

"Yeah, finally. Hey, I got another favor to ask."

"Not a problem if you want me to hang onto Morton for another night. We had a pretty good time."

"Actually, no. I'm dropping off a rental truck over at U-Haul. Can you pick me up and take me downtown to where my car is parked?"

"Yeah, sure."

"I'll be at the truck rental in about twenty minutes."

"We'll be there waiting for you."

I beat them there by five minutes, returned the truck, and was waiting outside when Louie pulled up in his

Ford Fiesta. Morton was in the back seat, barking a welcome. I opened the passenger door, picked up the empty pork rinds bag from the seat, and settled in.

Morton leaned forward and began to lick my face as Louie pulled back into traffic. "Good to see you, Morton. Did you miss me?"

"Hey, he really likes beer," Louie said as he made a U-turn at the sign that said, 'No U-Turn.'

"Mike gave him a beer at The Spot?"

"No, I gave him one when we got home last night. How did things go for you?"

"Beyond crazy, but I think I've just about got everything settled down. Just one more thing I have to take care of tomorrow morning. By the way, I'm parked in the ramp next to the Hotel Confidential."

"Whoa, pretty pricey night. Was it worth your while?"

"Not the way you're thinking, but ultimately, yeah. I got Barbie's collection back to her along with her car. I put Ken on a plane back to L.A. Now, all I have left to do is get Tubby Gustafson off of Nancy's back, and things will hopefully begin to settle down."

At the mention of Tubby, Louie shot me a look.

"Hey, we'll meet you at The Spot after you drop me off, and I'll fill you in. Run a tab. I'm buying."

"I'm liking the sound of that," Louie said. He pulled across the street from the Hotel Confidential a few minutes later. Morton and I climbed out. Louie headed off to The Spot, and we headed into the parking ramp.

As we crossed the street, I waved to the guy in the top hat in front of the hotel and got a wave back.

Forty-five

Morton and I drove over to The Spot to meet Louie. Mike was behind the bar, and he nodded at me and raised an empty beer glass as we walked in. I said, "Yes," and attempted to keep up with Morton as he headed toward Louie.

"Miss me already, Morton?" Louie asked. Morton sat alongside Louie's barstool with a mournful look on his face.

Louie opened the bag of pork rinds, poured close to half the bag into his hand, and leaned down. It took Morton about three seconds to inhale them all. Mike set my beer on the bar and a fresh drink for Louie. I checked my wallet, but it was empty and I looked over at Louie..

Louie shook hie head, and handed Mike a twenty. He raised his glass to me and said, "Here's to you. Congratulations on recovering the Barbie collection and getting her car back as well."

We clinked glasses, and I said, "Nancy's staying with Barbie for the moment. I'm going to talk to Tubby tomorrow and hopefully get him to lighten up on Nancy."

"She give you a date on when the article is going to come out?"

"No, in fact, I'm not even sure she's written it yet. Now she's getting into Barbie, and the hospital, and the stolen collection. Who knows? I'll just be glad to get the two of them out of my life and back to a semblance of whatever normal is. Anything going on with you the last day or two?"

Louie shook his head, drained his glass, and pulled the fresh drink closer.

"No, same old, same old. Nothing new. I enjoyed having Morton for the night. It's always fun, and he was there just long enough to remind me I have no business owning a dog."

"Did he screw something up?"

"No, not at all. It's just that it requires a degree of responsibility that I choose not to possess."

We chatted on for another hour. I had to step over to the ATM and get another twenty bucks for Mike before Morton and I headed home. I woke up just after sunrise the following morning, obsessing about talking to Tubby Gustafson. I was on my third cup of coffee when my computer alerted me to a new email coming in.

I clicked on the site, and there was an email from Jasmine.

'Made it through my shift. Pretty much fully recovered except for being so embarrassed. Sorry I was so stupid. I think we should talk, but if you don't want to, I understand. Jasmine'

I picked up the phone and called her.

"Hi, Dev," she said, maybe sounding a little nervous.

"Hey, I just got your email. Thank you, and yes, I would love to see you, too. Whatever fits your schedule."

"Is, umm, is Nancy still around?"

"No, she's not. I mean, I'm not seeing her if that's what you're asking." I went on to tell her about being followed and her car being shot up by Fat Freddy. I filled her in on getting Barbie's collection back and dropping Ken off at the airport.

"Mmm, Ken, yet another opportunity missed due to the Prosecco."

"Well, if it's any consolation, Nancy said it was only sixty seconds."

"Guess I'll never find out. You ever think maybe that was her fault? Oh, say, by the way, we've got a new supplier for our PPE. They're supplying us daily, and it seems to be working much better. No problems I'm aware of, although it's only been a few days."

"Long may it last. Do you know how they found the new supplier?"

"No, I don't, well, other than the union alerted the hospital. But I would guess, since they're statewide, your friend at Virus Protection—"

"Tubby Gustafson."

"Yeah, that's the name. My guess is he'll be out of business sooner rather than later."

"Good to know. I was planning on talking to him later this morning."

"Oh?"

"Nothing major, just regarding an invoice I sent him," I lied.

"Okay," she said, sounding like she didn't believe me. "Well, I suppose I should let you get on with your day."

"Can I give you a call on the weekend?" I asked.

"Yes, that would probably be a good idea. Thursday is my day off."

"I'll call you when you have more time," I said, making a mental note to get in touch on Wednesday and suggest she come over for breakfast Thursday morning.

I debated calling Tubby and decided it would go better if I just went over to his mansion. I sent Louie an email, let Morton out into the backyard, and headed over to Tubby's just before 10:00. I went through the usual routine at the front gate and finally pulled into the secure compound and parked. As I drove past the two thugs at the front door, I noticed they were staring at my Crown Vic.

There was a black SUV parked off to the side. The passenger side was dented and scraped. The side door was severely buckled and looked like if probably wouldn't open. White streaks ran across the damage, and I was pretty sure it was from Nancy's SUV. I pulled a pen out and wrote the license number in my pocket notebook before I climbed out of my car.

As I approached the front door, the two thugs did their usual routine of spreading apart and stepping out of the shade. I kept my arms at my side and held my car keys in my right hand. One of them held the yellow and black wand they always waved over me to check for items, and I walked toward him.

Usually, they gave me a hard time. Once in a while, they were downright rude. Today they didn't say anything. After he'd waved the wand and patted me down, he nodded at his partner, who opened the front door and indicated with a wave of his hand that I could go in.

I was patted down by a new guy inside. I didn't see a comic book or a skin magazine anywhere, so I guessed he just sat in the entry all day and stared at the door. He led me to the small room beneath the staircase and opened the door for me.

"You know how to access Mr. Gustafson on the computer?"

"Yeah, I've been through this a couple of times."

"Okay, just give the word when you're finished," he said and closed the door once I stepped in. I heard a lock click a moment later. I pushed the button on the keyboard and settled into the chair. A half-minute later, the screen flashed on, and suddenly, there was Tubby Gustafson, dressed and seated at his desk. He was wearing a black mask with an evil grin across the front.

A blonde woman in a white nurse uniform from the previous century was in the process of taking his blood pressure. The skirt barely covered her thighs, and the top revealed a canyon of cleavage.

"What is it, Haskell? You're interrupting my morning workout."

"Good morning, sir. Thanks for seeing me."

"Haskell, you finished with that doll business?"

"The doll business. How did you know about that, sir?

"I happen to own the storage facility, Haskell, where your friend Mr. Carson skipped out on his contract. It's my business to know. I spotted you on the security tape. Now, is there a point to this interruption?" Tubby asked as the woman took his temperature with one of those forehead thermometers.

"Well, sir, I picked up some information I thought might be of interest. My friend down at the hospital told me they have a new supplier for PPE that's working out really well."

"What in the hell does this have to do with me?"

"Nothing really, sir. I just thought you would like to know, in case some friend or family member becomes ill."

The woman looked at his blood pressure readout and shook her head.

Tubby waved her off and said, "None of that concerns me, Haskell. What the hell is this?" He held up my invoice and slowly waved it back and forth.

"That looks like it's my invoice for the three nights of security at your clubs, sir."

"Security? I'm thinking of charging you for overnight accommodation. You never fail to disappoint, Haskell. I introduce you to a new stream of revenue, and you want me to pay you for the privilege. You'll never get ahead."

"Does that mean you're not going to pay me, sir?"

He smiled and actually sounded nice. "Why no, Haskell. I intend to pay you in full. I'll have the check sent today, as a matter of fact." His face suddenly turned red, and he shouted, "And after that, I'm going to invoice your stupid ass for overnight accommodation. And believe me, it will be a hell of a lot more than this nonsense." He crumpled up my invoice and threw it at the screen.

"Perhaps we could just call things even, sir."

"That would be a very wise idea on your part."

I nodded.

"Anything else?" he asked and motioned the nurse toward him.

"No, sir."

"Perfect. Cece, I suddenly seem to have a pain in my neck," Tubby said as the woman in the sexy nurse outfit appeared on screen. Tubby leaned forward, and she began rubbing his shoulders just as the screen went blank.

I waited a minute before standing and called, "Okay I'm all fin—"

The door suddenly opened, and the guy smiled and said, "All set? You're free to go."

I hurried toward the front door and stepped outside. "Take care of yourself, Haskell," one of the guys said.

How strange. No one called me a name. No one threatened me. I nodded and hurried to my car.

I checked in with Nancy twice over the next few days. She seemed to be doing fine and was getting plenty of information from Barbie about the collection and her plans for the hospital. Wednesday night, I sent Jasmine an email.

'If tomorrow is your day off, can I prepare breakfast for you Thursday morning?'

I received a reply a few hours later. *'I can only stop for a few minutes.'* No doubt, still feeling guilty about the Prosecco.

Forty-six

Thursday morning finally arrived, and I was up early. I had the decaf coffee on, the caramel rolls on a plate, and I mixed up blueberry pancake batter with fresh blueberries. Jasmine arrived right on time. It was the first time I'd seen her since I'd dropped her off after the pink Prosecco disaster.

I had been watching out the window, and I opened the door as she stepped onto my front porch. "Hey, Jasmine. Thanks for coming."

"Thanks for asking me, Dev. I wasn't sure how—"

"That's all behind us. Let's go back to the kitchen. I've got blueberry pancakes, caramel rolls, and decaf coffee," I said and began to go back inside.

"Wait just a minute, Dev. There's something I need to tell you," she said.

"Look, about the Prosecco. It doesn't matter. You were finally able to relax after your first week working full time. I get it. It's not a problem. Let's just put it behind us and—"

"That's just it, Dev. See, there isn't any us."

"What?"

"You can be really nice, and I'll always appreciate the fact that you didn't turn me over to Mr. Gustafson, but the truth is I've met someone at work."

"Someone at work? Another nurse?"

"No, Dev, he's a doctor, and he's kind and gentle, and, well, I'm sorry, but I want to be with him."

"Well, you want some pancakes, and you can tell me more about him?"

She smiled and shook her head. "I don't think that would be a very good idea. Thank you, but I better get going."

With that, she turned and hurried to her car. No kiss, no wave. She just got in and drove off. I watched her until she disappeared before walking back to the kitchen. I poured the pancake batter into the trash and tossed the caramel rolls on top of it. Morton and I headed down to the office an hour later, and I sat and stared out the window. Nancy phoned me in the middle of the afternoon.

"Hi Nancy, you still over at Barbie's?"

"Hi Dev," she laughed. "No, I fled the scene. A little too crazy, although I was able to get all sorts of information. I'm not going to do an article. I'm going to write a series."

"A series on Barbie? That sounds really interesting. Hey, if you're not too busy, I was thinking, maybe we should do dinner tonight, and we could catch up. I'd love to hear all about the Barbie series," I lied. "I can grab some steaks. What kind of wine do you—"

"Oh, thanks, Dev, but I'm actually at the airport right now. I sent my Barbie idea out to some publications, and one of them responded. They're going to run it."

"What about the article on Tubby Gustafson?"

"He shut down the business two days ago, and in todays' world, my article suddenly became old news."

"Did he shut things down because the bottom fell out of his business?"

"Yes, apparently another company came on the scene with better equipment and more of it, and Gustafson was out of business overnight."

"Sounds like the perfect ending," I said and heard a loudspeaker voice in the background. "Where are you going?"

"I'm on my way to Washington. The Post wants to talk to me about taking a position."

"Really? You mean the Washington Post?"

"Yeah, they're going to run my Barbie series."

"That's wonderful. Congratulations."

"Thank you. I'll see what they have to say. Hey, I need to ring off. They're getting ready to board."

"Okay, thanks for the call, Nancy. Wishing you all success and—" but she'd already hung up.

Epilogue

Jasmine continued working at the hospital and was on the news a few weeks later. She and her fiancé had developed a virus testing device that could reduce the virus test result time to minutes rather than days.

I never did hear back from Nancy. I learned that she took the position with the Washington Post and moved out to Virginia. Her Barbie series actually ran in the Washington Post. The six-part series went viral on the internet, which led to a GoFundMe platform and allowed Barbie to set up her Dream House hospital. The first patients at the hospital were the dolls belonging to Devan Riley's wife, Denise. A video was made of Barbie, wearing sexy blue scrubs, delivering the dolls to the Riley home in her recently repainted pink convertible. Now she's getting customers from all over the world and is helping women to travel back to a much simpler time, if only for a few moments.

As for Tubby, after he closed down his Virus Protection company, he paid an online news source to promote a counter version to the negative reviews he'd gotten, calling the reviews fake. He made a generous donation to a local couple developing a virus testing innovation, and any negative online comments quickly disappeared. Ever the entrepreneur, after Nancy's six-part series on Barbie went viral on the internet, Tubby paid for a woman to have plastic surgery to look like Barbie. His clubs are sold out seven nights a week wherever she performs.

"As for me, I'm just hoping my life will finally get back to whatever the new normal turns out to be. I, oh hang on a second, I have to take this phone call. Haskell Investigations…"

The End

Hope you enjoyed the read. Thanks for taking the time to read **Dream House.** If you enjoyed the read and would like to leave a review, just click on the appropriate link. I'm indie published so your review really helps. Thank you, much appreciated…

Check out this sample of **Alley Katz**, the next book in the Dev Haskell series.

Sneak Peek

Alley Katz

Second Edition

MIKE FARICY

Prologue

For once, Taylor Cummings woke to the smell of something delicious. At first, he thought it might be the restaurant across the alley. He looked at his watch, just after five in the morning, way too early for them to be cooking. He pulled off the jacket he used as a blanket, rolled off the mattress on the floor, and stood. He hadn't eaten since lunch at school yesterday, and his stomach growled. Whatever he smelled was definitely coming from the other room.

He tucked his shirt into his jeans, tied his shoes, and tiptoed out of the room. The scent grew stronger as he moved down the short hall toward the light. He peeked around the corner and focused on his uncle Eli stirring a pot on the hot plate. His stomach growled again at the scent of whatever was in the pan.

Without turning around, his uncle said, "Sit your butt down, buddy, and I'll dish you up a bowl of your grandma's secret chili recipe. It'll be ready in four minutes. What would you like to drink?"

"What do we have?"

"I'm not sure. Give a look in the refrigerator."

"The refrigerator's empty."

"Well then, we'll just have water. I guess you could add a couple of ice cubes and make it ice water. Your choice."

Taylor took the glass and the coffee mug from the cabinet and turned the water on. There were two empty chili cans in the sink, and he filled them under the faucet. He let the water run for a good long minute until it looked clear enough to drink before filling the glass and mug. He placed them on the table, actually a section of sheetrock resting on a pair of sawhorses, and sat down on the lawn chair.

"Where have you been, Eli?"

"Working. Been coming up with a formula to—"

Taylor shook his head. "You mean you've been gambling again and lost whatever you had. Where'd you steal that stuff you're cooking?"

"Now, why are you starting out so negative? I told you this is your grandmother's recipe. I been cooking this for a couple of hours."

"Eli, I saw the cans in the sink."

"Yeah, well, that company heard about your grandma's recipe, and they stole it from her. They've been making all sorts of money off it. I just figured the least they could do was give me a couple of cans. Now here, this is just about ready to—"

The door suddenly burst open and a very large man with a shaved head and a tattooed neck burst into the room. "Eli Cummings, it's time for you to pay up," he shouted as he stormed past Taylor.

Taylor sat glued to the lawn chair, too frightened to move.

"Now calm down and hold on a second, Lyle. I got your payment right here. Let me just turn this off," Eli said. He suddenly grabbed the pan and tossed the boiling contents into Lyle's face.

"Ahhh-ahh," Lyle screamed and staggered backward a step or two. Eli wound up and hit him on the forehead with the pan, sending him backward. He crashed through the sheetrock table and landed on the floor.

Taylor sat wide-eyed as Lyle groaned and slowly moved his head from side to side. Eli bent down and pulled a wallet out of the man's pocket along with a set of car keys. "Time to go, Taylor, now!" he said, as he pulled a twenty-dollar bill from the wallet and handed it to Taylor. Taylor ran back to the bedroom, grabbed his jacket, and hurried back to the kitchen.

Eli was gone, and Lyle was attempting to sit up. Taylor decided it might be a good idea to leave. He hurried out the door just as Eli backed a shiny red car with two white racing stripes out of the driveway and sped down the street.

One

I was behind the wheel, shouting obscenities at the Mercedes in front of me because they hadn't turned on their left-hand blinker until after the light changed. I couldn't drive around them due to the bus that had just pulled to the corner. I needed the car to pull four feet into the intersection, but apparently, that wasn't about to happen. My curse words and shouting didn't seem to have any effect, but then with my windows rolled up, they couldn't really hear me. A half-dozen cars, an ice cream truck, and some college kid on a motorized scooter drifted past in the oncoming lane, and still, the Mercedes didn't move.

I leaned on my horn, as did two of the cars behind me. The traffic light changed to yellow, the Mercedes finally moved, and I accelerated through the intersection. It was raining, and it took a moment to get any traction. Some jerk waiting on the cross street honked at me.

I was hurrying to the grocery store to buy cut flowers for Gladys. She was cooking dinner tonight, and if I was the least bit late, it would be another night of one-word answers. I figured the flowers would set the mood for an enjoyable dinner and, with any luck, breakfast.

I sped up Grand Avenue just in time to wait for the traffic light on Lexington. At least there was a left turn lane at this intersection, not that it really mattered. The light was exceptionally long, and I was beginning to think it was broken when it finally turned green. I accelerated up the hill past the entrance to the grocery store parking lot and took a right at the corner. Experience had taught me parking in the overflow lot was actually the quickest way to park and run into the store.

I passed the rear entrance into the lot and pulled into the overflow lot, screeching as I turned and sped into the lot. A red SUV, paying no attention, suddenly backed out of a parking place. I slammed on the brakes and leaned on the horn, but with the wet pavement, I slammed my Crown Victoria Police Interceptor into the rear of the SUV.

I sat behind the wheel for a long moment looking at the damage to the SUV, thinking, *'Oh God.'* I got out of my car and hurried over to the driver's door. The window lowered as I approached. A woman with trimmed gray hair and glasses turned toward me. She did not look happy.

"Are you all right, ma'am?"

She seemed to study me for a minute before she answered, "Yes, but what exactly do you think you were doing?"

"What was I doing? I was going to park my car in the parking lot until you backed into me."

"First of all, you were driving at a rather high rate of speed. Was that you I heard screeching around the corner? Secondly, you were traveling in the wrong direction."

"Wrong direction?"

"You entered through the exit."

"Exit?"

She pushed her door open, forcing me to jump back as she climbed out of her car and hurried to the rear. "Oh dear, will you look at this, a broken taillight, my bumper is dented, and that rear quarter panel is going to need replacing. All because you entered through an exit."

"What do you mean an exit? This is the way I always go when—"

She stormed back toward my entrance to the overflow lot, stood in front of the sign, frowned, and signaled me with her index finger. "Would you mind stepping over here, please?"

As I headed in her direction, I said, "Look, lady you backed into me and—"

"I presume you can read," she said, pointing to the sign.

I stepped in front of the sign, ready to protest. Unfortunately, it read,

EXIT ONLY!
DO NOT ENTER

"So, now what's your excuse?"

That last comment prompted a flashback, and for a brief moment, I was back in the hallway outside my high school English class getting yet another lecture from Ms. Wright, my teacher.

She must have recognized the blank look on my face because she suddenly said, "Wait just a minute. Don't I know you from somewhere?"

"I, I'm sure we've never met. I didn't think I did anything wrong, and if you hadn't backed into me, I—"

"Oh. My. God. You're not Haskell, are you? Devlin Haskell? The young man I had senior year? The student who was more interested in the girls in the classroom than what we were discussing in class? I believe I gave you a 'D' just so I wouldn't have to deal with you that final semester. Devlin Haskell?"

"Oh, hello, Ms. Wright."

She glanced at my Crown Vic. "Oh dear Lord, don't tell me you're a police officer now."

"Actually, no, ma'am, I purchased that car at a police auction."

"What on earth are you up to? I've wondered about you for years. You were so... Well, probably best we don't go there. How have you been?"

"Pretty well, thank you. Well, at least up until a moment ago. I still live in the city."

"And you're not a police officer?" she asked and looked over at my car again.

"No, ma'am, I'm a private investigator. Are you still teaching?"

She smiled and shook her head. "No, I retired a few years back. I still hear from a lot of my former students. I volunteer part-time tutoring. I see some things haven't changed with you," she said, glancing at the Exit Only sign.

"Yeah, umm, sorry about that. How about if I give you my details and you contact your insurance company? Your car looks like it should be okay to drive. Here's my card," I said, pulling out my wallet and handing her a card.

"Haskell Investigations. Your office is over on Randolph Avenue?"

"Yes, ma'am."

"Interesting. I remember you very well, Mr. Haskell. I felt I could never quite get through to you."

"I'm guessing all of my teachers would say something like that. I remember there was one guy who would tell his class on the first day that he didn't want any Dev Haskells in the room."

"Oh, yes, Mr. Kennedy. We had a few words about that. Now here, you stand next to this sign and let me get a picture," she said, taking her phone out. Before I knew what was happening, she'd taken two pictures of me. She walked back to our cars and began photographing the damage from a number of different angles.

"Let me check with my insurance company, and I'll be in touch once I hear from them. I'll phone them as soon as I get home. Interesting to meet you again, Devlin. Somehow, I'm not surprised it's under these circumstances."

I held the driver's door for her as she climbed into her SUV. "It was nice to see you again, Ms. Wright. Sorry about the damage."

She smiled and said, "Some things never seem to change, Devlin. Maybe take a moment to read the sign. As I've told you many times before, we all have to follow the rules. I'll be in touch."

As I watched her disappear around the corner, I was thinking back to my high school days. A horn honking brought me back to the here and now. I pulled into the spot she vacated and hurried into the grocery store.

TWO

I was more than twenty minutes late when I parked in front of Gladys' house. I grabbed the flowers, her favorite, cut mums, and hurried up to the front door. I had to ring the doorbell three times before she finally opened the door.

"Oh, finally, it's about time."

"Yeah, sorry I'm late, but I can explain. A woman backed into me on the way to get these flowers for you," I said and held out the bouquet of yellow mums. I figured I still might have half a chance if I splurged and got the large bouquet, twenty bucks worth of cut mums.

"Well, come on in. I've had to keep the dinner warming in the oven for the last half-hour. Steak filets wrapped in bacon, except they're probably all dried out by now," she said as she hurried back to the kitchen.

I opened the screen door and stepped inside, then, in an effort to catch up, I quickly slammed the front door closed, cutting off the bouquet of mums about two inches below the flowers. "Damn it," I whispered and watched the flowers fall to the floor as I opened the door up.

"Dev, what are you doing? I'm putting our overdone dinner on the table."

"Coming," I called and quickly scooped up the flower blossoms and dumped them back into the cellophane wrapper.

"Dev? What are you doing? Get in here."

I hurried into the kitchen. Vintage Gladys, the table was set with her grandmother's china. Sterling silver place settings were arranged on embroidered linen napkins. A Waterford crystal wine carafe was on the table, and Gladys's Waterford wineglass was almost empty. The wineglass at my place hadn't been filled.

"Just put those flowers in the sink, and I'll deal with them later. God, this meal is going to be an absolute disaster."

I couldn't argue, and as it turned out, that was probably the best choice. After the dozen or so one-word responses to my questions, I gave up and focused on my overdone, dried out steak fillet, scorched green beans, and the crusty, overcooked scalloped potatoes.

When Gladys set her knife and fork down signaling she had finished eating, I jumped to my feet and cleared the dishes, arranging them on the counter the way she liked before washing them by hand.

"As long as I'm up, can I get you a dessert?" I asked.

"Sure, Dev, what did you bring?"

It was the most she'd said to me in the past forty minutes and served to remind me that I had offered to bring a dessert. "Actually, I was thinking of pouring you another glass of wine and just listening to whatever you have to say.”

“Thanks, but I can pour my own wine, and I don’t really have anything else to say.”

I glanced at the clock on the wall. If I hurried, I could probably catch my office mate, Louie Laufen, down at The Spot bar. “How about this, Gladys. I know you’re upset with me being late, and I don’t blame you.” Even though I did. “How about you just relax and take it easy after doing all the work on this, this very lovely dinner? And I’ll clean up the kitchen. How does that sound?”

“It sounds like you’re hoping to spend the night with me, and that’s not going to happen, Dev. You were a half-hour late, and because you apparently didn’t care enough to call, the dinner I spent the better part of the afternoon preparing was ruined.”

“Gladys, I told you. A woman backed into my car, and I had to deal with that.”

“Yeah, sure, you probably gave her your phone number. Tried to sweet-talk her.”

“Well, for your information, she turned out to be a teacher I had back in high school. I just wanted to make sure she was okay and to get her information, so when I report the accident to my insurance company, they’ll know—”

“You know, Dev, I think it would be best if you just leave. I don’t want you anywhere near my grandmother's china or my crystal. If you hurry, you can probably still catch that Louie character at that dreadful bar where you two waste so much of your lives."

"You sure I couldn't—"

"Thank you for the flowers. At least you remembered how much I love mums. I'll put them in a vase once I've finished cleaning up."

That was definitely my traveling music.

"All right, Gladys. Thank you for dinner. Hope to talk with you later." I bent down to give her a kiss, but at the last minute, she turned her head, and I ended up kissing her hair. Anything else I said would just add to the problem, so I headed for the front door. There were two mums lying on the floor next to the front door. I picked them up, closed the door behind me, tossed the flowers into her front garden, and hurried to my car.

Three

I drove home and pulled Morton off the couch. We went for a quick walk around the block then hopped in the car and headed down to The Spot. As we pulled up, two guys were standing outside smoking cigarettes. We nodded hello to one another, and Morton and I headed into the bar. Louie was seated on his usual stool at the end of the bar.

Mike was bartending, and when he saw us step in, he grabbed a bag of pork rinds from the rack and tossed them in front of Louie. Louie looked up from the newspaper he was reading and watched as Morton began picking up speed, making his way along the bar.

"I thought you were having dinner with that Glad Ass woman tonight. What happened? She get tired of trying to deal with you and sent you on your way?" He tore open the bag of pork rinds, dumped half the bag into his hand, and then leaned down and gave them to Morton. For his part, Morton was careful not to knock any onto the floor. Once finished, he sat and patiently looked up at Louie with mournful eyes.

"Does the word disaster have any meaning? One word answers. Overcooked food, and an unhappy woman pretty much sums up the entire evening." I went on to tell him about the car accident, the ruined bouquet of mums, and the dreadful dinner.

"If memory serves, this isn't the first time you've ended up on 'Glad Ass's' bad side."

"Yeah, I know. I'm not even sure she believed my story about my high school teacher backing into me. I figured there was no point in hanging around, waiting for her to discover how I ruined the bouquet of flowers. That'll probably serve as the icing on the cake and give me about a five-day cold spell before she'll be willing to put up with me again."

"Dev, did you ever think that this might be one of the reasons she's available? Based on the stories you've told, it sounds like she can get pretty negative in a very short amount of time."

"Yeah, there is that, but she's got some good points. She really likes to—"

"Too much information. Buy you a beer?"

"Yeah, at this point, it certainly can't hurt and might just help."

We chatted on about everything and nothing for another round of drinks when Louie said, "Say, maybe just a warning, but I was out of the office this afternoon, and just as I was pulling up, a black SUV pulled away from the curb. I can't be sure, but it looked an awful lot like your close personal friend, Tubby Gustafson, and that Fat Freddy character—"

"Fat Freddy Zimmerman?"

"Yeah, that's the guy. It looked an awful lot like those two. I'd guess they didn't just happen to pull over to make a phone call outside our office."

"The way the day has gone, that's about the last reason they would be there. Bad things seem to happen in threes. I had the car accident, slammed the bouquet in Gladys' front door, and now Tubby Gustafson is looking for me. The perfect end to an already lousy day."

"Sorry to be the bearer of bad news, but I figured it would be better to let you know than to have you blind-sided."

"Yeah, thanks, Louie. I do appreciate the heads-up. Maybe I should just head up to someone's lake place and hide for a couple of days."

"You know someone who has a place you could use for a bit?"

"Actually, no, I don't. I'll just have to hang around tomorrow and see what day brightener Tubby has for me."

Louie took a sip and said, "I'll be in court for most of the morning. Don't think I'm avoiding you, or Tubby, for that matter."

"Not to worry. I think we better head home. I may as well rest up for whatever tomorrow is planning to bring."

Louie nodded, poured the rest of the pork rinds into his hand, and said, "Okay, Morton, a little reward to you for having to put up with Dev. Keep at it. Sooner or later, he's bound to catch on."

I waited a couple of seconds for Morton to devour the pork rinds before we headed out the door. Once home, we settled in front of the TV. I stretched out on the couch, and Morton stretched out on the floor. We fell asleep partway through a movie about pirates. I went up to bed a little after midnight.

Morton woke me about five minutes before my alarm went off. I let him out the kitchen door then went back upstairs to shower and shave. Once I was dressed, I unplugged my cellphone and read the message from Gladys that had come through while I was in the shower. *'Flowers ruined. Thanks for nothing.'* Probably a good idea I left when I did.

I was just dishing up my breakfast when Morton barked at the back door. I let him inside, and forty-five minutes later, we were parking across the street from the office.

It wasn't until I unlocked the door that I remembered Louie had told me he would be in court all morning. I made coffee and settled in at my desk. I began reviewing a pile of job applications I'd received from a friend at an insurance company. I'd be making phone calls checking on previous jobs the applicants had listed. It was slow-moving, boring, no thought required work that paid the bills.

I heard the stairs creaking around 11:30 and glanced out the window to see if Tubby Gustafson's SUV was parked on the street. Instead, I saw Louie's faded orange Ford Fiesta parked at the curb, and a moment later, the door opened and a red-faced Louie stepped into the office.

I knew better than to try to start a conversation just after he'd climbed the stairs to the second floor. So, I said, "Hi Louie, didn't think you'd be back this early. Let me get you a coffee."

I grabbed the mug from his picnic table desk, dumped the remnants down the sink, and refilled it. Louie was seated at this point. Still red-faced and breathing as if he'd just finished a five-mile run. Once I set the mug on his picnic table, he pulled it in front of him, and took a series of sips over the course of the next three or four minutes. Eventually, he sat back in his chair and said. "Any visitors this morning?"

"You mean like Tubby Gustafson?"

"Yeah or Gladys. I was thinking she might come down and return that ruined bouquet you left for her."

"I guess the good news is, so far, neither one has made an appearance."

"Well, the day isn't over yet," Louie said as he pulled a stack of files from his briefcase.

"Things go your way in court this morning?" I asked.

"Yeah, pro-bono work, three cases, just initial hearings, but it takes time. It serves as a reminder to me that

I really don't have anything to complain about. All I have to do is look out the window to find someone who has it worse."

Four

The afternoon passed quickly, and in no time, Louie asked, "Hey, I'm at a stopping point. You thinking about going over to The Spot for one?"

"I could make time in my busy schedule for at least one. Let me take Morton around the block, and we'll join you in a couple of minutes."

Louie headed over to The Spot. Morton and I headed off in the opposite direction. Morton seemed interested in every tree and fence gate along the way. It took the better part of fifteen minutes before we rounded the corner and came in sight of The Spot. We also happened to catch a black SUV pulling away from our office building, heading up the street to the interstate entrance, and disappearing. My first thought was Tubby Gustafson looking for me again.

I debated jumping in the car and heading out of town, but fortunately, a cooler head prevailed, and we made our way over to The Spot. Louie must have seen us through the window because he was in the process of pouring half a bag of pork rinds into his hand. Morton knew there were pork rinds waiting for him at the end of the bar and almost tore my arm out of the socket in an effort to get to Louie. He had Louie's hand emptied and licked clean in a few seconds.

Mike arrived with a beer for me and a fresh drink for Louie as Morton sat and stared at Louie. I pulled a ten from my wallet, the only cash I had, and set it on the bar. Mike smiled and took it.

"Here's to you. Glad you two finally made it," Louie said, raising his glass for a half-second before he took a sip.

"Thanks to Morton taking his time, we missed Fat Freddy and Tubby Gustafson going up to the office. God only knows what they want."

"You think you should give him a call?"

"Tubby? I'm not sure he'd even answer. If he did, he'd probably tell me to get over to his place so he could listen to whatever awful message he has in person. No, thanks."

"Call him and tell him you're out of town. He won't be able to do anything about it, and if he does let you know what he wants, it will give you a day or two to figure out how you're going to deal with it."

"Actually, that kind of makes sense."

"Surprise, surprise. How long ago did you see him?"

"Just a few minutes ago. They headed up the street and onto the interstate."

"Maybe wait an hour and call. Tell him you got word from someone in one of the offices on the first floor, and you wanted to get in touch."

"Great idea, Louie, that's what I'll do, call him in an hour."

We sat and traded stories for the next hour and a half before Louie said, "You going to give Tubby a call?"

"Yeah, like you said, I want to wait for an hour before I call him."

"It's already been an hour and a half."

The jukebox was playing an oldie by the Rolling Stones. "Mmm-mmm, okay, but I better step outside. Order me another beer. This shouldn't take too long."

I stepped outside and speed-dialed Tubby's number. He answered on the third ring. "Just where in the hell have you been, you worthless piece of—"

"I'm out of town, Tub— err, Mr. Gustafson."

"Oh really, out of town. Where? Chicago? Kansas City? New Orleans?"

"No, sir, umm, I'm up in Finland, sir."

"Finland?"

"Yes, sir. Finland, Minnesota. Visiting a friend in the hospital. He's got some rare communicable disease. He's on his death bed, and now that I've seen him, I'm going to head back to town tomorrow, but it might not be safe to see me for a few days. I wouldn't want to risk getting you sick."

"I understand, Haskell, and I appreciate you showing some concern for my health. Wishing you a safe journey home, hope your friend recovers, oh, and one more thing…"

"Yes, sir, what's that?"

"Get your dumb ass over to my car now, you idiot!" With that, the headlights flashed on a black SUV parked across the street and down about two doors. The tires screeched as the vehicle leapt forward into the oncoming traffic lane and pulled up and over the curb, forcing me to jump out of the way.

A thug I didn't recognize slid out from behind the wheel. He was muscular looking, with a shaved head, a tattooed neck, and a face with red blotches and what looked like blisters. He opened the rear door, and I could see Tubby shaking his head, looking like he was ready to explode and still holding his phone.

"Lyle, you have my permission to break every bone in Haskell's body," Tubby shouted.

"Might be a good idea to get in here, dumb shit," blotchy faced Lyle said.

"Oh, nice to see you so soon, Mr. Gustafson. Thank you for making the time to see me," I said as I slid into the backseat.

Lyle slammed the door closed as I was climbing in, pushing me even closer to Tubby. A tray on the back of the passenger seat was pulled down, and it looked like Tubby was in the process of eating a large piece of chocolate cake.

He placed a large forkful in his mouth and said, "Why Haskell? Why? After all I've done for you. Is it any wonder you're nothing but a failure?"

"Good evening, sir. How are things?"

"Not good. Certain people seem to think they can get away with lying to me."

"Oh, umm, I wasn't lying, sir. I knew you were parked across the street. I was just about to walk over, but you saved me the trouble."

"Silencio, you moron," he shouted, spraying bits of chocolate cake in my direction. "God save me. Frederick, give this idiot the Cummings file."

Fat Freddy Zimmerman turned around in the front passenger seat, smiled, and raised his eyebrows, suggesting he was laughing at my predicament. He shoved a manila file folder in my direction.

"Well, take it, for God's sake," Tubby shouted.

"Thank you," I said, hoping I sounded polite.

"Thank you? For God's sake. You idiot, you don't even know what's in there. Open the damn thing and take a look."

"Oh, yes, sir. I was just about to do that, but I thought, you know, being polite and all. I thought it—"

"One more word. One more stupid utterance on your part, and I'll strangle you myself. Now open the damn file," Tubby shouted.

I opened the file and stared at a black and white photo of a nice enough looking guy with dark, curly hair. I studied the photo for a long moment.

"Well," Tubby growled.

"You said you didn't want me to talk, sir."

Tubby closed his eyes, exhaled, and muttered something. I only caught the last word, which was 'Frederick.'

"Haskell, do you know who the hell that is?" Fat Freddy asked.

I studied the image for another moment and shook my head. "He doesn't look familiar. I'm pretty sure I don't know him."

"His name is Eli Cummings, and he owes Mister Gustafson money."

"A lot of damn money," Tubby growled.

"You want me to pay his debt? I just gave my last ten-dollar bill to the bartender. How 'bout I go back in and see what I have for change. It's all I've got, but you're welcome to it, Mr. Gustafson."

Tubby's breathing increased audibly, and his eyes glared. He suddenly shouted, "Get out. Get out. Get out!"

I opened the door and jumped out of the back seat. Tubby threw the file out the door after me as Lyle hit the accelerator. The SUV bounced off the curb and ran the red light at the corner.

"Find him, you idiot, or I'll—" Tubby screamed as they sped down the street.

An oncoming car skidded to a stop, and the driver leaned on the horn. I watched them disappear, wishing this time it would be for good.

Louie looked at me as I stepped back into The Spot. I tossed the file onto the bar and said, "Check this out. That guy ring any bells?"

"You went back to the office?"

"I wish. No, I stepped outside to make Tubby's call. I told him I was up north visiting a dying friend, but unfortunately, he just happened to be parked across the street. They almost ran me over when they pulled up onto the sidewalk. Go ahead, open the file. I'm supposed to find that guy," I said as Louie took the file and opened it.

He studied the black and white photo for a second then lifted it up and read the piece of paper beneath it, mostly addresses. "You know this Eli Cummings guy?"

"Fortunately, no. Not sure I want to if Tubby is looking for him. If they want me to find him, that suggests he's probably hiding somewhere or has left town. With Tubby looking for him, leaving town sounds like the better option."

"What are you going to do?"

"Well, I'm not going to spend a lot of time looking for someone who has probably fled to parts unknown. I'll check around just so Tubby gets the word I'm looking, but I'm not going to waste my time."

"What do you think he did?" Louie asked.

"My guess is Tubby lent him some money at about a two hundred percent interest rate. Now the guy can't be found, and Tubby expects to be paid. Serves Tubby right."

To be continued . . .

Thanks for checking out the sample of **Alley Katz**. Dev involved in an "interesting conversation" with that Wright woman? It doesn't make any sense. She's got something planned that's probably going to cost him. Things are about to go crazy, better grab your copy and check it out.

Books by Mike Faricy
Crime Fiction Firsts

A boxset of the first four books in four crime fiction series:

Russian Roulette; Dev Haskell series
Welcome; Jack Dillon Dublin Tales series
Corridor Man; Corridor Man series
Reduced Ransom! Hot Shot series

The following titles comprise the Dev Haskell series:

Russian Roulette: Case 1
Mr. Swirlee: Case 2
Bite Me: Case 3
Bombshell: Case 4
Tutti Frutti: Case 5
Last Shot: Case 6
Ting-A-Ling: Case 7
Crickett: Case 8
Bulldog: Case 9
Double Trouble: Case 10
Yellow Ribbon: Case 11
Dog Gone: Case 12
Scam Man: Case 13
Foiled: Case 14
What Happens in Vegas… Case 15
Art Hound: Case 16

The Office: Case 17
Star Struck: Case 18
International Incident: Case 19
Guest From Hell: Case 20
Art Attack: Case 21
Mystery Man: Case 22
Bow-Wow Rescue: Case 23
Cold Case: Case 24
Cash Up Front: Case 25
Dream House: Case 26
Alley Katz: Case 27
The Big Gamble: Case 28
Bad to the Bone: Case 29
Silencio!: Case 30
Surprise, Surprise: Case 31
Hit & Run: Case 32
Suspect Santa: Case 33
P.I. Apprentice: Case 34
Rebel Without a Clue: Case 35

The following titles are Dev Haskell novellas:
Dollhouse
The Dance
Pixie
Fore!
Twinkle Toes
(*a Dev Haskell short story*)

The following are Dev Haskell Boxsets:
Dev Haskell Boxset 1-3
Dev Haskell Boxset 4-6
Dev Haskell Boxset 7-9
Dev Haskell Boxset 10-12
Dev Haskell Boxset 13-15
Dev Haskell Boxset 16-18
Dev Haskell Boxset 19-21
Dev Haskell Boxset 22-24
Dev Haskell Boxset 25-27
Dev Haskell Boxset 28-30
Dev Haskell Boxset 1-7
Dev Haskell Boxset 8-14
Dev Haskell Boxset 15-19
Dev Haskell Boxset 20-24
Dev Haskell Boxset 25-29

The following titles comprise the Jack Dillon Dublin Tales series:
Welcome
Jack Dillon Dublin Tale 1
Sweet Dreams
Jack Dillon Dublin Tale 2
Mirror Mirror
Jack Dillon Dublin Tale 3
Silver Bullet
Jack Dillon Dublin Tale 4
Fair City Blues

Jack Dillon Dublin Tale 5
Spade Work
Jack Dillon Dublin Tale 6
Madeline Missing
Jack Dillon Dublin Tale 7
Mistaken Identity
Jack Dillon Dublin Tale 8
Picture Perfect
Jack Dillon Dublin Tale 9
Dublin Moon
Jack Dillon Dublin Tale 10
Mystery Woman
Jack Dillon Dublin Tale 11
Second Chance
Jack Dillon Dublin Tale 12
Payback Brother
Jack Dillon Dublin Tale 13
The Heist
Jack Dillon Dublin Tale 14
Jewels To Kill For
Jack Dillon Dublin Tale 15
Retirement Scheme
Jack Dillon Dublin Tale 16
The Collector
Jack Dillon Dublin Tale 17

Jack Dillon Dublin Tales Boxsets:
Jack Dillon Dublin Tales 1-3
Jack Dillon Dublin Tales 4-6

Jack Dillon Dublin Tales 1-5
Jack Dillon Dublin Tales 1-7
Jack Dillon Dublin Tales 6-10

The following titles comprise the Hotshot series;
Reduced Ransom! Second Edition
Finders Keepers! Second Edition
Bankers Hours Second Edition
Chow Down Second Edition
Moonlight Dance Academy Second Edition
Irish Dukes (Fight Card Series)
written under the pseudonym Jack Tunney

The following titles comprise the Corridor Man series:
Corridor Man
Corridor Man 2: Opportunity knocks
Corridor Man 3: The Dungeon
Corridor Man 4: Dead End
Corridor Man 5: Finger
Corridor Man 6: Exit Strategy
Corridor Man 7: Trunk Music
Corridor Man 8: Birthday Boy
Corridor Man 9: Boss Man
Corridor Man 10: Bye Bye Bobby

Corridor Man novellas:
Corridor Man: Valentine
Corridor Man: Auditor

Corridor Man: Howling
Corridor Man: Spa Day

The following are Corridor Man Boxsets:
Corridor Man Boxset 1-3
Corridor Man Boxset 1-5
Corridor Man Boxset 6-9

All books are available on Amazon.com

Thank you!

Contact the author:
- Email: mikefaricyauthor@gmail.com
- Twitter: @Mikefaricybooks
- Facebook: Mike Faricy Author
- Website: http://www.mikefaricybooks.com

Published by

MJF Publishing

Dream House ✦ 329